Trouble in Threes

The first time Stephen kissed her, Jane knew he was foxed—and she could put his flaring passion down to too much brandy drunk too fast.

The second time Stephen kissed her, he clearly was in need of comfort, reaching to her on the brink of despair, and clinging to her for dear life.

But now there was no mistaking the naked desire in his eyes as he said, "Jane, I cannot resist you." There was no denying the unbridled hunger of his kiss when he drew her to him with arms as strong as steel, bringing her against the full length of him, and making her melt in that embrace.

Then she heard the words she so dreaded . . . the words she feared to face. . . .

"Marry me," he whispered—and she thought, no, not again. . . .

SIGNET REGENCY ROMANCE
Coming in November 1997

Mary Balogh
A Christmas Bride

Allison Lane
The Unscrupulous Uncle

Emily Hendrickson
Lord Ware's Widow

A Marriage
of Convenience

Barbara Allister

Ⓞ
A SIGNET BOOK

SIGNET
Published by the Penguin Group
Penguin Putnam Inc., 375 Hudson Street,
New York, New York 10014, U.S.A.
Penguin Books Ltd, 27 Wrights Lane,
London W8 5TZ, England
Penguin Books Australia Ltd,
Ringwood, Victoria, Australia
Penguin Books Canada Ltd, 10 Alcorn Avenue,
Toronto, Ontario, Canada M4V 3B2
Penguin Books (N.Z.) Ltd, 182–190 Wairau Road,
Auckland 10, New Zealand

Penguin Books Ltd, Registered Offices:
Harmondsworth, Middlesex, England

First published by Signet, an imprint of Dutton Signet,
a member of Penguin Putnam Inc.

First Printing, October, 1997
10 9 8 7 6 5 4 3 2 1

To Sandy Jacobs,
her 1995–96 health science class,
and Dr. Mitch Jacobs.
Thanks for all your research on rabies.
And to George Ann Alford,
who read for errors and listened
to my worries.

AUTHOR'S NOTE
Although today we think of England as a country that is rabies free, it was not until 1924 that the disease was eradicated there.

Chapter One

The late afternoon sun cast dark shadows on the still-green lawn as the men and dogs returned from an afternoon's hunting. The dogs swirled around and under the men's feet, tripping them occasionally.

Stephen Middleton brushed his brown hair out of his eyes, handed his gun to a waiting servant, and bent to pull a spaniel away from his boots. To his surprise, the dog snapped at him, catching his hand between her teeth. He pushed the creature away, muttering a curse.

"Are you all right?" Adolphous Beresford, Lord Langston asked, pulling himself from the brown study he had been in for most of the day.

Stephen stripped the glove from his hand. "She just broke the skin. Rather surprised me." He smiled and shook his head as if in disgust with himself for showing any emotion. He wondered not for the first time why he had accepted Langston's invitation.

"Glad it was not worse." Langston called the groom in charge of his hounds to him. "Take the dogs back to their kennels and watch that brindled spaniel. She bit Mr. Middleton."

"She has been off her feed recently. I will have one of the grooms keep an eye on her while I am gone," the man said quietly.

"Gone? Oh yes, I remember. The dog trials," he said, cutting off the man's explanation. "If you see any dogs you think would improve my pack, buy them. We may see you there if Mr. Middleton is interested and my mother leaves early," Langston went on, wishing that he had found some excuse to escape his mother's visit completely.

"There is a coach and four leaving the house," Middleton called.

Langston cursed underneath his breath. He glanced at the corner where the coach had just disappeared and wondered if he would face a stormy scene with his mother before long. For the last year, he had not been in her good graces. Stephen glanced at his friend, but Langston refused to acknowledge the curiosity that he knew was in his friend's eyes.

Stephen frowned, wondering exactly what was wrong. Since he had met Langston in London after spending the last eighteen months in Canada, he had known something was distressing his friend, but Langston, despite Stephen's many suggestions, had refused to burden his friend with his problems. Stephen, his mind filled with his own difficulties, had not asked many questions.

"Shall we go in?" Langston asked, careful that his uneasiness not show in his voice. "You were always one of my mother's favorites."

"Me?" Stephen asked, surprised. "How can you say that? Remember how she scolded us when she discovered that you, Jane, and I were the ones who had been stealing apples from Farmer Jones?" At the mention of the name Jane, he was startled to see his friend's face go blank.

"Did I mention that Jane is now my mother's companion?" Langston asked, his voice as expressionless as his face.

"Jane? But I thought you had simply postponed everything, that the two of you were to wed." Stephen could not keep the surprise and excitement from his voice.

"After her father's death last year, she released me from our engagement," Langston said carefully. He kept his brown eyes on the ground. "I thought I wrote you." Even after a year, he didn't like saying it.

Stephen looked at him, waiting for a further explanation, his heart racing. Jane was free. Langston did not continue.

"Your mother's companion?" he asked, still puzzled. He was careful not to reveal his elation.

"When Jane's father died, he left his affairs in disorder. After it was decided that we would not wed, Mama asked Jane to be her companion."

"And she agreed?" Stephen's disbelief rang in every syllable. "Surely Jane had some other choice."

Langston looked at him, his face set in immovable lines. "None," he said quietly.

"She lives here? With you?" His shock made him come to a complete halt. He had escaped to Canada as soon as he could after his father's death just to avoid attending their wedding. How could Langston bear to see her every day?

"Good gad, no! Mama decided to move to Bath. I thought I had told you she had bought a house there." Langston nodded to the footman who opened the side door for him.

"Bath? Do you actually visit her there?" Remembering his own visits to the city with his grandmother, Stephen gazed at his friend with horror. He wondered cynically whether Langston had indeed written or if the letters were only in his friend's mind.

Langston laughed and shook his head, but before he could say anything else, his butler appeared. Langston nodded. The older man cleared his throat and said quietly, "Lady Langston is waiting for you in the drawing room." Although the butler did not let his distaste show by anything but a slight flaring of the nostrils, Langston knew Smythe disapproved of the informal way that he and his friend were dressed.

Langston sighed. "Tell her that I will be with her as soon as I change, Smythe," he said. He turned to his friend. "You can wait until later to come down if you wish."

"Nonsense. I will be down as soon as I have changed. I am looking forward to seeing both your mother and Jane." Stephen smiled at his friend and bounded up the stairs, his heart racing. Jane was here.

"Do not forget to have Vernon look after that bite,"

Langston called after him. Stephen nodded. "How long have the ladies been here?" he asked his butler.

"They arrived only a short time ago." The butler waited for more instructions. Langston ignored him and walked up the stairs, his eyes on the marble steps just beginning to show wear from years of footsteps.

As he changed clothes, Stephen thought about what his friend had told him. He wondered what had happened in the eighteen months he had been gone to change a relationship that he had been certain would be one of the lifelong love matches; then Stephen smiled. Jane was free. Then he hesitated. Langston had seemed so strange. Surely his friend wasn't telling him everything; he was certain of that. And Jane a companion? Jane, who had slipped away from her governess time after time, following them until her mother finally agreed she could wander the countryside with Langston and him as long as the boys agreed. His eyes narrowed.

"Would you prefer the sapphire pin, sir?" his valet asked him, his wizened face puzzled.

"Jewels for an evening in the country?" Stephen asked, brought back to the present.

"Her ladyship will expect it," Vernon said firmly. His master sighed and allowed him to place the pin. He glanced in the mirror wondering if Jane would see a difference in him.

Stephen turned to leave. Then remembering his promise to his friend, he stopped. "What should I put on a dog bite, Vernon?"

"A dog bite?" The valet's face whitened, remembering the experience he had been through as he traveled with his master.

"A nip. But I promised Langston I would have you look at it."

With the familiarity of long service, Vernon complained, "Very wise of him, but you should have said something before I finished dressing you. Let me see it." He frowned at the break in the skin but said nothing more. In a trice, he had washed the hand and poured brandy over the wound.

"That stings," Stephen said, pulling his hand free and shaking it.

Vernon took his hand back into his grasp once more. He inspected the spot. "Do you wish a bandage?"

"A bandage? For this? Nonsense." Stephen walked toward the door. "Do not wait up for me. I can put myself to bed."

His excitement grew as he walked down the stairs. He was going to see Jane again. From the moment he entered the gold drawing room, Stephen could feel the tension. He glanced at his friend, standing near the fireplace, his face an expressionless mask. Hiding his own eagerness as well as his uneasiness, he crossed to his friend's mother. "Lady Langston, what a pleasure to see you once more. And what an attractive turban." His valet had been right. Lady Langston was dressed as she would have been for an evening in London, her gold silk gown set off by a topaz necklace and brooch.

She smiled and held out her hand to the man who had been in and out of her home since he had been a boy at Harrow. Stephen took her hand in his own, lifting it to his lips.

"You need not try to wheedle me, Stephen," she said with a light lilt as she patted his cheek affectionately. "Did you learn that in Canada?" She inspected him with her quizzing glass from the top of his brown locks, over his handsome face, and to the tips of his evening shoes, noting the new breadth to his shoulders and the sharp jaw approvingly. "It seems as though your visit there did you no harm." She turned to the young lady seated near her. "You remember Jane Stanfield, Stephen."

"How could I forget my partner in mischief?" Leaving Lady Langston, he crossed to stand in front of Jane. He smiled, determined not to let his surprise at her altered appearance and behavior show. Eager to see her once more, he had used the few moments before the butler announced him to look at her. It had taken all his skill to hide his surprise. The gray gown she wore seemed more than a symbol of mourning. All the life and sparkle that made her so delightful seemed to have drained away. "How are you, Jane?"

She smiled, lifting her once sparkling green eyes to his. Only with effort did Stephen keep back his exclamation of surprise at the sadness deep within them. "Well. Thank you so much for your letter when my father died." Her voice was as lifeless as the rest of her. Her light brown hair once glowing with golden lights was dull and pulled back from her face with no effort at style.

"I am sorry I was not here to be with you. By the time I received Langston's letter, several months had already passed." He longed to sit beside her, to tease her as he once had done, to soothe the sadness from her eyes.

She lowered her head to look at the needlework she held in her lap in an attempt to hide her eyes. "Did you enjoy your time in Canada?" she asked, glancing up at him once more. She kept her eyes focused on him although she longed to stare at her former fiancé.

"It was the most exciting place I have ever been. May I sit beside you and tell you about it?" She nodded, darting a look at Langston to see how he would react. Langston stared off into the distance. Stephen kept his smile only because he was as determined as ever to keep his emotions hidden. He took his seat beside her and caught his breath. Always slender and rosy cheeked, Jane looked faded.

"Tell us all," Lady Langston demanded. "I am certain my son will not mind hearing it again." She glared at her son, who refused to look at her.

Stephen started to explain that he and her son had not spoken of his travels but quickly stopped. The expression on his friend's face as he looked at Jane puzzled him. Did he still care for her?

"Well, was it as exciting as we have heard?" Lady Langston asked.

"What have you heard?" Stephen asked with a smile. He noticed that neither Langston nor Jane would meet the other's eyes.

"Savages, of course. The last time I was in London—we were there for most of the Season, staying with my sister at her son's. You remember him, Henry Fitzwilliam, Lord Ramsey; he was a year behind you at Harrow. Since Langston sold the town house, I must wait for an invitation to visit London," Lady Langston said petulantly. Stephen looked at his friend, startled by that information. He longed to ask what had happened to make his friend take such an action. Langston had always been happier in London than at the manor. "Now where was I? Yes, savages. One of the colonials had one as a servant. He became quite a conversation piece. Did you bring any back with you?"

"The only Indians I saw were peaceful. Although they are not as civilized as we, I would not call them savages," he said, his eyes never leaving Langston's face.

"You were always too kind, never finding fault with anything," Lady Langston complained. "How did they live?"

"Most were hunters and fishermen. Many of the furs that grace our lovely ladies in the winter are first purchased there. In fact, our beaver hats, Langston, are products of their enterprise—at least, the fur is." Stephen smiled at everyone, trying to ease the tension that was all too evident to him, although Lady Langston seemed oblivious to it.

"That is what you went to Canada to explore, the fur trade?" Langston asked, nervously adjusting the sleeves of his corbeau-colored coat.

"Yes, my uncle, my mother's brother, had invested in a series of trading posts there. When he died and I inherited, my solicitors suggested that I inspect them to see if I should sell my interest or keep it," Stephen explained, maintaining the story that had given him a reason to escape.

"And what have you decided?" his friend's mother demanded. Langston looked slightly scandalized, and even Jane looked up, her eyebrows raised. "Is that not the question everyone wanted to ask?" Lady Langston said decisively, refusing to admit that she was asking a question that was not any of her business.

"I have not yet made up my mind," Stephen said quietly. He smiled at her, more to relieve Langston's mind than anything else. "I had to return earlier than I had planned."

Before Lady Langston could question him further, the

butler entered to announce dinner. As she rose and shook her skirts free of wrinkles, Lady Langston said, "How nice to have escorts into dinner! I miss that in Bath. And have you ever seen such handsome gentlemen, Jane, dear! If I had been a young lady and seen them together, one so blond and the other with dark hair, I do not know which I would have chosen!" Oblivious to both her son's and Jane's frozen faces, she took Stephen's arm. "Have you been to London yet? How is that stepmother of yours? I saw her once or twice during the Season. Didn't I mention that I saw her, Jane?" she asked, not even turning her head to listen for a reply.

Carefully separated by a space large enough for another person to walk between them, Jane and Langston followed the other couple into the dining room. "Yes, you did," Jane murmured when the question was addressed to her once more. She allowed Langston to seat her but kept her eyes down. He took his seat at the head of the table, his mother at the foot. Stephen sat opposite Jane, his eyes on the top of her head.

As soon as the first course had been served, a soup made from the turtle the gentlemen had caught the day before, Lady Langston continued her quizzing of her son's friend. "What did you think of London? Was it dreadfully thin of company? We were forced to leave earlier than usual when my sister left to visit her youngest."

"I was there only a short time, and most of that was spent with my agents. When I finally had some time to go into company, I saw Langston at our club, and he invited me to visit him," Stephen said pleasantly. He and Langston exchanged a glance. He had gone to his club to get away from his stepmother and her problems. When he saw his old friend, Langston had pulled an explanation from him and then offered him a temporary refuge from his worries.

"Langston? In London?" The older lady's voice grew sharp. She started to say something but thought better of it. Stephen stared at his friend, but Langston refused to meet his eyes this time. "Well, I am certain Langston was happy to see a friendly face. How long do you plan to stay?" she asked and rushed on without waiting for his answer. "Jane and I will be here for at least a week. Then we will be visiting Mary in Scotland. Did Langston tell you that she has three children now? They are dears but so exhausting. Fortunately, Jane does not mind them."

Remembering that Lady Langston saw only what she wanted to see, Stephen looked across at Jane to see if she agreed, but the younger lady kept her head down and her face hidden. In the year she had spent with Lady Langston, she had evidently become adept at hiding her thoughts.

"She is so good to take care of them so that Mary and I can visit. When we visited Lucinda—you remember Lucinda. She was presented the year you and Langston were sent down from Cambridge." Lady Langston continued, totally absorbed in her own thoughts. She prattled on, oblivious of their lack of response.

By the time the ladies finished their tea and the four of them had played a few hands of whist, Stephen was ready to say good night to the ladies and to seek some answers. When Langston proposed a game of billiards, he agreed.

"Sorry about my mother, Stephen," Langston mumbled as he set the balls up. "Had no idea she would be visiting me anytime soon when I asked you to visit."

"Would it make it easier if I left? I could say I had received—"

"No!" Langston took a deep breath and said more calmly, "You will make the visit more bearable."

"What has happened? When I left here eighteen months ago, you and Jane were in one another's pockets. Now you are not even talking. And Jane. She has changed so much." Stephen broke the balls and stood back for his friend to make his shot, his blue eyes curious.

"Jane's father died. I told you that." Langston bit the words off as though he didn't want to say them.

"And what did that have to do with the way the two of you felt?"

"Jane's father was not the only one whose affairs were in disarray," Langston said quietly. He put down his cue and walked over to the table where a bottle of brandy and glasses sat. Stephen stared at him, not certain what to say, not willing to interrupt. Langston's explanations meant too much to him. Pouring two glasses, Langston handed one to Stephen and motioned him to the chairs that were nearby. "During the Little Season shortly after you left, I began playing deep. I lost." He held up his hand as if to silence the exclamations he knew were coming. "I could have covered those losses. Of course, I would have had to reduce my spending, but I could have recovered most within a year or two."

He stared at the paste buckles on his evening slippers, unwilling to look at his friend. "My further mistake was investing in some shares Mr. Stanfield was touting. Although I plunged deep, I at least didn't involve my mother. Or perhaps I should say that, fortunately for me, my mother's jointure was never in my control. Jane and her family were not so lucky. Mr. Stanfield believed in the stock so much that he mortgaged his lands and invested most of his wife's jointure and his daughters' dowries in order to buy more shares."

"What? Everything? Langston, is there anything I can do to help . . ."

Langston continued as though he had not heard him. "By leasing the hall in order to pay George's school fees and the mortgage, they are managing. Jane took the post with my mother, and her mother and younger sister make their home with Jane's uncle." He frowned. "After Stanfield's death when their situation became known, they came to me for help." He laughed bitterly. Stephen stared at him, not knowing what to say. "Me! To survive myself, I had to sell the town house and one estate that was not entailed. And they wanted my help!" He closed his eyes but could not escape the memory of the look in Jane's eyes when he had explained what had happened, when he had said they could not marry. "After a frank discussion of our situations, Jane and I decided we should not suit.

"Fortunately, my title is still worth something on the marriage mart. In a few weeks, I will announce my marriage to Miss Lydia Thackeray." He sank back in the chair as though the life had flowed out of him with his words.

"Why did you not write me? Is there anything I can do?" Stephen asked, his face concerned. Then Langston's words sank in. "Who is Miss Lydia Thackeray? Have I met her?"

"She had left town on a brief visit before you arrived. She is lovely." He paused. Stephen leaned forward. "But even if you had arrived before the end of the Season, I doubt that you would have met her. She has small acquaintance among the *ton*." He took a deep breath and forced the words out. "Her grandfather's a Cit. Money but little else."

"Have you told Jane?" When Langston said nothing, Stephen stood up and refilled his brandy glass. "You would not let her read about your engagement in the paper." His face revealed his shock. Langston had always been rather self-centered, but he had not been unfeeling. Stephen sat down again, thinking about Jane's reaction.

His friend ran his hand over his face, trying to keep his emotions in check. "I have not yet mentioned my engagement to my mother. Oh, she knows I have to find a wealthy bride to restore my fortune, but I had hoped to present her a *fait accompli*. And when I tell her, she will tell Jane."

"Langston!"

"I know that is taking the coward's way out, but I can't face Jane. You did not see the horror in her eyes when I explained why we could not marry," his friend explained. His jaw set firmly. "I will not endure that again."

Once more, Stephen looked at his friend, wondering at the changes he could see. "Is there nothing I can do to help?" he asked again. His mind raced. Langston and Jane were no longer betrothed.

"Nothing except stand between me and the ladies. My mother was horrified to learn what happened. She continues to blame me for the broken engagement and the loss of the London house. Since Jane consented to be her companion, all she has complained about is the loss of the town house." He picked up his cue once more and walked to the table. "I suppose when I marry Miss Thackeray and purchase a new house in town on one of the more popular squares she will look on me with favor once more." He laughed bitterly. "Shall we finish the game?"

Stephen, his heart pounding, walked to the table and picked up his cue, carefully hiding his emotions. "How can you bear to have Jane live with your mother?"

"I refused as long as I could." Although Langston's words were very quiet, Stephen could tell from the tiny quiver in his voice that he was disturbed. "However, when my mother decided to remove to Bath, there was little I could do. Jane did need a position, and Mother has the money to hire her. This is the first time I have seen her in a year." The last sentence was said so quietly that Stephen had to listen carefully to catch it.

"But you were both in London for the Season."

"According to Mother, Jane rarely went out in the evenings since she was still in mourning. Then, too, we were in different circles. I could avoid her. Come, let us finish the game." Langston took his shot, watching the balls carefully. For the rest of the evening, Langston refused to allow any more questions, his good humor seemingly restored. By the time he retired, Stephen had even more questions than before.

As he prepared for bed, Stephen had only one thought on his mind—how to convince Jane to consider him.

Chapter Two

When Jane entered her room and closed the door behind her, she sighed with relief. Crossing to the dressing table, she picked up a brush and stared at herself in the mirror. What she saw there brought a frown to her face. "No wonder Stephen hardly looked at me," she whispered to herself. The walls that she had so carefully erected around her feelings were crumbling.

From the first moment that Lady Langston had announced her plan to visit her former home, Jane had prepared herself. But how could she have known that Stephen would be here at the same time?

She was pleased at the way she had reacted to Langston. He had not been able to meet her eyes, but, like her, he was determined not to embarrass his mother. After weeks of dreading their first meeting, Jane was relieved but also a little sad. She laughed at herself bitterly. What had she expected? That Langston would fall to his knees in front of her and ask her to take him back?

And if her dream had come to fruition? Jane turned away from the question she was not yet ready to answer. She glanced in the mirror again and frowned. What must Stephen have thought of her, her hair pulled back from her face and fastened tightly into a coil on her neck? She pulled at the neck of the dress she wore, remembering the last time she had seen Stephen. They had been dancing when he told her he was going away. She still remembered how lost she had felt. But she had hidden her feelings quickly and wished him a speedy voyage. "You will be present for our wedding, won't you?" she had asked, smiling up at him.

His eyes had grown dark. As the music came to an end, he had led her from the floor and back to her mother. "I fear that will be impossible." He watched her glance around the room until she found Langston. He smiled wryly. "I hope you will always be happy," he said so softly she almost missed his words. He made a bow and was gone.

"Poor boy," her mother had whispered, looking after him, her eyes sad.

"Stephen? Nonsense, he will have a great adventure. How I wish I were a man and could go where I wanted." Her mother had merely looked at her, a tiny frown creasing her forehead.

This afternoon Stephen had looked so different, so mature. Why hadn't she noticed how much like a little boy Langston had remained? Would he have still been wearing that petulant little frown had they married? Jane took the pins from her hair and began to brush it. Although she told herself she should be thinking about Langston, it was Stephen who occupied her mind. As she drifted off to sleep after spending hours reliving the moments of the evening, Stephen filled her dreams, too.

Rising early was a habit that Stephen had been unable to break since his return to England. Knowing that his friend rarely emerged from his room until late, he dressed and made his way to the breakfast room. To his surprise, he was not the only early one in the household. He smiled. "Good morning, Jane. Did you sleep well?" The conventional greeting was out of his mouth before he thought.

Jane's head jerked up, her sadness evident before she carefully made her face a mask. "As well as can be expected," she said quietly. Realizing that her words gave too much away, she rushed on. "I never sleep well when I am traveling."

"Luckily that is not a problem with me. I would never have survived my travels if it were. There were times when the only bed I had was the hard, rocky ground. I often wished that you and Langston were with me. You would have enjoyed the fishing."

"Fishing." Her voice was wistful. "I have not been fishing in a year."

"Go with me this morning. Langston will not be up for hours, but he made me free with his stream." Stephen smiled, his blue eyes twinkling much as they had done when he was a boy and making some outrageous plan for their amusement.

"Fishing," Jane said excitedly. Then her shoulders, which had been thrown back and squared, slumped. "I cannot. Lady Langston will expect to see me with her breakfast tray." The touch of color in her cheeks faded.

Refusing to allow her to escape him, Stephen thought quickly. "Then will you walk with me through the gardens? We will tell the servants where you are so that they can call you when she sends for her tray." Once more he coaxed her with a smile, determined to make her notice him.

"A walk in the garden." Once more Jane's voice was wistful. She smiled at him, remembering the adventures they had shared. He had always been kind to her, kinder than Langston she realized with surprise. It had been Stephen who had always included her in the boys' plans.

"Come. I promise we will not wander far from the house."

Yielding to his blandishments, Jane nodded. Stephen sat back in his chair, pleased with her agreement. Jane and he talked as he quickly finished his breakfast.

A short time later they entered the garden. The once carefully pruned flowers and bushes were in disarray, only those perennials still blooming wildly. As Stephen looked around curiously, he realized that the garden looked much like his friend's home, neglected. How could I have missed this? he wondered.

Jane, who had been longing to take a turn about the garden since her arrival the day before, breathed deeply. Too happy to be in the country once more, she didn't notice the shabbiness around her. She smiled. Stephen noticed that the bodice of her gray gown was filled out quite nicely though the color did little to enhance her pale face. "Are you certain you will be warm enough? I could ask a servant to bring you a shawl."

"I shall be fine," she said with a smile. "You always did worry about me. I can assure you that a little fresh air will not harm me now any more than it did when we were younger." She took a deep breath. "Tell me more about your travels," she suggested.

"It was green, a different green from here. Wilder. I enjoyed the hunting though I am sure you would not. Remember how you insisted that we let the fox go? Has Master Huntsford ever forgiven you?" he said, his eyes dancing as he remembered their antics.

"He asked for a country dance at one of the balls we held after a hunt and assured me that I was a delight to partner on the floor." Her smile faded slightly as she remembered a happier time. Refusing to sink further into melancholy, she pushed her emotions aside and looked up at her escort.

"He did not recognize you when you were dressed in a ball gown. Of that I am certain. Had he done so he would have sent for his whip as he threatened to do the day of the fox incident."

"Whip a young lady? The colonies must indeed be uncivilized. No Englishman would dream of raising his hand to his dancing partner," she said, laughing. For the first time in many months she felt young again. As she had done when she was younger and had escaped her governess, she untied the ribbon that held her hair in place, letting it fall down her back. She shook her head much the way a wet dog shakes itself.

"Now you look more the rebel who followed Langston and me through this valley and into trouble. I was afraid that you had cut your hair," Stephen said with a smile.

"My hair? You noticed my hair?" she asked, stopping in place and pulling him to a stop. She looked up into his blue eyes, her own green ones wide.

"I have always noticed you," he said quietly, turning so that he could look at her. Although he was above average in height, just over six feet, she reached his chin, only needing to tilt her head slightly to look into his eyes. Something she saw there held her frozen. Stephen started to speak.

"Here you are. Jane, Smythe asked me to tell you that Mother has called for her tray," Langston's cheerful message hid the uneasiness he had felt when he had seen them standing, staring into one another's eyes, Jane's hair cascading down her back.

"Take this with you," Stephen said, bending to pick one of the hardy flowers in the bed. Jane smiled at him and hurried off. As she disappeared, Stephen cursed and shook his hand.

"What is wrong?" Although he tried to make his voice cordial, Langston was certain Stephen could sense his displeasure.

"The spot where the spaniel bit me is sore," Stephen said, looking at the angry red bite.

"Did you have Vernon look after it for you?" Langston asked, his brow creased as he looked back at the house, his annoyance at seeing Jane looking into Stephen's eyes forgotten.

"Yesterday. But I shall have him look at it again if it will please you," Stephen said, his voice dry.

"It would please me more if it had never happened," his friend said. "That spaniel did nothing worthwhile yesterday, and she is usually such a good hunter." He smiled at Stephen. "I have a few letters I must write first, but my valet said he heard last night that there was to be a mill only a few miles away. Shall we go?"

"But what about your mother and Jane?"

"When I visited Mother this morning, she informed me that she and Jane would be renewing their acquaintance in the neighborhood and that they would return in time for tea." Langston grinned broadly. "Shall we make good our escape?"

"Lead on!" Stephen followed his friend back into the house. A short time later they left, leaving word that the ladies were not to wait meals on them.

In the company of his friend and acquaintances from the countryside, Langston became the man that Stephen had known for years. For a few hours both managed to forget the tensions that were part of their lives.

Although the gentlemen could escape, Jane was not so lucky. Visiting in homes where she had once been an equal, she faced a gauntlet of questions, some well-meant, others prying. Resolutely, she kept a smile on her face and answered her inquisitors quietly. As soon as Lady Langston and she left each house, she knew the gossip would start. She had heard it in London when people thought she had left the room.

"Have you ever seen someone so much changed?"

"How does she manage to hold her head up? I heard—"

"What can you expect from a girl who chases after the young men? What can her mother have been thinking of to allow it? Disgraceful."

"Lady Langston must be a saint. To take Jane into her household once she had refused Langston."

"Refused him? I heard Lady Langston agreed to have her as a companion because . . ."

To her surprise, however, neither the gossip nor her seeing Langston for the first time in a year was what bothered her most. Instead, it was seeing her old home. When they drove by the gates to her home and realized once more that someone else lived there, she wanted to cry. Blinking quickly to prevent the tears from falling, she reminded herself that she, her mother, and George had made the decision together. They had known the consequences of their decision only too well. Oh, Papa, why did you get involved in that insane scheme? she wondered as she had so many times before. Her eyes on her family's land, she did not see the sympathetic glance that Lady Langston sent her way.

"Do you have my vinaigrette, Jane? The motion of this coach is making me ill," she demanded, successfully drawing the young lady's attention back to her and diverting her thoughts.

"I did not put it in today. You told me you would not need it. Shall I tell the coachman to hurry? We are only a short distance from the manor."

"No. I shall manage since we are so close to home." She

waved her handkerchief in front of her face. "On the trip to Scotland be certain to have it with you at all times."

Jane nodded and wondered if the return to her former home had been as difficult for Lady Langston as it had been for her. The question of why the lady had chosen to remove to Bath had puzzled her for months. It was obvious that the older lady enjoyed seeing her friends here as much as she enjoyed the society in Bath and London. She also thought of the two men she had known since childhood and wondered at the changes in them. Langston seemed so surly and Stephen so mature. Had they noticed differences in her? The last year had not been easy for her, and she sometimes didn't recognize herself in the quiet and unassuming woman she had become.

By the time they arrived at the manor, Lady Langston had revived. When they discovered that the gentlemen were absent and did not intend to return before bedtime, Lady Langston suggested, "I plan to have my tea and supper on a tray in my room. Tell Smythe what you want. I am certain that you will want to write your mother and tell her how everyone asked about her. Give her my best regards."

Relieved, Jane agreed. Asking Smythe to have her tea brought to the library, she sat down at the table and began her letter, skillfully concealing her distress from her family as she had done in every letter since she left them. Her mother had been so relieved when Lady Langston had offered Jane the job as her companion. If Jane had to take a position, at least it would be with someone Mrs. Stanfield knew, someone who would be kind; her mother's words had done much to make her decision for her. And in spite of her own questions why the lady had offered the position, Jane knew that Lady Langston cared for her. Except for this week, the year had been bearable.

Jane paused, thinking of the agony she had suffered when Lady Langston had announced that they would be visiting her son. She did not want her mother to know what this visit had cost her. Her face brightened. At least Stephen had been here. As he had done when he was a boy, he smoothed her pathway, making her laugh. Telling her mother about his adventures, she filled the page.

Her letters finished, Jane returned to her room and washed her hair, letting it dry before the fire in her bedroom. Then she brushed it, letting the waves fall over her shoulder. Ready to curl up in bed and read until it was time to sleep, Jane realized that she had left the book she had been reading in the coach. Pulling on her robe and slippers, she crept downstairs to the library once more. Intending to find a book and hurry back to her room, Jane glanced around the room. Many of the books there were old friends. She picked up three of them and sat down in a chair, trying to decide between them.

The candles by which she had been reading were mere stubs when a noise in the hallway pulled her away from her book. Placing her books on the table, she crept to the door and opened it a crack. To her dismay there seemed an army of people around.

"Let them help you up the stairs, Langston," Stephen said in a voice that was slightly slurred, transferring his friend from his support to that of two sturdy footmen. "It is time for bed." He turned to Smythe, who was looking at his master with a frown on his face. Jane opened the door wider, unaware that the candle behind her revealed her presence. "Can they manage him?" he asked the butler, stepping around the footmen until all the servants faced away from the library.

"Certainly, sir." The butler's frosty tones revealed that Stephen was overstepping his bounds.

"Good. Lady Langston home?"

"Both ladies have been abed for hours."

"I can see myself to bed. No need to wait up," Stephen said, walking carefully toward the library. Jane quickly closed the door and, remembering how informally she was dressed, frantically searched the room like an animal trying to escape a trap.

"Yes, sir." Smythe stuck his chin in the air and went to lock the front door, his disapproval evident.

As soon as the butler disappeared, Stephen opened the library door. "You can come out now," he whispered loudly.

Jane, certain that he would bring every servant in the house to the library, tried to quiet him. "Shsh!"

"I know you are in here, Jane. Come out, come out, wherever you are." The chant from his childhood slipped off his lips, only slightly slurred.

She moved behind the chair where she had been sitting, using it as though it were a shield. "Go away." Although her words were urgent, she was not sure what he would do. She had never been able to second-guess him.

"Not until you tell me good night," he said as though he were a small child making demands on his parents, peering around the door looking for her. When he caught sight of her behind the chair, he smiled.

"Good night, Stephen," she said firmly.

"Not that kind of good night." He walked toward her.

"What kind of good night are you talking about? Stephen, are you foxed?" She peered over the back of the chair and pulled her robe more firmly around her, hoping that he did not come any closer.

"A bit on the go. Langston's foxed," he said smugly. "Never could hold his liquor as well as I could."

"Stephen, you need to go to bed. Vernon will be waiting for you."

"Told him not to wait up."

"You tell him that every night, and he still stays up waiting for you." Realizing that her words might be misconstrued as interest in him, she hurried on. "At least the servants say he does."

"Not since Canada." His honesty caused him to add, "At least not every night. Smythe said you were in bed. What are you doing up?" He glanced around as if aware of where he was for the first time. "You have been reading!" he exclaimed.

"Yes, and now it is time to go to bed," Jane said firmly, determined to reason with him as she would have done with her younger brother. She edged around the chair and headed for the door.

"No. You cannot go yet." Stephen put his hand out and grabbed her arm, his grip tighter than he realized.

She froze. "Stephen. You are frightening me. Let me go!" Jane, thoroughly warned by her mother, knew all too well what advantages gentlemen of the household might take of companions.

He released her arm. "I am sorry." He sounded so much like the boy he had been all the fear inside her disappeared. "All I wanted was a kiss." He smiled at her wistfully.

"A good-night kiss?" He nodded. Jane sighed and reached up to brush his cheek with her lips as she did with her brother. Stephen, however, had other ideas. He bent his head and pressed his lips to hers, pulling her so close to him that she could hear his heart pounding.

Finally, he pulled his lips away from her. "Good night," he murmured and walked out of the room.

Jane stood there for some time, her heart beating rapidly. She touched her lips gently and shivered, the tingling she had felt when his lips pressed hers leaving her weak. "Oh, Stephen," she whispered.

Chapter Three

The next morning the breakfast room stood empty for hours. Jane, the first one down, looked in cautiously before she entered. Although she had finally convinced herself that Stephen had kissed her simply because he had had too much to drink, she still didn't want to see him until she had had more time to think. In spite of her outward calm, she breathed a sigh of relief when she realized that she was the first one down. She sat at the table, determined to be finished before anyone else came in.

Her plans were dashed. A short time after Jane accepted a cup of chocolate and some toasted bread, Stephen walked in, his eyes clear and his face rested. "Good morning, Jane," he said as though the kiss the evening before had never happened. Only his determination enabled him to appear calm.

Maybe he didn't remember anything, Jane thought as she echoed his greeting, glancing at him surreptitiously under her long lashes. He was as neatly dressed as ever. Even during their rambles through the countryside, he was the one who always remained presentable while she and Langston were the despair of their households. Dressed in a dark brown coat, Stephen accepted his plate of eggs and beef and waited impatiently until the footman had left the room. "Did you sleep well?" he asked innocently, his eyes dancing.

"Yes, thank you," she murmured, her eyes fixed on her plate.

"What were you reading when I interrupted you?"

She gulped, almost choking on the mouthful of chocolate

she had just drunk. Stephen moved rapidly around the table, pounding her on the back. "Are you all right?" he asked anxiously, his hands still on her shoulders. She nodded, expecting him to return to his seat. Instead, he stayed where he was, his fingers caressing her neck. She tingled wherever he touched her. Startled, she turned and looked up at him. Staring into her eyes, he bent his head.

The door of the breakfast room flew open. "Coffee," Langston snarled. Startled, Stephen stepped back, moving to the sideboard where the food was laid out.

Jane rang the bell, noting Langston's red eyes and less than impeccable grooming. Her eyes returned to Stephen, who was as fresh as though he had never had a drop to drink. When the servant appeared, she had him bring a fresh pot of coffee. "Do you want anything else?' she asked her former fiancé, her disapproval giving her words a slight edge.

"No."

Determined to make her escape quickly, Jane returned her attention to her food, missing the angry look that Langston sent Stephen. Stephen raised his eyebrow questioningly. Langston took another gulp of coffee and put his cup into the saucer with a clink. The silence in the breakfast room grew.

Before it could become unbearable, the door opened once more. Relieved, all three of them looked up. Smythe stood there, his displeasure written on his face. "The head groom insists that he must speak to your lordship at once."

"Now?" Langston asked, surprised.

"At once, he said," his butler explained. "A matter of some urgency."

"Show him in," Langston said wearily. He looked at his friend and shrugged.

When the groom appeared, he was plainly disturbed. He twisted his hat in his hands. "Well, what is so urgent?" Langston demanded. The groom glanced at Jane and shuffled his feet. Realizing that the man did not want not speak before her, Jane drank the last of her chocolate and made her escape from the room.

"Well?" Langston asked again, his impatience evident.

"It's the dogs, your lordship." The man twisted his hat in his hands, trying to find the right words.

"You interrupted my breakfast to discuss the dogs?"

"The boy had to put down two of them," the groom exclaimed.

"Put down? You mean he killed them?" Langston got up hurriedly, his chair overturning behind him.

"He had no choice. They were frothing at the mouth."

Both Langston and Stephen froze. When the silence had grown so uncomfortable that the groom shifted from one foot to another, Stephen asked the question on both their minds. "Which dogs?"

"The brindled spaniels your lordship gave him orders to watch . . ."

Neither of the men heard the rest. Stephen stood up, his chair joining Langston's on the floor. "The brindled spaniel," he whispered and looked at the bite on his hand.

Langston quickly joined his friend, his hand on his shoulder. "You cannot be sure. We will call the doctor." Stephen moved away from him. Langston asked the groom, "Tell me once more what happened."

"The new boy. Jones's youngest. You remember you told me that I could hire him," the groom explained.

"Yes, but what about the dogs?" Langston asked, his face serious. He kept his eyes on the groom, not wanting to look at his friend.

"When the boy saw them frothing at the mouth like they were, he got a gun and shot them just as he would have done on his pa's farm. Then he came and told me about it. And I told you."

"How long ago was this?"

"Very early. The lad has been so excited about working for you that he arrives shortly before daybreak." The man twisted his hat in his hands once more. "I thought you should know."

"Thank you," Langston said. "Tell the lad that if anything like this happens again to call you first and you will take care of it. And, Harris, check to see that neither bit any of the grooms." The man nodded his head and hurried from the room, relieved that Langston had not demanded the boy's dismissal. Langston turned to face his friend.

Stephen's face was white. Langston took a deep breath. "The boy could have been wrong."

"Your groom did not think so." Those few words took an effort for Stephen to produce. His mouth was dry and his heart was beating rapidly. His legs started trembling so much that he grabbed Jane's chair and sat down before they gave way completely.

"I will send for the doctor." Langston crossed to the bell and pulled it vigorously.

"He can do nothing," Stephen said through clenched teeth. His hand closed around Jane's cup so tightly that it cracked.

Refusing to believe that Stephen was right, Langston gave the footman his orders. "And get him here soon," he demanded. He crossed to stand behind his friend, wanting to put his hands on his shoulders once more but afraid of Stephen's reaction. Neither man spoke.

The sound of the door opening broke the stillness. Both men looked at the doorway, hoping that the fears of the last few minutes were to be erased. Jane entered.

"Did you see my book?" she began. Then the shock on their faces registered with her. "What has happened?"

Stephen swallowed and tried to say something that would reassure her, but he could only croak. She looked at Langston. He only shook his head and closed his eyes, his hand clenching the back of Stephen's chair so hard that his knuckles were white.

Realizing that something dreadful must have happened, Jane acted quickly. Crossing to the bell, she pulled it hard. "Bring some brandy. Quickly!" she demanded when the footman appeared. As soon as he returned, she poured each of them a glass. "Drink this!" she told them. As soon as they had picked up the glasses, she sat down, determined not to leave until she found out what was wrong. Langston had a look in his eyes that she had seen only once before— when he had told her they should not suit. And she had never seen Stephen look as he did now, a green tinge under his tanned skin.

Langston gripped his glass in both his hands and managed to get it to his mouth. Stephen picked his up, but his hands were shaking so badly that he spilled most of the brandy before it reached his lips. Jane looked from one to the other. Neither would meet her eyes. Stephen kept his eyes on the glass in his hand. Langston stared off into the distance, his face set.

The breakfast room door swung open with a crash. All three of them jumped. "Langston, you must stop these rumors at once. My maid has demanded that I allow her to return to London," Lady Langston said angrily.

"What rumors?" Jane asked, her eyes on Stephen's face.

"The silly woman has some idea that we have rabid dogs on the estate. She is certain she will be bitten and will die. You simply must do something." She glared at her son as if he were the cause of the problem and took her seat at the table.

Jane's eyes widened. "Is it true?" she asked, looking from one to the other. She stared at Langston, waiting for his denial. He simply nodded. She closed her eyes for a moment. "What's wrong? Were you bitten?" she whispered, her voice so low that Lady Langston didn't hear.

The silence that followed confirmed her fears. "Who?" she asked, afraid of the answer. Lady Langston continued to complain. Jane looked from one man to the other.

"Stephen. His hand," Langston said, his voice as soft as hers had been.

Then Jane looked at Stephen, at his hand with the small red wound already fading. She wanted to go to him, to put her arms around him to protect him, but even as a boy he had refused all offers of comfort when he had been injured. As she looked at him, he shuddered.

Lady Langston continued to complain until her son spoke up. "Mama, tell your maid that the dogs are dead. There is no danger to her."

"You mean . . . ?" Lady Langston could hardly force the words out.

"Yes, Mama. It was not a rumor."

"What do you mean?" The older lady put her hand to her throat as if protecting it. She gazed at her son in horror as if expecting him to collapse instantly.

"The youngest groom killed two dogs that were frothing at the mouth this morning."

"This morning, but—"

"Mama, please be quiet." the firmness in Langston's voice surprised even himself.

"How—how dare you!"

Stephen made a strangled sound in his throat and dashed out of the room.

"Why, whatever is the matter with him?" Lady Langston said. She turned to look after him, too surprised by Stephen's actions to continue her harangue with her son.

Langston turned to glare at his mother. "One of the dogs bit Stephen," he said through clenched teeth.

In spite of what she already knew, Jane's heart sank as she heard him say the words aloud. Lady Langston stared at her son and sighed. Neither Jane nor Langston realized that she had fainted until she started to slide out of her chair onto the floor. Both rushed forward, their hands tangling as they reached to help the lady back into her chair. Langston jumped back away from Jane as if he had been scalded. Jane, her attention completely focused on her employer, said quietly, "Send for her maid and her smelling salts. She will be all right shortly."

"I wish I could say the same for Stephen," Langston said hoarsely as he slipped from the room during the commotion that followed.

Her employer once more ensconced in her bed, a cold compress on her head and her maid with smelling salts close at hand, Jane left the room, satisfied she could do nothing more for the older lady. Determined to find Stephen, she hurried downstairs. After searching the library and the study, she questioned the servants. But no one had seen him.

Langston, arriving just in time to hear the last of the servants' responses, said quietly, "I will check the stables. Perhaps he went for a ride."

Jane stared at him in disbelief. Stephen close to the dogs? Then she nodded and sighed. Wandering into the library once more, she remembered how happy Stephen had been the evening before and hurried out. Restlessly pacing the hallway, she stopped every time someone rushed through it. Finally, unable to contain her restlessness any longer, she slipped out into the garden, wandering its paths. For the first time she noticed its generally unkempt appearance, turning around to get a complete view. It was then she saw Stephen sitting on a marble bench, his head in his hands.

She moved so quietly that he did not hear her approach. The touch of her hand as she brushed back his dark hair from his forehead startled him. "Stephen, my dear—" she began. Then she choked.

He grabbed her hand as though it were a lifeline and he a drowning man. "Jane," he sighed. Moving over, he made room for her on the bench, keeping her hand tightly in his. Silently, she sat down beside him, wondering what she could say to him. The easy platitudes had no place here. Her fingers curled around his. They were still sitting in silence when the footman found them.

"His lordship requests that you come to the study." The once calm servant stumbled over the next words. "The doctor has arrived."

Stephen's grip on her hand tightened until Jane had to bite her lip to keep from crying out. Her pain ignored, she whispered, "You must see him, Stephen."

"Why? I know what he is going to say." He stood up and pulled her to her feet beside him. The servant took a step backward as though afraid of being too close to him. "The dog was rabid. When I was in Canada, I saw two men who were bitten by rabid animals. The first, an Indian, had an easy death; his medicine man gave him poison. The second, a Frenchman, was not so fortunate. He died a slow and painful death. Vernon knows. He shared his last hours."

"Stephen, talk to the doctor. If it is as hopeless as you

say, Langston and I will be here," Jane promised, her voice too soft for the servant to hear. "We will not desert you."

He turned so that he could stare into her eyes, his own eyes cloudy and full of pain. What he saw strengthened him. "For you, Jane. Only for you," he said in a shaky voice.

Sending the servant ahead to say they were coming, Stephen and Jane walked slowly back to the house, stopping occasionally. Stephen glanced around as though afraid he would never see the world again.

"The doctor is in the library," Smythe said, his face as impassive as usual, but his voice was as sympathetic as it had been when, as boys, Stephen and Langston had incurred Lady Langston's wrath.

Stephen's hand tightened on Jane's. Then he took a deep breath. "Maybe you and Langston are right. I could be worrying without reason," he said, trying to comfort her. "Will you come with me?" She nodded. He opened the door into the room where the doctor and Langston waited.

The sight of the two of them together made Langston freeze, his face set in somber lines. The doctor walked forward. "Lord Langston has told me about the problem. May I see the bite?" Stephen stepped forward and held out his hand. The doctor adjusted his glasses and inspected the almost healed wound. "Hmm. Not much of a injury. Fortunate for you."

"Does that mean he is in no danger?" Jane asked, her eyes brightening. Langston smiled. Even Stephen stood straighter.

"No, Miss Stanfield." The despair that filled their eyes was greater for the few moments of hope. "You always jump to a conclusion. This will take more time," the doctor scolded. "Let me see your hand again."

Stephen, his hand trembling this time, held it out again. "Hmmm." The three friends could not look at one another. "Tell me how this happened and when," the doctor demanded, poking the edges of the injury. Stephen winced.

Quietly Stephen and Langston gave him the details.

"You say you were wearing gloves, Mr. Middleton? And

you washed your hand with soap and water and rinsed it with brandy?" The doctor pushed his glasses up on his nose and cocked his head to one side. Stephen nodded. "Hmmm. Are you certain that the dogs were rabid?" He turned to look at Langston, his thick bushy brows raised.

"That is what my grooms said, Dr. Clarke," Langston told him, hoping for a contradiction.

"Strange. I have not heard of any other cases in the county. In fact, I do not believe there has been a case of rabies in this area since I arrived. They were certain?" He dropped Stephen's hand and stared at Langston. Once again the three friends felt a frisson of hope run through them.

"Would you like to talk to the lad who found them?" Langston asked, his voice carefully neutral. The doctor nodded. "I will send for him."

"Nonsense. The boy would be frightened to death. One of Jones's boys, isn't that right? I will step down to the stables and have a word with him. Might as well check for any other injuries those dogs may have caused," the doctor said, pushing his glasses up on his nose once more.

"I will go with you," Langston said.

"And I," Stephen added. Jane, left behind, watched them go. Then she closed her eyes and prayed before going upstairs to her employer. With every step she took, she realized how little the doctor had said.

When she entered Lady Langston's suite, the lady was sitting up in bed, her maid hovering nearby. "Well, you have certainly been gone a long time," the lady said waspishly. Then she relented. "Has the doctor arrived? What does he say? Are we in any danger?"

The last question sent a wave of anger through Jane. Biting her lip, she took a deep breath, fighting for control. When she thought she could speak calmly, she said, "He has said little. Lord Langston, Mr. Middleton, and he have gone off to speak to the groom who killed the dogs."

"Now why would he do that? Well, who can tell. He is a man after all. He said nothing?"

"Very little. He did say there were no other reports of rabies in the county."

"That is something to be thankful for." She closed her eyes for a moment. Jane sat down at the secretary, picking up the pen and penknife in order to sharpen the quill so that she could begin the correspondence. She jumped and stabbed the end of her finger with the knife when Lady Langston commanded, "Go downstairs at once." Sticking her bleeding finger in her mouth, Jane nodded and stood up. "I am simply too distraught to go down myself." The lady leaned back on her pillows, one hand to her brow. Then forgetting her pose, she leaned forward. "And the boys will probably tell you more than they would me. They always did."

Her reference to the boys made Jane smile. Lady Langston sometimes refused to acknowledge that her son and his friends were now grown men. "As you wish," she said with a curtsy.

"And, Jane," the lady added. Her companion stopped and turned around. "Once you have found out the details I insist upon knowing everything." She once again but her hand to her head. "This is just too terrible, too terrible. How will I ever be able to face Middleton's stepmother again?"

Wishing that her own mother were nearer to hand to give her advice, Jane made her way downstairs. "I will be in the library, Smythe. Please tell Lord Langston and Mr. Middleton I am waiting for them." Jane wandered around the room, picking up first one book and then another, too nervous to settle down. She found a feather duster, left in the turmoil of the morning, and began dusting the tops of the books she could reach. When the door opened, she whirled around. Catching sight of the maid, she sighed.

"May I have my duster, miss?" the girl asked nervously.

Wordlessly, Jane handed it over and watched as the girl hurried from the room. Hearing noises in the hall, she opened the door and peered out, seeing her friends and the doctor. One look at their faces told her that the news was not good. She followed them into the study, Smythe on her heels. He poured the men each a brandy and then waited for other orders. Jane sank into a chair near Stephen, taking his hand in hers. Langston noticed but for the first time felt no resentment.

When the doctor had finished his brandy, he wiped his face with his handkerchief and pushed his glasses up on his nose. When the silence had grown uncomfortable, Langston asked, "What do you think?" He could not look at his friend.

The doctor stared at him. Then he turned to Stephen. "I hope you have your affairs in order, Mr. Middleton."

Jane gasped. Stephen's fingers tightened around hers so much her fingers turned white. "Are you saying—" she began in a voice that did not sound like her own.

"I am saying I do not know," the doctor said. "If the groom was right, and I am not saying he was, then there is a problem. Mr. Middleton, I would put your affairs in order just in case."

Langston poured himself another glass of brandy and downed it in one gulp. "I'll get rid of the damned dogs," he muttered.

"Not so hasty, my lord," the doctor cautioned. "If those two were rabid, some of the others will be infected. Better to keep them under watch. If others show the symptoms within the next few days, then Mr. Middleton will have his specific answer."

"What?"

"Are you telling me I simply have to wait?"

"Can nothing be done?"

The doctor listened to the babble of voices for a few minutes. Then he said in a firm voice, "Be quiet, please." When a surprised silence fell, he turned to Stephen. "Mr. Middleton, I wish I could give you better news. But do not give up! In a few days, we will have our answer."

Stephen, who had known from the first moment the groom had brought the news what the answer must be, took a deep breath. "And if I have the disease? How long do I have?" His voice was so low, so controlled that his two friends exchanged worried glances. When Stephen hid his emotions, he was in deep pain, pain he did not allow anyone to share.

Langston listened to the doctor explain that if Stephen had the disease he would begin to show signs in seven to ten days if it progressed in a normal fashion. He thought about the first time he had watched Stephen hide his pain from the world. They had been at school, eagerly awaiting the summer holidays. Then Stephen had received a letter from his father telling him that his new stepmother was too nervous to have a boy his age underfoot all summer. He would have to go to one of their other estates. Instantly, Langston had declared Stephen would spend the summer with him. Even though Stephen had agreed, it had taken Langston and Jane all summer to overcome his feeling of rejection.

He pulled out of his reverie to hear Stephen say, "I will leave for London as soon as Vernon packs."

"Nonsense." Langston and the doctor looked at each other. Then the younger man signaled the older to continue.

"You cannot leave." Both Langston and Jane let out the breath they had been holding. "I want you here where I can keep an eye on you. You may make your condition worse by traveling. And you will want to know what happens to the dogs," the doctor said firmly.

"But you told me to get my affairs in order."

"A figure of speech," the doctor assured him. "Besides, the mail coaches can deliver a letter very speedily these days. I want you to stay here."

"What if I am a danger to those around me?" Stephen asked, his eyes on Jane, whose hand he still clasped tightly.

"It will not come to that," the doctor assured him. He gathered his belongings. "Call me if there is any change or if the dogs show any signs of the disease."

Langston walked him to the door, closing the door to the study behind them carefully. "Is there anything else I should know?" he asked the doctor.

"Do not let him brood too much. Keep him occupied. And if there is any change, call me at once!" The doctor accepted his hat and cane from Smythe. He pushed up his glasses once more. "Keep those dogs penned and watch them carefully."

When Langston returned to the study, Stephen and Jane were still sitting in the same positions, neither speaking. Stephen, his face as white as newly fallen snow, had his eyes closed. In Jane's large green eyes, tears welled, threatening to spill over. At the sound of the door closing, Jane turned around, blinking rapidly to try to control her tears. Langston took his seat, staring at his friend, wondering how a man who looked so full of life and health might be dying. "It is not fair," he burst out.

Stephen opened his eyes, let go of Jane's hand, and stood up. He brushed back the lock of hair that persisted in falling on his forehead despite his and Vernon's best efforts. He swallowed. "What? Life?" he asked wearily.

"You did nothing," his friend explained. "It should have been I. They are my dogs." Jane, her eyes full of pain, shuddered at the thought of losing either of them. Curiously, she noted and then pushed to the back of her mind the information that the loss of either would bring her pain.

"This is not your fault, Langston," Stephen said firmly. "You could have easily been the one bitten."

"But I was not." Langston got up once more and walked toward his friend. Putting his hands on Stephen's shoulders and ignoring his attempts to pull away, he demanded, "Tell me how I may help."

"Help?" Stephen laughed bitterly, thinking of the fate that awaited him. "Help?" He laughed again wildly.

"Stop it!" Jane cried, jumping up to face him. "You heard the doctor. He is not sure you have rabies."

"No? Then why did he tell me to put my affairs in order?" Stephen asked angrily. He stormed out of the room.

"Follow him, Langston. He should not be alone," Jane ordered. Her former fiancé nodded and hurried off. Jane sighed. Then she rushed upstairs.

Chapter Four

The next twenty-four hours were difficult. For much of the time, Stephen stayed in his room, refusing to see anyone except Vernon. When Langston tried to get him to open the door, Stephen ignored him, continuing his pacing around the room like a tiger in a cage at the Royal Exchange. The last time Langston tried to gain entrance, Vernon opened the door and slipped out. A crash sounded against the door, and the two of them jumped.

"You had best leave him to me, my lord," Vernon suggested. "He is in no state for company."

"What is he doing?"

"Mostly pacing. Sometimes he writes and then tears the paper to pieces. And I am sorry to report, my lord, that he has broken some of the ornaments about the room," Vernon said, hanging his head.

"A few ornaments are nothing." Langston turned around to walk away and then paused. "He will not do anything to harm himself, will he?" he asked, his voice breaking on the last word. He turned back around so that he was facing the valet.

"Not Mr. Middleton!" Vernon's voice was sharp. He glared at his master's friend as if indignant that anyone would even suggest such a thing.

"Good." Langston breathed a sigh of relief. "Stay with him. And send for me as soon as he will see me." He waited until Vernon had slipped back into the room and then made his way to the sitting room where the ladies waited.

"How is the poor boy?" his mother asked, raising a lace-edged handkerchief to her eyes. "You did tell him, did you not, that he is not to give in to despair?" Her son did not answer. She asked again, her voice sharper, "Well, did you?"

"He would not talk to me," her son admitted.

"Not talk to you. You are his host. Of course, he will talk to you. Go right up there again!"

"No, Mama. I will not." Langston turned to face her, his face set in harsh lines. "Stephen has asked to be left alone, and I, for one, will respect his wishes. Good night, Mama, Jane!"

"Good night? Where are you going? Langston? Jane, Jane, stop him!" the older lady demanded.

Watching the man whom she had once thought her whole world practically run from the room, Jane wished that she too could escape. As soon as she had returned to the older lady's suite, Lady Langston had pried and poked until she knew everything that Langston and Jane had observed. Then she had begun speculating. With Langston gone, Jane realized that she had several nerve-wracking hours before her. Although her own imagination was quite vivid and had already presented her with several shocking conclusions to Stephen's problem, Lady Langston persisted in inventing several more lurid ones.

"Jane, did you hear what I said?" Lady Langston asked peevishly. "Make him come back."

"I cannot do that, my lady," Jane mumbled.

"Of course, you can. You were always able to make him listen to you." Lady Langston tapped her cheek with her fan. "In fact, I was quite jealous of you and Stephen for some time."

"Jealous of me?" Jane turned to look at her employer.

"Years ago. The first summer Stephen came to stay with us. Langston never wanted to be with me," Lady Langston said wistfully. Then she smiled. "Later I realized that he was simply growing up. I blamed it on his school, too. I never wanted him to leave home, but his father had put his name down at Harrow as soon as he was born. If his executor had not insisted on his going, Stephen would not be here today in the situation he is in."

"You cannot know that. He and Langston might have met in some other way," Jane said quietly, surprised at the lady's revelations.

"I suppose. But it is quite lowering to think of that handsome boy at death's door."

"The doctor is not certain." Jane realized that she was trying to convince herself as much as Lady Langston.

"Stephen seems to be."

"We must hope for the best and pray," Jane reminded her, wishing that she could believe her own words.

"Always positive. You are a joy to me, Jane. I only wish my son were so supportive." Before she could continue her complaint, Smythe entered and announced dinner. "Have I told you how much I enjoy having you with me?"

Jane blushed and shook her head, wondering at Lady Langston's unusual manner. Busy with her friends and correspondence, the lady rarely shared more than the latest gossip.

"If we two are to be the only ones at dinner, we must not keep Cook waiting. You know how she dislikes having her meal grow cold," Lady Langston said with a laugh as she took Jane's arm. She continued as though the revelations of a few moments previous had never happened. "I wonder if she will be willing to come to us when we return to Bath? Although Jacques's meals were quite good, I have missed Cook's way with the simple dishes."

Persuading Lady Langston that having two chefs was not a good idea took Jane most of the evening and kept her mind off Stephen. Only when her employer was arrayed in her nightdress and comfortably resting in her bed, did Jane have time to consider Stephen's dilemma. Before she sought her own bed, she crept down the hall to Stephen's room.

Raising her hand to knock, she dropped it, realizing the impropriety of her action. She put her cheek to the door as if by touching the wood that divided Stephen from the world she could take away some of his hurt. As Langston had told her earlier, he was still pacing. Or someone was. She sighed. Hearing a noise behind her, she turned.

"What are you doing here? Mooning over him?" Langston asked, his voice bitter and slurred. "It will do you no good."

"What?"

"I have seen you with him, laughing, letting him told your hand. He is not such a good catch now, is he?" Langston's once impeccable garments were wrinkled, and his neckcloth was untied. He stared at her with reproach in his brown eyes.

"What are you talking about, Langston?" Jane asked, not certain that she wanted an answer. Although she knew that he and Stephen drank, she was surprised to see him castaway for the second night in a row. She pulled him away from the door.

"Do not want him to hear, do you? Well, I could tell him things," Langston laughed harshly.

"I will talk to you in the morning," Jane said, turning to walk away, wondering if Langston had changed in the year they had been apart or if she simply had been too blinded by emotion in the past to see him clearly.

He grabbed her arm and pulled her toward him. "You will talk to me now," he said, his voice rising angrily.

"Not here," she said firmly, trying to pull away from his painful grasp. She was frightened, but she was determined not to show it. Somehow he seemed more dangerous than Stephen had the evening before.

"Where?"

"The study?"

Releasing her, he stepped back but stayed between Jane and the hall to her room. Having no other choice, she walked down the stairs, Langston only a step behind her. She rubbed her arm, knowing that she would have bruises there the next day. As soon as he closed the study door behind them, Jane asked, "What is this about?"

"You know."

"If I did, I would not be asking," she said angrily. She crossed the room and took a seat in a chair facing him, her gray skirts drawn in carefully as though by controlling them she was controlling herself.

"You and Stephen." Langston sat on the arm of a chair across the room and glared at her. The rage he had felt that morning as he entered the breakfast room threatened to swamp him.

"Stephen and I? What do you mean?"

"I saw you yesterday and this morning. You were holding his hand."

"And?" Jane's voice grew icy with indignation. She glared at him, not wanting to believe that he would deny their friend her company or that he would dare criticize her actions.

"And I do not approve!" Langston pulled another chair close to hers, sat, and reached for her hand. Jane moved back as far as she could and kept her hands tightly clasped together.

"I believe you gave up any rights to approve or disapprove of my actions a year ago," she said bitterly.

"I explained." He ran his hand through his blond hair, completely destroying any semblance of order that it had. He seemed to shrink into the chair.

"And I said money did not matter to me. But you disagreed." She took a deep breath, trying to gain mastery over her still lacerated emotions. "Now if you will excuse me, it is time I went to my own room. I do not see that we can accomplish anything by continuing this conversation." She stood up and put the chair between them. He stepped toward her, his hand out. "Do not touch me again, my lord," she said between clenched teeth.

Langston stepped back, his eyes anguished. "I will not have it. Remember that!" He watched as she walked from the room, her shoulders set angrily.

Then he picked up the brandy decanter. Seeing it almost empty, he pulled the bell.

"Another bottle," he demanded when the sleepy servant appeared.

The night was long for all three of the friends. Stephen paced his room. From the moment the doctor had acknowledged that his fears were valid, he had wanted to run away, to hide, to pretend that nothing had happened. But he could not leave. Once that evening he had even told Vernon to pack his belongings. His valet had looked at him and started to say something. Then he changed his mind. Pulling the portmanteau from its storage place, he pulled open one drawer.

"Put that away," Stephen said a few minutes later, his voice breaking. He lay down on the bed for a moment, staring at the curtains above his head. "I do not want to die, Vernon," he said softly.

The valet did not know what to say. He simply nodded.

"Go to bed, Vernon," his master ordered, tired of the sympathetic glances the valet kept giving him.

"But, sir!"

"Go to bed."

"Yes, sir." The valet walked toward the door, his face sad. Taking advantage of the fact that he had served Middleton since the lad had been at Cambridge, he turned. "Do not give up hope. Remember, even the doctor was not certain."

His reminder echoed in Stephen's mind for the rest of the night. By morning he had made up his mind what he was going to do.

When Stephen appeared at the breakfast table the next morning as though nothing had happened, Jane was startled. She choked on her chocolate, only able to stammer, "M—morning" to his greeting. Looking as though he had had a good night's sleep instead of pacing around his room, Stephen helped himself to a slice of beef and some rolls.

"Is there ale?" he asked the footman who had filled his plate.

"Yes, sir." The footman filled his mug to the brim. Jane, still struggling with what to say, watched as he downed one mug and requested another.

"Stephen, is there anything I can do?" she finally got out, her voice still uneven.

"No. I have decided that Dr. Clarke is right. I must wait to see how the dogs are doing. When I visited their kennels a few minutes ago, all of them were fine," he said firmly. Then he looked at her again. As she had been every day since she had arrived, she was dressed in a dull gray gown. "Do you have anything that is not mourning?"

"I beg your pardon?" Jane's voice grew cold. Although Lady Langston had often begged her to wear brighter colors, she was unaccustomed to anyone else's questioning her apparel.

"It was only a suggestion. Surely you know that those gowns do little to enhance your beauty." For once Stephen was not thinking about how his words would affect his listener. "You look much better in green or blue."

"I am sorry that my gown does not meet with your approval. But my wardrobe is limited," she said angrily, putting her cup down with a clink. She wondered how she had ever admired him. Her voice and her glaring eyes warned Stephen to choose his words carefully. Instead, he ignored the hints.

He downed another mug of ale and signaled for a third. "Sorry. I forgot your changed circumstances." He lifted his mug and drank deeply. "How are your mother and brother and sister? Will you have a chance to visit them while Lady Langston is visiting her daughters?" Jane stared at him, wondering if she were hearing him correctly. He drank deeply again and then, as if her silence spurred him on, broached the question he had wanted to ask since he had seen her again. "Why did you not let me know about your broken engagement?" he asked after the silence had stretched uncomfortably between them.

Although she had not dreamed it would be possible, Jane was pleased when Langston came into the room only moments later. Still feeling out of sorts, he made his way to the table and took a seat next to her. "I believe I owe you an apology," Langston said as he sat down.

"An apology? For what?" Stephen asked as he emptied his mug once more. He motioned to the footman.

"Is that ale? Give me some," Langston demanded. Squinting, he inspected his friend. "Any symptoms?"

"Langston!" Jane protested.

"I am sure you wanted to know, too," her former fiancé replied. He took a deep drink of ale, closed his eyes for a moment, savoring its richness. "You seem more in spirits today, Stephen."

"Ale, my lad, ale," his friend laughed, holding up his mug for more. "And the dogs seem healthy." He glanced at the small mark on his hand and then put his hand in his lap so that he would have no reminders. "Shall we ride this morning?"

"Ride?" Langston asked, marveling at his friend's attitude.

"The morning is too beautiful to stay inside." He smiled at Jane. "Will you join us, Jane?" he asked, ignoring Langston's frown.

"No, thank you. Lady Langston will have need of me," she said, grateful that she could escape both Langston's frowns and Stephen's questions. As if her words were a signal to summon him, a footman entered and approached her.

"Lady Langston requests your presence, Miss Stanfield," he said with a bow. Jane made her farewells and slipped away.

"Well, it will be just you and me, Middleton," Langston said, drinking the last of his ale. His formality made Stephen raise his eyebrows. "Have you any place you want to go?"

"No. I just do not want to stay inside another minute," Stephen said, his hand closing tightly around his mug of ale.

"Then, we're off."

By the time they returned late that afternoon, they were both less than steady on their feet. Riding through the village, Stephen had insisted that they stop for something to drink. They had stayed all afternoon, drinking and gambling. Stephen's resolve of the morning to ignore his problem quickly faded before the villagers' curiosity. "He don't look sick," he heard one man say, his voice booming.

The barmaid, a buxom woman who liked to flirt, refused to come near him once she realized what had happened to him. "What if he touches me? I don't want no rabies," she told the innkeeper.

"Would he be here if he was sick? Serve the gentlemen!" ordered the innkeeper.

"Serve him yourself," the barmaid said, tossing her head and taking a deep breath. "Or don't expect to visit me tonight." Looking around to see if his wife had heard the girl, he nodded.

"Innkeeper, some food," Langston ordered, finally realizing that Stephen intended to stay where they were. Still angry with his friend for his attentions to Jane, he was feeling guilty, too. It was his dog that had bitten Stephen. That thought remained with him during the ride home and dinner.

By the time the ladies left the dining room after dinner, Stephen could no longer keep his worries at bay. "We need to inspect the dogs," he said, slurring his words so that Langston could hardly understand what he said.

"Nonsense. Anything wrong and we would have been told," his friend reminded him, pouring him another glass of port.

"Must see the dogs," Stephen said again, standing up and pushing his chair back so that it fell on the floor. He held on to the edge of the table to steady himself.

"Cannot walk that far, old man," Langston said apologetically after he had tried to stand and could not.

The footmen who had come in to clear the table looked at one another but were careful not to allow their emotions to show. Stephen took a few steps, wobbling so much that he sat down again in the chair Jane had recently vacated. "I am dying," he said in mournful tones. "Cannot walk."

"Neither can I."

Stephen stared at him, his eyes wide. "Don't want you to die, too."

"Fetch Mr. Smythe," one footman whispered to another.

Before the ladies finished their tea and decided to retire for the evening, the gentlemen were safely in their rooms in the hands of their valets.

Vernon undressed his master, shaking his head.

When he arrived with hot water to shave Stephen the next morning, he was still shaking his head. He pulled the curtains back from around the bed and at the windows, waiting for his master's complaint. It never came. Stephen just lay there, his eyes open, his face bleak.

"The dogs are still well, sir," the valet said, hoping to break his master's mood. Stephen's only response was a nod. "Shall I lay out riding clothes, sir?"

Stephen closed his eyes for a moment. Then he sat up in bed. Ignoring the problem by trying to drown himself in liquor the day before had not made it go away. "No."

His valet waited for other instructions. When the silence grew uncomfortable, he asked, "Shall I shave you?"

Stephen ran a hand over his chin and nodded. He swung his legs over the bed and stood up. "Did you put me to bed last night, Vernon?"

"Yes, sir." The valet's voice was steady and calm, hiding his worry. "If you would sit down?" he suggested.

By the time he was dressed in the dark blue jacket and fawn pantaloons, Stephen's calm had been replaced by carefully controlled anger. Had he not accepted Langston's invitation, this would never have happened. His head still pounding from his excesses the evening before, he walked downstairs and into the breakfast room. He accepted a cup of coffee but refused anything else. Soon he retired to the study.

Sometime later, Langston found him there, surrounded by crumpled paper. "The grooms tell me the dogs show no signs of illness," he said with a smile.

"Vernon told me," said Stephen as calmly as he could, his anger boiling just below the surface.

"What are you doing?" his friend asked curiously, no more aware of the undercurrents than he had ever been.

"Doing? Why do you not see? I am taking my emotions out on paper."

"Did notice you had created quite some disturbance. Shall I send for more paper?" Langston asked, looking around the room at the crumpled masses.

"Why?" His friend's voice was cold.

Langston looked at him curiously, wondering what was going on in Stephen's head. The behavior Stephen had been showing the last few days was not one he was familiar with. "You must be running out," he said calmly.

"Of time?" Stephen asked, his words cold with suppressed anger.

"No, paper." Langston paused, "You did hear me. The dogs are doing fine. What is wrong?"

"Wrong? Other than the possibility that I am dying?" Stephen asked, his face contorted with anger.

"It is still just a possibility," his friend said soothingly. "Shall I send for the doctor? Are you ill?"

"No more than yesterday. Except for this cursed head." He ran his fingers through his hair, pushing the lock that fell on his forehead back into place. Although he was not sure he wanted it to, Stephen felt his anger receding.

"I know. Mine is pounding. Always say I will never drink that much again." Langston sat down, eyeing the brandy decanter longingly. "What do you want to do today? According to the grooms, the trout are biting."

Stephen considered the idea for a moment and then shook his head. The motion did nothing to ease his pounding headache. "I must make plans."

"Plans? Thought you were going to stay with me for a while," Langston asked, frowning.

"For what may happen."

"Thought you said nothing could be done."

"Not that kind of plan. I need to contact my agents and my solicitor. Just in case," Stephen said quietly.

"In case of what?" Langston looked at his friend and then murmured, "Oh."

As though he had not heard what Langston had said, Stephen continued, "I start but cannot finish." He nodded at the crumpled papers strewn around the room. "What I need to do is go to London."

"You heard the doctor. He wants you to stay here," Langston cautioned.

"I could be back by tomorrow night if I traveled on horseback," Stephen reminded him. Getting away from the manor, even if only for twenty-four hours, had great appeal.

"But what if something happened? You cannot go." Before they had finished discussing the situation, Smythe called them to luncheon.

Unlike her two gentlemen friends, Jane had time to think the day before, and she had been up early that morning. As she walked in the garden, she thought of the way Langston had treated her two evenings before. Her mouth narrowed and her eyes flashed. How dare he try to control her behavior! Even his apology had done little to soothe her. In fact, their absence had allowed her anger to build.

Whenever Lady Langston had sent for her, she erased her anger from her face, but it simmered beneath the surface. Finally finished with the correspondence that morning, she and Lady Langston made their way to the sitting room, each working on a piece of needlework. The quiet time gave her time to rehearse her grievances.

During luncheon, she ignored Langston, keeping her attention focused on her employer and Stephen. Langston tried to catch her eye, but she refused to look at him. Stephen looked from one to the other of his friends, his eyes narrowing. Lady Langston, realizing that something had happened between her son and her companion, chose to ignore the situation.

"Jane and I will be making calls in the neighborhood this afternoon. Would you two gentlemen care to accompany us?" she asked coquettishly.

Langston's no was so loud that his mother stared at him. "I think Stephen and I should stay here. In case something happens," he added quickly, trying to cover his hasty words.

Stephen stared at him, opened his mouth to disagree, and then realized that if he were going to London, he could not accompany them. "I think Langston is right," he said quietly, glancing at Jane. Only the smallest hint of disappointment marred her face. She hid it quickly. Langston's lips smiled at his friend's answer, but his eyes did not.

A short time later, Stephen handed Jane into the carriage, his hand hesitating before releasing hers. He stepped back. The two gentlemen watched as the carriage pulled away.

"She is not for you," Langston said quietly, too quietly, his eyes were filled with anguish.

"Who?"

"Jane."

Stephen followed his friend into the manor, too conscious of the servants to answer him. As soon as they were once more in the study with the door closed, he turned. "What did you mean?" he asked, his tone revealing his anger.

"About what?"

"Jane." He waited until the silence grew. Then he said, "Do not do this, Langston. We have all been friends too long."

"Too long for you to forget that Jane is mine."

"I thought you said you were marrying someone else. Have you changed your mind?" Stephen asked him, wondering not for the first time how much his friend had changed.

"No. That does not change anything. Jane is mine," Langston said, his voice sharp.

"Langston! Listen to yourself, man. Do you plan to make her your mistress? Is that why you had your mother hire her as her companion?" Stephen's words lashed his friend. Langston winced as he realized what he had said.

"No. I did not want Mother to hire Jane. I tried to persuade her the idea was wrong, but she insisted." Langston's voice was frantic. He buried his face in his hands.

"And now?" Stephen took several deep breaths to calm himself and forced the disgust from his voice. "What are your plans for Jane now?"

"Nothing, I promise you. I never knew how much I missed her until I saw her again." He sighed, closing his eyes. "She will have nothing to do with me."

"Langston, you made your choice," Stephen said as calmly as he could. He thought of Jane and wondered what would happen to her, forced as she was to keep on seeing her former fiancé. "You cannot do this to Jane."

"To Jane. You mean to you," Langston said angrily, the

remorse he had felt just seconds before evaporating. "I have seen the two of you together."

Stephen flinched. Had Langston seen him kiss Jane a few days before? "What are you talking about?" he demanded.

"Holding her hand, catching her eye, smiling at her. You did all of those things," Langston accused him. "I saw you in the garden, in the breakfast room. What are your intentions?"

"Have you forgotten that Jane and I are friends?"

"Only because you came home with me." Once more Langston's tone was petulant.

Stephen took another deep breath. "You are right." He paused as an idea came to him. "Have you changed your mind about your engagement to Jane? Do you plan to ask her to accept you again?" He walked over to the window, trying to achieve a degree of calmness. Even if Langston said no, he had no right to claim her.

"I cannot," Langston murmured, his face an anguished mask. "But she has always been mine."

"That never bothered you in London. Have you given up your ladybird?" Stephen reminded him, his eyes and tone censorious.

"You never understood. A man must have variety."

Stephen frowned. "Langston, I do not want to quarrel with you. And if I stay here, I probably will. I think I should return to London," he said when he could trust himself to speak again.

"No. You cannot. Dr. Clarke insists that you remain. You heard him," Langston said frantically. "I will say no more. You are right. It is simply the strain of having Jane in my house. I will be fine once she is gone. There is no one in London to care for you if you are ill. I cannot let you go."

"Vernon will be with me. Besides, I need to make arrangements in case the worst happens," Stephen said, his eyes reflecting his sadness. "I must solve my problems with my stepmother," he reminded him.

"Stay here. My dog bit you; therefore, the problem is mine." Langston cajoled. "Let me help—" He stopped, a crafty look crossing his face. "You stay here. I will go to London for you."

"You cannot make the arrangements."

"No, but I can send your solicitor or agents down to see you. And they will come more quickly for me than if we merely sent a groom with the message," Langston said. He smiled, the same persuasive smile that he had used when he wanted someone to do something for him.

"And you will escape once more," Stephen said softly, his eyes on his friend's face. Langston's smile faded, and he nodded.

"Even Mama will not be able to find fault with my actions," Langston added, his face set in uncompromising lines. "Let me go!"

After thinking for a few minutes, Stephen realized that Langston had offered the best solution. "By the time you are changed and ready to leave, I will have the note for my solicitor ready. He will contact my agents." He watched his friend cross the room. When the door closed behind Langston, he took a seat at the desk. Dashing off a note to his solicitor, Stephen signed his name with a flourish. Then a peculiar look crossed his face, a militant light lit his eyes, and he added another line.

Chapter Five

By the time the ladies returned from their afternoon with friends, Langston had been gone for several hours. During that time Stephen had sat first in the study and then in the library, consumed by thoughts of what might happen. Unable to concentrate on reading, he began pacing again.

Although he knew he needed to stay at the manor, Stephen worried what would happen to his family if the worst were to happen. His stepmother, he knew, cared only for herself: the events of the last eighteen months certainly proved that. She would complain about the need for mourning and then adhere to it strictly, too interested in the opinion of the *haut ton* to ignore its dictates. His half-sister Caroline, however, would be devastated.

He smiled as he remembered the letters he and Caroline had exchanged during the time he had been in Canada. She was interested in everything. When he remembered the quick trip he had made into the country to take her the gifts he had brought her, he frowned. Although Caroline was twelve, almost thirteen, her clothes had made her seem younger. And she was so much alone, left to the care of her governess and the servants. Perhaps he should send her to school. Her mother would resist the idea, but he was the child's guardian. Once again he frowned. What would happen to Caroline if he died?

The sounds of a carriage arriving brought him out of his dark thoughts. He walked into the hallway as Lady Langston and Jane entered the house. "Did you have an enjoyable afternoon?" he asked casually, as though he had no worries at all.

Lady Langston smiled at him and handed Smythe her shawl and bonnet. "How satisfying to see old friends," she said. "Since they did not come to London this year, I was able to give them all the news." She beamed at him. Then, as though she had just remembered his problem, she asked, "How are you feeling, dear boy?" Her face and her voice were suitably somber.

"Very well." His words restored her happiness. "I am simply bored with my own company," he explained, looking at Jane.

"Your own company? Where is Langston?" Lady Langston demanded, her voice sharp.

"He is on his way to London."

"London! Why how dare—" Langston's mother began.

Stephen cut her off. "To run errands for me. I need to talk to my solicitor, and Langston has gone to get him." Watching Jane's face, he saw her relax slightly.

"Just as he should. At least the boy has some sense left," the older lady declared. "Jane, I will go to my room. I am simply exhausted. I must rest before dinner." She swept up the stairs.

When Jane would have followed her, Stephen reached for her arm. She flinched when he inadvertently touched one of the bruises that Langston had left on her arms. He stepped back. "Do not go," he suggested.

She looked up at him, confused. As Lady Langston had preened and displayed herself to the neighborhood that afternoon, she had sat quietly. Most of her former neighbors did not know what to say to her. She was a too vivid reminder of the vagaries of human existence. Although Langston had consumed most of her thoughts, Stephen had also played his part. Since her father's death and Langston's desertion the year before, she had convinced herself that no man would ever look at her again. But Stephen had proved her wrong. Was he merely flirting with her? The words hung on her lips unspoken.

"Please," Stephen begged, surprised at how willing he was to let her know he wanted her company. Once again she was draped in gray that dulled the brightness of her hair and eyes. He longed to see her in blue, any color but gray or black.

"Stephen, I do not think . . ."

"Just for a short time. Pour my tea. You always know just how I like it," he pleaded, surprised at his own persistence.

Already awash with tea, Jane agreed, shocked by her acceptance. "For just a little while," she said quietly. Smythe, an interested observer, made his way into the kitchen and gave the order for tea.

"Do you have any of Miss Jane's favorite biscuits?" Smythe asked. When the engagement between his master and Miss Stanfield had been dissolved, he had been as shocked as anyone. Jane had always been a favorite of his. Her quiet demeanor as Lady Langston's companion had simply added to his admiration. "And put some bread and butter on the plate. Master Stephen ate little at luncheon."

While Smythe was giving his orders, Stephen led Jane into the sitting room. He sat beside her on the settee. "Has this visit been difficult for you?" he asked, longing to take her hand in his.

Jane, her eyes carefully downcast, brought her head up sharply, staring at him. Deciding that he was simply trying to make conversation, she took a deep breath. "Everyone has been very kind," she said quietly.

"Even Mrs. Marston?" he asked, surprise in his voice.

"Lady Langston has not yet visited her," Jane said primly. Her eyes danced.

"Lucky you. Do you remember how she caught us swimming?"

"Us? As I remember, you and Langston were the ones in the water. I was merely dangling my feet over the edge," she reminded him, her voice amused. She smiled wistfully, wishing that those days were not gone forever.

"Your mother did not accept that argument then, as I remember. You spent two weeks in your room."

"And you and Langston merely went without dinner," Jane said as indignant now as she had been then.

"But a lady must always—"

"If you say another word, Stephen Middleton, I will leave you alone." Her eyes sparkled, and indignation made her cheeks rosy.

"Not that. Never that," he begged, his smile mischievous. Then suddenly he was serious once more. "I can never tell you how much your company means to me now," he said quietly, his face somber.

"Oh, Stephen—" She could not go on. She glanced down at her clasped hands and blinked fiercely to keep her tears from overflowing. "Are you certain you are all right? Do you wish me to have Smythe call Dr. Clarke?"

"I am fine. It is the uncertainty. I have never liked to wait," he said soothingly.

"You were always better than Langston. Remember how he used to search for his birthday presents?"

"He was terrible. He would find them and then be disappointed when he had no surprises for his birthday," Stephen said. He smiled at her, enjoying her animation. Before he thought his words out carefully, he asked, "What went wrong?"

All of Jane's brightness disappeared, and her polite mask reappeared. But she didn't pretend to misunderstand his question. "I do not know," she whispered. Once again she blinked back her tears.

"He has changed." She nodded, unable to say anything. "Was I so unobservant before I left? Or has this happened just while I was gone?" he wondered. When she did not answer, he continued his musings. "I always knew he resented having his money tied up in trust."

"And as soon as it was released, he gambled it away," she said bitterly.

"I was surprised when you did not marry after your second Season," Stephen added.

"Both he and my father thought I was still too young and that a long engagement would be best. Langston said that was the only way he could make a proper settlement on me," she said, her voice lifeless as she repeated an explanation she had given many times. "Mother and I tried to convince them that it was foolish to wait, but it did no good.

Knowing what I do now, I realize that Father had invested my dowry in one of his money-making schemes and was hoping to have time to retrieve it." Surprised at her honesty, she was silent for a moment, staring at her hands clasped in her lap. Stephen picked up her hand, holding it tightly in his own. She took a deep breath and added, "After you left, Langston spent most of the year in London. I heard rumors of his behavior—you know what gossips are like. But I never believed that he would break—" Realizing she had said too much, Jane cut off her remarks, cursing herself under her breath.

"Then it was not a mutual decision?"

"Mutual? I had loved Langston since I was old enough to be interested in boys," Jane said, relieved to have someone with whom she could be honest. It had been so long since she had talked with her mother. Even though Lady Langston was sympathetic, Jane had to watch her words. Langston was her son. "But now." She paused. Surprise flitted across her face as she thought about her feelings. She pulled her hand loose and moved farther away from him.

"Now?" Stephen prodded, intrigued by her tone.

Fortunately, Smythe entered with the tea tray at that moment, saving Jane from a reply. As she poured the tea and handed Stephen his cup, Jane pondered what she had been about to say. Was she fickle? Only a year ago she had wanted to marry Langston. When Stephen urged her to continue, she asked, "Now it is your turn. How is your sister?"

The question was the opening that Stephen had been waiting for. After telling Jane about the girl, he paused and sighed. "I worry what will happen to her if I am not around to check on her."

"What do you mean?"

"Apparently my stepmother resents having a daughter as old as Caroline. And in the eighteen months I was gone she managed to waste a large portion of Caroline's inheritance on herself. She is very good at twisting the trustees around her fingers. Fortunately, my solicitor let me know what was happening, and I returned to take charge." He frowned. "What will happen when it is time to present Caroline I do not know." He sighed again and frowned, his eyes on his cup of tea. When he looked up again, he was pleased to see the concern on her face.

"Can't you do something?" she asked.

"If I am here, certainly. I am her guardian. If I am not . . ." He paused dramatically.

"Surely there is someone in your family—" Jane began.

He interrupted her with a bitter laugh. "Surely you have not forgotten. I am singularly unblessed with family. My stepmother, Caroline, an old cousin who retired from the world years ago, and I are all that are left. And I do not trust my stepmother's relatives. They are too interested in themselves."

"What are you going to do?"

"Perhaps my solicitor will think of something." He frowned and looked at his hand, no longer trying to win her sympathy. "This damned bite. It has destroyed everything."

"Nonsense. As long as the other dogs are healthy, surely you must be, too," she reminded him.

"That is assuming the spaniel bit one of them," he told her. That idea had disturbed his afternoon.

"It must have. Think about the way they bite and snap at each other," she said.

"Perhaps you are right," he said, handing her his cup for more tea. He took a bite of bread and butter. "How comfortable this is." He smiled at her. She smiled back.

She picked up her needlework where she had left it that morning. As she worked, she glanced at him under the cover of her long lashes, noting the breadth of his shoulders and the way his tanned skin made his eyes seem bluer than usual. She wondered why she had never noticed how handsome he was.

As he finished his tea, Stephen was aware of her glances. Using no pretenses, he stared at her. Although dimmed by the mourning that she wore, she was still a beautiful woman, lovelier by far than the latest bevy of beauties who had graced the *ton*. Even though he had avoided parties while he was waiting for Weston to complete his new clothing, he had ridden in the park. Every mother with an unattached daughter in tow had arranged an introduction. None suited him as much as Jane. The idea that had been on his mind since she had arrived and Langston had made it clear he had given up claim to her pushed its way forward once more. "I had planned to marry," he said into the comfortable silence.

Jane stuck her finger with her needle and hurriedly put it in her mouth. "Are you all right?" he asked, a frown creasing his brow.

"Just careless. Have I met the young lady?" she asked carefully, only the tension in her shoulders revealing her interest.

"What young lady?"

"The one you planned to marry. I did not read of your engagement in the gazettes," she explained.

Stephen laughed. "There is no young lady. At least not yet. But if the crowd of flibbertigibbets I met in London is an example of the current crop, I may remain single," he explained, noting with satisfaction when she dropped her needlework on her lap and smiled at him.

"I am certain you are too critical. I met some pleasant young ladies during afternoon calls this spring," she said.

"You have one thing right. They are young. Were we ever as silly as they?" he asked, turning slightly so that he could look at her more closely.

"We must have been. Remember . . ." The rest of the afternoon passed so pleasantly that they were both surprised by the bell to dress for dinner. As Stephen walked up the stairs toward his room, he smiled, forgetting the uncertainty in which he lived.

That pleasant mood remained until the following morning. Once again the head groom interrupted them while they were lingering over breakfast. He entered, his hat in his hands, his face worried. "What is wrong?" Stephen asked, certain he knew the answer.

"It's one of the dogs, Mr. Middleton. Before he left, my lord gave me orders to let you know if any of them hounds acted peculiarly."

Jane gasped and covered her mouth with hand. Stephen's face hardened. "Well," he demanded.

"One of the pups is sickening for something. Won't eat," the groom told him. "Put it in a pen by itself as Dr. Clarke said."

Stephen thanked him, his voice expressionless. "Let us know what happens," he said quietly as though the man's words had not dashed what little hopes he had had.

"Should I send for Dr. Clarke?" Jane asked, her eyes wide. The thought of losing Stephen was more than she thought she could bear. She wanted to go to him, to put her arms around him, but she knew she could not.

"No!" Stephen bit off the word and closed his lips so tightly that they became a thin white line. He sat at the table, staring at the jam pot and empty teacup as though they could reveal an answer. The silence stretched uncomfortably between them. Jane pushed back her chair, getting up. "Do not go," he begged.

Startled, she sat back down. "Lady Langston expects me," she said quietly.

"I do not want to be alone," Stephen told her, his voice breaking on the last word.

"I will talk to her and come right back down. I will meet you." She paused. Then, as though she had come to some decision, she said, "In the garden?"

"Do you promise?" His voice was more like that of the boy she had known than the man he had become.

"I promise," she whispered, hoping her employer would understand.

Fortunately, Lady Langston, horrified by the news, had insisted that Jane bear him company. "I worry about Stephen, Jane," she said. "He is too much alone. That stepmother of his has much to answer for. Go to him. If only Langston had not gone to London."

Once again Jane found Stephen in the garden, seated on a bench, his head in his hands. She sighed and walked toward him, wondering what she could say. When she realized that she was there, he reached out and took her hand, pulling her down to the bench beside him, much as he had done when he was a boy and she needed assistance up a tree or a bank. She turned slightly so that she could see his face. Involuntarily, her free hand rose to brush back the lock of hair that had fallen on his forehead.

Capturing that hand as well, he held them tightly. "Oh, Jane," he murmured, his voice shaky.

"Stephen." The one word conveyed all her sympathy and despair. For a time they were silent. Then Jane asked, "Have you sent for Dr. Clarke?"

"Why? He can do nothing."

"Stephen, remember. He told us to send for him if any of the dogs showed signs of illness," she said, freeing one of her hands to trace his mouth, remembering the kiss they had shared only a few days ago.

Stephen caught his breath. Then he turned his face so that his lips burned into her palm. Startled, she pulled away, blushing. "Jane," he whispered, pulling her back to him. Before she could resist, he had captured her lips. Although the kiss began softly, Stephen deepened it, coaxing her to respond. She started to pull away and then leaned closer, her arms encircling him. "Jane," he whispered against her lips. Having tried to convince herself for the last year that no man would ever find her attractive, Jane resisted and then relaxed.

Her lips parted slightly. He plundered the depths that she offered. She gasped and pulled back, freeing her hand. Startled by her own emotions, she stood up. "Jane," he pleaded, holding out his hand to her. She did not respond. "Jane, do not leave me alone!"

"I cannot stay," she whispered.

"Why?" He stood up.

She turned to stare at him. "You know. Stephen, you must not. What if one of the servants should see and report it to Lady Langston?"

"What is wrong with my kissing my friend?" he demanded.

"I am Lady Langston's companion. And do you kiss all your friends? Would you kiss Langston?" she asked, trying to make light of the situation in spite of the fact that she only wanted to stay by his side.

"Langston is a man," he reminded her.

"And I am a companion."

"And a lady, a lovely lady. Or you would be if you were dressed properly."

"Good day, Mr. Middleton," she said stiffly, turning to leave him.

In two paces he was beside her, his arms around her. She stood stiffly, not fighting his embrace. He lowered his forehead to hers and stood there, staring into her eyes until she closed them. "Do not leave me alone," he begged. Remembering the anguish in his eyes, she hesitantly agreed. She pulled free and stepped back.

"But you must send for Dr. Clarke," she insisted.

Agreeing finally, Stephen led her back into the house where she asked Smythe to send for the doctor. "What shall we do now?" he asked, his voice once again revealing his unhappiness.

She smiled. In moments like these he reminded her of her brother. Then, remembering the way he had kissed her, her eyes widened and her breath grew short. Forcing her thoughts away from the sweetness of his lips, she asked, "Did I tell you that Langston taught me to play billiards?"

"When? Are you any good?" Stephen asked, imagining her stretched to make a shot across the table.

"Shall we find out?"

"Lead on."

When Smythe showed the doctor into the billiard room sometime later, they were both laughing. But as soon as they saw him, their faces grew somber once again. "I am sorry to spoil your mirth," he said, his eyes moving from one to the other. "Is Lord Langston here?"

"He had business in London," Stephen said shortly.

Jane hastened to fill the gap. "We sent for you, Doctor. One of the pups is ill." She took a seat and urged the doctor to sit also. Stephen racked their cues and then stood behind her chair.

"And you, Mr. Middleton? Any headaches, stiffness in your neck?"

"None that I did not bring on myself."

Quickly the doctor jumped up and crossed to him. He took Stephen's head in his hands and forced him to look at him. He stepped back when the symptoms he sought were not present. "Explain," he demanded.

Stephen flushed angrily, looking at Jane, who lowered her eyes demurely. "If you must know, I had too much to drink," he said in a voice that he hoped only the doctor would hear.

"That was foolish, Mr. Middleton, most foolish but only to be expected. Probably would have done the same myself," the doctor admitted. "I would not advise it for a regular habit."

"Nor I," Stephen agreed. "Do you want to see the dog?" The doctor nodded. Jane rose to accompany them, but Stephen stopped her and asked, "Will you wait here in case my solicitor arrives?" He did not want her present when the doctor gave him the bad news. She nodded, her face as serious as his own. He squeezed her hands tightly in his own and then left. She stood staring after him for several minutes and then hurried from the room.

"Smythe, I will be with Lady Langston. Let me know as soon as Mr. Middleton and the doctor return." She realized that Stephen's request was merely an excuse to exclude her.

As she entered the older lady's room, Lady Langston looked up, put her chocolate cup back on its saucer, and laid the novel she was reading beside her. "How is he?" she asked, her normally happy voice worried.

Taking a deep breath, Jane squared her shoulders. "A bit sunk in despair," she admitted.

"Why I would wonder if he were not. And what have you two been doing?" Even though Lady Langston had sent her companion down to Stephen, she realized that her actions might bring her censure, especially from Jane's mother, one of her oldest friends. Jane would have been horrified to learn how much Lady Langston told Mrs. Stanfield in her letters, letters that Jane never got to see although she handled most of the lady's correspondence.

"We talked. And played billiards."

"Billiards! Why Langston ever taught you that game, I will never know. In my day only gentlemen played," Lady Langston complained.

"Even my mother had no objection to it," Jane reminded her.

"Well, if it keeps Stephen occupied, I suppose it is fine," the older lady said with a sigh. "Where is he now? And why are you not with him?" She sat up in bed and looked around as if she expected to see him somewhere.

"Dr. Clarke and he are inspecting the sick puppy."

"You go right back downstairs and wait for them. Then come up and tell me what you found out." Jane had reached the door when the next order came. "And tell Smythe I wish some tea. My chocolate has grown quite cold."

Jane nodded and slipped from the room. Giving Smythe Lady Langston's instructions, she made her way to the library, one of her favorite rooms in the house. Picking up the book she had been reading a few days before, she settled into a deep leather chair, forcing herself to concentrate on the words and not on memories of the way Stephen had reacted then. She had only read one page when the door opened.

"Jane?" Stephen looked around and then caught sight of her. "Do not get up."

"What has happened?" she asked, noting the smile in his eyes and on his lips. "Isn't the dog sick?"

"Oh, the poor thing is quite sick, but Dr. Clarke does not think it is rabies. He thinks the pup ate something that disagreed with him."

Jane smiled, her eyes sparkling. "Is he certain?"

Stephen frowned. "Have you ever known him not to qualify his remarks?" he reminded her.

Her smile faded slightly. "No." Then she thought again. "When my brother and sister had measles, he was very sure," she told him. Looking at him, she wished the situation now were as simple as measles. "What did he say?"

"To keep an eye on the pup and the rest of the dogs. If it was something the dog ate, it should be well in a day or two." He paced around the room, his face serious. "You should have seen the way those grooms acted, Jane. It was as though I had leprosy." He sank down in a chair near hers. "Only the head groom was willing to come near me. And those poor dogs."

"What about the dogs?"

"It was obvious that no one had groomed them in days. The men had just thrown their food over the fence, letting them fight among themselves for it. Gad, I wish Langston were here." He ran his hands through his hair. "I do not think they will obey my orders to treat them more carefully."

"Is there anything I can do?" she asked. "I know most of the men. I am certain they are merely frightened."

"Yes, of me."

"You know how suspicious they are of strange situations. You did not mention Dickson, the man who takes care of Langston's dogs. How did he react?"

"I asked for him, but the head groom said he was away. Langston gave him leave," Stephen said. He sat down and drummed his fingers on the chair.

Jane smiled at him. "At least the doctor had good news," she reminded him.

Stephen got up again and began to pace about the room. "Yes," he said shortly. He frowned.

"What is wrong now?" Jane asked, standing up and crossing to stand before him. She longed to soothe the frown from his forehead.

"Nothing." He sighed and then contradicted himself. "Everything."

"Explain." She laid her hand on his arm. His hand covered it. Taking a deep breath, he led her to the chair in which she had been seated.

Pulling his chair in front of hers, he took a seat. Capturing her hands, he stared deep into her anxious green eyes. "It's the waiting, the not knowing," he began. "If only I knew for certain."

"But every day that goes by without your showing any symptoms makes your chance of not having the disease greater," she reminded him, tightening her fingers around his. Unconsciously, he stroked her palm, sending tingles throughout her body.

"Perhaps." He sighed.

"What?"

"You are so good to listen to me, to bear with me," Stephen whispered, his blue eyes serious.

She blushed. "You would do the same for me," she reminded him. "I would be a poor friend if I deserted you now."

"And you never give up on anyone," he said quietly. The idea that she would be as supportive to any of her friends who were in trouble irritated him. Unconsciously, he tightened his hands around hers until she winced. "I am sorry," he said, bringing first one and then the other hand to his lips.

Her eyes grew wide, and her breath came quickly. She ran her tongue around her lips.

He leaned forward and captured them, his lips soft against hers. He stood up, pulling her upward with him and into his arms. Surprised, she at first tried to pull free, but he would not let her go. He kissed her more deeply, his arms wrapped around her, molding her to him. Her struggles to escape ceased. They did not hear the door open and then close again quickly.

They did hear Lady Langston ask in a clear, ringing voice, "Where are they, Smythe?"

"In the library, my lady." He held open the door and ushered her inside. By the second time she entered the room, Stephen and Jane were standing on opposite sides of the room, only their increased color and Stephen's crushed neckcloth testifying to the embrace of a few moments before.

"Well, what news did the doctor give?" Lady Langston demanded, well pleased by what she had interrupted.

As Stephen explained, Jane retreated to a chair well away from the ones where they had been sitting. Although she tried to convince herself that Stephen had kissed her merely because he needed comfort, she longed to go to her room and investigate the emotions that burned through her. She glanced at Stephen and found he was staring at her, his blue eyes warm and glowing. She blushed. He smiled and turned his attention back to Lady Langston.

After luncheon Lady Langston and Jane retired to complete their neglected correspondence. Stephen, feeling enclosed in the house much as the dogs were enclosed in their kennels, ordered his horse saddled. Leaving word that he would return before dinner and that his solicitor, if he arrived, be given a room, he galloped across the countryside. The afternoon sun warmed him and helped him clear his mind. By the time he returned, he had made a decision.

Hurrying into the house, he asked the footman who held open the door, "Where is Miss Stanfield?"

"Lady Langston and she recently retired to dress for dinner." When Stephen frowned and turned to head up the stairs himself, the footman cleared his throat.

"Yes?" Stephen turned to face him, his foot on an upper step.

"The man you were expecting arrived a short time ago. Lady Langston invited him to join her for dinner."

Stephen nodded at him and made his way to his own room. Opening the door, he walked in. "Vernon, I must change quickly," he said as he untied his neckcloth. Pleased to see his master in better spirits, the valet rushed to pour the water in the bowl.

A short time later, Stephen, dressed in an elegant blue evening jacket with his sapphire pin in the folds of his Oriental tie, brushed back the lock of hair that kept falling on his forehead. "I am not overdressed?" he asked, taking one more look in the mirror. Vernon shook his head and handed him a fresh handkerchief to tuck in his sleeve. Stephen glanced at the mirror once more and took a deep breath, feeling more nervous than before his first appearance at a *ton* party. Quickly, he made his way downstairs to the sitting room where everyone gathered before dinner.

"Is Miss Stanfield down?" he asked the footman who held the door open for him.

"You are the first, sir."

Stephen paced about the room, too nervous to sit down. The door opened, and Jane walked in, more rested than she had been that morning. Still dressed in gray, she made a vivid contrast to the gold and white of the room. Stephen walked toward her and took her hands in his, looking down into the depths of her green eyes. "Jane," he began. The door opened once more. He stepped back and dropped her hands as Abercrombie, his solicitor, walked in.

"Mr. Middleton, I have been so worried since Lord Langston informed me what has happened. Have you had any additional news? What has the doctor said today?" the man said as he hurried to stand before Stephen.

Covering his disappointment at being interrupted before he could talk to Jane, Stephen greeted the man cordially. "Where is Langston?" he asked, looking around as if expecting the man to enter the room at any moment.

"Lord Langston asked me to deliver this to you," his solicitor said as he handed Stephen a letter.

Lady Langston, who had arrived in time to hear the last statement, frowned. "And I imagine that my son has found something that requires his attention in London. Is that not right, Stephen?" Her voice was dry and raspy. She cleared her throat. "Do not try to put a good face on it. My son does not wish to see his mother."

"No, that is not true," Jane said quietly, taking her arm and leading her to a chair. "You know it is I who has driven him away." She spoke so softly that only Lady Langston could hear. Stephen quickly engaged Abercrombie in conversation, probing to discover exactly what Langston had told him.

Before the situation became too emotion laden, Smythe announced dinner. Stephen offered his arm to Lady Langston, and Jane followed with his solicitor.

Even though Cook had quite outdone herself with the dinner, saying as she did to Smythe that it might be that nice Mr. Middleton's last, only Abercrombie gave the meal the attention it deserved. Even the freshly poached trout, usually a favorite with everyone, was hardly touched. By the time the ladies withdrew to the sitting room, Cook was frantic. "What more can I do?" she wondered, mentally reviewing recipes for the morrow.

"Mr. Middleton never thinks of food when he is worried," Vernon reminded her. The others all agreed with him, each who had known Stephen Middleton as a boy supplying some story until her hurt feelings were soothed.

Stephen, sitting with his solicitor over wine, allowed the man time for only one glass. Asking a question and receiving the answer he had hoped for, he led the way to the sitting room where the ladies were drinking their tea. Jane was sitting behind the tea service while Lady Langston put a few stitches in her needlework. Looking up, Jane stared into Stephen's eyes, surprising a proprietary look. He smiled at her and refused a cup of tea, choosing a seat beside Lady Langston, leaning over to whisper something in her ear. Her eyes grew wide and worried. Then he whispered something else.

Lady Langston rose. The gentlemen stood. Taking Stephen's arm, she said, "We will return shortly," offering no explanation for her strange behavior. Jane glanced curiously at Stephen, wondering what was so important that he must speak to her employer immediately. Then a horrifying thought crossed her mind. Was it Langston? What had he done?

Left behind, Jane struggled to make conversation with Abercrombie, all the while wondering what was happening.

When they returned a few minutes later, Lady Langston was beaming. She arranged herself on the settee and picked up her needlework once more. "Do you enjoy card games, Mr. Abercrombie?" she asked.

"Yes, Lady Langston, I do." The solicitor looked around the room, recognizing that something was happening.

Engaging him in a few moments of conversation, finally, she called to Jane, "Find us some cards, dear girl, so that Mr. Abercrombie and I can play."

Jane nodded and slipped from the room. In a few seconds, Stephen followed her, his eyes watchful. Lady Langston beamed. "He will be much better for her than Langston would," she said regretfully. Then she remembered the uncertainty of Stephen's future. Her face grew somber.

"You cannot be suggesting?" Abercrombie asked, looking toward the door. His face wore a horrified expression as he remembered one item he had been asked to supply. "He would not."

"And what is your objection?" Lady Langston asked, her voice cold. As the solicitor sputtered a few words about too hasty decisions, she raised her glass and inspected him as though he were a piece of meat for the morrow's luncheon. Abercrombie fell silent, realizing that he had said too much.

While Lady Langston and Abercrombie sat in a strained silence, Stephen and Jane were alone in the billiard room. "I know there must be cards about somewhere," she explained as she searched one drawer after another, keeping her eyes fixed on the task at hand.

Stephen, on the other hand, did not take his eyes off her, watching as she moved gracefully from one table to another. Finally, he stepped forward, putting his hands on her shoulders and turning her to face him. He brushed her curls back from her forehead and then bent to brush his lips across hers.

"You must not," she murmured, feeling guilty for enjoying the look in his eyes. She took a step or two backward. He followed.

"Jane, I cannot resist you," he whispered, stepping closer to her. She sighed. Taking the sound as a signal, he kissed her again, his lips taking possession of hers once more, his arms pulling her tight against him. At first she was stiff against him, her arms held close to her sides. Then she wrapped them tightly around his neck. Finally, he raised his head and stepped back. She sighed once more but did not follow. He ran one finger down her cheek and under her chin, forcing it up so that she could look into his eyes. She blushed and closed her eyes tightly.

"Look at me," he said softly, caressing her cheek once more. Her eyes glowing like emeralds stared into his. "Oh, Jane," he whispered once more and plundered her lips. He felt her trembling against him and knew his own control was at an end. He stepped back, keeping hold only of her hands. When their breathing had steadied, he spoke again. "Marry me," he pleaded.

Chapter Six

Surprise made Jane pull away from Stephen. "What did you say?" she asked, raising her hands to her breast as though she were some saint facing martyrdom.

"Marry me." Realizing that he had not handled the situation well, Stephen stumbled on. "We suit, you and I. I have always cared for you. You must know that. And you will have a life of your own instead of being at Lady Langston's beck and call."

His words, designed to make her accept, or so he thought, instead brought tears to her eyes. She blinked rapidly, trying to hide the disappointment she felt, a disappointment she didn't understand. She was confused. She tried to speak, but her throat was too tight for words.

The longer she was silent, the more nervous Stephen grew. "I promise that I will provide for you even if the worst happens." He paused, and his voice grew hoarse. "And now that Langston has deserted me you are the only one I can turn to." He longed to pull her into his arms and kiss her senseless but feared she would run away if he did.

Jane stared at him, longing for something more. "I—I," she stammered.

"I know it is sudden. But I do not have the time to wait," he said, taking her hands in his. "Jane, say you will marry me."

"But I have nothing . . ." she began.

"What difference does that make?" he asked. She flinched, remembering what a difference those words would have made in her life if Langston had only said them a year before. "You have always known that I am wealthy.

I do not need a dowry from you. In fact, I will make a settlement on you that will enable you to help your family," he said, his eyes never leaving her face. He was willing to promise anything to get her to accept his proposal. And the fact that Langston had stayed in London might be his good fortune. "Marry me," he urged again. Langston would accept the deed; he would have to.

"Why?" she asked, her eyes large. Tell me how you feel, she silently begged.

He smiled at her, not at all put off by the fact that she did not instantly accept his offer. He had known that getting her to agree would not be easy. "We are friends," he began. She nodded. Leading her to the settee, he seated her and took his place beside her. Once again, he captured her hands in his. "If the worst happens, I know I can leave my sister to your care. You are strong enough to resist my stepmother's designs. And your mother will help you."

Her eyes widened as she realized what he was saying. "But if you do not . . ."

"Then we shall live happily together for many years. You cannot say we do not suit. Can you?" he asked, a frown crossing his brow. Reluctantly, she shook her head as she remembered how well they had always gotten along. "I thought not. We know each other very well." He paused, his face serious. "Is it Langston?" He held his breath, waiting for her reply.

Jane shook her head and then added, "No. There can be nothing between Langston and me. We can never go back to what we once had. And he does not want that," she added quietly, wondering why saying those words aloud did not cause her more pain. She turned to face him. "I understand the benefits to me," she said. "But I do not see what you will gain. I do not love you."

"But you do." She frowned and started to say something. He hurried on. "Oh, I know it is not in the same way you cared for him. But others with happy marriages have begun with less than friendship." He smiled at her, daring her to contradict him. She nodded. "I have told you about my problems with my stepmother. You would solve some of those. And, if Dr. Clarke is right, I will have a wife with whom I can discuss my problems, my interests, not one of the brainless beauties renowned for surface beauty only. A wife who will be loyal." He cupped her face in his hands, smiling at her. "A wife whose kisses make my heart pound." He bent his head and kissed her, letting his lips brush hers and then deepening the kiss until it seemed he would drink in her soul.

Jane's heart raced. Leaning toward him, she returned his kiss. Finally, breathless, she pulled away, still confused. She looked at him, seeing with fresh eyes the man he had become but also the boy he once was, a boy who had encouraged her to dream, to dare. "Are you sure?" she whispered, her hands tightly clasped in her lap so that she would not wind them about his neck. That thought surprised her. He nodded, his eyes on hers. She smiled slowly. And his heart began to hope.

"Jane?" he whispered.

She would have a home of her own, a dream she had abandoned a year earlier. She thought of the years she had known him, the kind way in which he had treated her. Only her own guilt at using him held her silent. She pushed that feeling away. "Yes," she answered. Exhaling the breath he had been holding, he smiled and reached for her, pulling her close.

"Mine," he whispered against her lips as he kissed her again. When they returned to the sitting room sometime later, Jane was blushing. Stephen, his neckcloth slightly disarranged, smiled at Lady Langston. "Wish us happy," he said.

"My dears. What wonderful news! I can hardly wait to tell your mother, Jane. She will be so pleased!"

"Mama." Jane put her hand to her mouth, her eyes wide.

"I will write her immediately," Stephen promised. "Do you think she will refuse her permission?"

"You are so droll." Lady Langston laughed. "She will welcome you with open arms, as I am sure you know. Now we must start planning the wedding. Will you be married at

St. George's in London?" Abercrombie, a silent witness to the announcement, frowned.

Stephen stood perfectly still, his eyes on Jane. "I thought here," he said quietly, his face somber. Something in his manner communicated itself to Jane. Her eyes widened as she remembered what had happened, what could happen. She tightened her fingers on his. "Will that be acceptable to you?" he asked her, looking deep into her eyes.

"Yes," she murmured, wondering if she had made the right decision. Would she have the strength to bear him company to the end if necessary? Her fingers tightened about his once again. "We can speak to the vicar tomorrow."

"Abercrombie arranged for a special license," Stephen admitted. "I know it was presumptuous of me, but I hoped you would agree. It should arrive soon."

"Soon? A special license? I simply cannot agree. Why, what would people think?" Lady Langston complained. "And your bride clothes. You would not have time to order any."

"As much as I would love to see Jane in brighter colors, I must insist," Stephen said, looking down at the almost healed bite on his hand. Lady Langston followed his gaze. She sat back, her face losing some of its animation.

"I suppose you are right," she said, remembering what had happened. "But, Jane, what will you wear for your wedding? Half-mourning will not do. Come and sit beside me so that we may discuss this."

"I suppose we cannot wait for my mother to arrive," Jane suggested, looking at Stephen. Reluctantly, he shook his head.

"If everything goes well, I promise I will take you to see her," he said. He raised her hand to his lips. "While you and Lady Langston discuss the wedding, I need to make arrangements with Abercrombie."

Taking her seat, she let go of his hand and watched him leave the room. Lady Langston, already mentally composing her letter to Jane's mother, smiled. "So handsome. Such wonderful manners," she said. Her face grew serious.

"Only one thing would have made me happier. But that was not to be. Langston's loss, my dear." Jane's glowing look disappeared. "Now, none of that; everything will work out for the best," Lady Langston told her. "Let us retire to my room to discuss your clothes. I refuse to allow you to be married in gray."

While Lady Langston and Jane planned her wedding dress, Stephen met with his solicitor. An unwilling participant of the events of the evening, Abercrombie had no hesitation in expressing his disapproval. "I do not believe this marriage is in your best interests, Mr. Middleton. It is obvious that the lady has no expectations," he said in his dry voice.

"Nor do I," Stephen reminded him, his voice sharp. Mr. Abercrombie looked at him, noting the anger in his eyes, and retreated.

"If you are certain this is what you want—" he began.

"It is. Here is what I need you to do," Stephen said, his face stern. Over the next two hours, the men discussed the changes in Stephen's will and the details to be included in the marriage settlement. "You are certain my stepmother will not be able to have my will overturned?" Stephen asked, looking at the document in front of him.

"I can assure you, Mr. Middleton, that none of the wills I have drawn have ever been overturned." Abercrombie paused. He cleared his throat. "Does the future Mrs. Middleton know what you have planned?"

"Vaguely. If it becomes necessary, I will explain it to her."

"If you are certain?"

"I am." Realizing that the man was trying to keep his best interests in mind, Stephen explained. "I have known Miss Stanfield since I was eleven years old, Abercrombie. In all that time she has never betrayed me."

Startled, the lawyer looked up. Satisfied with what he saw in his employer's eyes, he said quietly, "In that case, I have no further objections."

When they had finished all they could do that evening, they made their way up to bed. Stephen longed to knock on Jane's door just to see her again but entered his own room.

"Wish me happy, Vernon," he said as his valet handed him his nightshirt.

The valet paused and then smiled. "Miss Stanfield accepted you?" he asked.

"You knew, did you?" his master asked with a laugh.

"Only that you had a partiality for her," the valet explained.

"Never could keep anything from you," Stephen complained good-naturedly. He climbed into bed and put his hands beneath his head, a smile on his face. The valet folded the discarded clothing and left the room, his face thoughtful.

Although Stephen drifted off to sleep rather quickly, Jane was not so lucky. Despite Lady Langston's approval, she was not certain about her decision. She wished that her mother were nearby. If she could only talk to her. The longer she lay in bed, the more restless she became. Finally, she got up. Taking the candle beside her bed, she walked to the small desk. Lighting the candles there, she took out a piece of paper and picked up her pen. *Dear Mama*, she began.

She hesitated. How was she to explain what had happened? She had been so careful during the last year to hide her unhappiness from her family. Would they understand? She thought of the events of the last few days and began to write. When she finished, she read it through once more, made a few alternations, and sealed it. Sitting back with a sigh, she looked at it.

Even though she had not been completely open with her mother, the essentials were there. Once more Jane thought about the way she had changed in the few days she had been at the manor. Or had the change happened more gradually?

She had not wanted to accompany Lady Langston on her visit to the manor but had not thought of any logical reason to escape it. Now she was glad that she had come. Langston's attitude during the last few days had been more like a boy who is determined not to share his belongings.

Once again she grew angry as she thought of the way he had threatened her.

The thought made her grow cold. When would he return? What would he do when he discovered her engagement? Jane got up, wrapping her arms around herself. She shivered as she remembered the way his hands had gripped her arms. Langston was fiercely possessive of some things. Then she gave herself a shake. Langston was the one who had decided that money was more important to him than she was. Surely, he would wish them happiness.

She crawled back into bed, pulling her covers up to her neck in hopes of stopping her shivers. She curled up in the middle of the bed, her heart beating loudly. How soon did Stephen intend for them to marry? She shivered again, though not from cold, as she thought of his lips on hers, his arms around her. Surely he did not intend that they stay at the manor? The question worried her as she drifted off to sleep.

Her sleep filled with disturbing dreams, Jane awoke later than usual the next morning. She sat up in bed, surprised to see Lady Langston's maid in her room.

"Good morning, Miss Stanfield," the maid said, handing her a washcloth to take the sleep from her eyes.

"Good morning, Miller," Jane mumbled. "What are you doing here?"

"Lady Langston suggested that you might need my help this morning. She wants you to look your best. I believe she is expecting callers."

"Callers?"

"Yes, miss. She suggested that you wear this gown." Miller displayed a blue sprigged muslin.

Recognizing the dress as one of those they had selected from Lady Langston's wardrobe the evening before, Jane gasped. "How did you ever finish the alterations so quickly? You must have worked for hours!"

"The neckline could be tightened by the ribbons. Then it only took a short time to tighten the bodice. Fortunately, you are only a trifle taller than Lady Langston," the maid assured her, pleased at Jane's reaction. "I will finish the other dresses sometime today."

Jane slipped from her bed, picking up the dress and holding it in front of her. She remembered Stephen's complaints about her gray clothing and smiled as she thought of his reaction to this dress.

When she entered the breakfast room sometime later, she was pleased when he reacted just as she had expected. Jumping up from his seat, he crossed to her side, leading her to the chair across from him. "I like your new gown," he said, taking his seat once more. He smiled at her, and her heart fluttered.

"Thank Lady Langston. She insisted. She even sent her own maid to oversee me today," Jane said, lowering her lashes.

"I will." Once again Stephen inspected her, noting the more elaborate hairstyle held in place with blue ribbons that matched her dress.

Jane smoothed her skirts nervously. After wearing black and gray for so long, she did not feel like herself. "What are your plans for today?" she asked, taking a sip of chocolate.

Stephen raised his eyebrow. "I thought we were to visit the vicar," he reminded her. "Have your plans changed?"

She blushed, and he smiled. "No," she whispered.

Stephen longed to get up, go around the table, and take her in his arms. At that moment, a footman walked in with the muffins Stephen had requested. "May I serve you?" he asked Jane.

Her cheeks still flaming red, she gave her orders, her eyes not leaving Stephen's. Not until Mr. Abercrombie entered the room a few minutes later, did their gaze drop.

"A fine morning," the solicitor said, his eyes going from his employer to the lady across the table. "Have you had any word about the condition of the dogs this morning?"

Stephen and Jane looked at him and then back at each other. "None," Stephen said quietly, hiding the rush of fear the question had sent through him. Jane dropped her eyes before his, hoping he had not seen the pain in hers.

Realizing that the question had changed the atmosphere,

Abercrombie hurriedly ate his breakfast. Neither Jane nor Stephen broke the silence, but neither ate much, pushing the food from one side of their plates to another.

When the footman had cleared their plates, Stephen asked, "Will Lady Langston wish to accompany us to see the vicar?"

"Shall I ask her?" Jane suggested, rising.

"Yes. Abercrombie and I will be in the study," Stephen told her, pulling down the sleeves of his dark green coat. "Send word when you are ready to leave."

As soon as Lady Langston had finished her toilette, the three of them left, leaving Abercrombie to work on the settlements and to wait for the license. Except for the older lady's determinedly happy chatter, the coach was silent. Abercrombie's question at breakfast had reminded Stephen and Jane just how brief their marriage might be. Their reserve remained with them through the interview with the vicar.

When their coach drew up in front of the manse, Stephen handed the two ladies out and followed them up the walk. The maid who opened the door recognized them immediately. She dropped a hurried curtsy, her eyes wide. "I will tell Reverend Wickersham you are here," she said, showing them into the best parlor.

When the vicar entered a few minutes later, a wide smile on his face, Stephen stood up. "It is good of you to see us, sir, on such short notice."

After greeting Lady Langston and Jane, the vicar stood back. "Now tell me what I can do to help to make this difficult time easier," he suggested to Stephen.

Jane and Stephen exchanged rueful glances. Lady Langston frowned slightly. "I should have known you would have heard about my problem," Stephen said with a slight smile. "The three of us never could keep anything from you for long."

"Have things grown worse? Dr. Clarke told me he thought it was merely a bumblebroth and would soon disappear." Wickersham frowned. He looked at Jane and

Stephen, both of whom had been his students during the summers. His soft brown eyes were sympathetic.

"No," Stephen hurried to assure him. "But the situation has led us to a decision." He looked at Jane, who smiled at him. The vicar caught his breath but did not reveal his uneasiness.

"Do not be so mealymouthed, Stephen," Lady Langston interrupted. "Mr. Wickersham, Stephen and Jane wish to be wed." She beamed at the three of them as though the decision were her own.

"Married?" The vicar took one look at Jane, who was gazing at Stephen, and said no more.

"I think it is an almost perfect match," Lady Langston said. "They are such good friends." She dabbed her eyes with her handkerchief, wiping away a few tears.

Longing to ask what her son thought of the match, the vicar listened quietly as Stephen explained the details of the situation, his eyes serious. Only when he looked at Jane did Stephen smile. "What does your mother think, Jane?" he asked when he had heard them out.

Jane blushed and lowered her eyes, letting Stephen explain. "I have sent an express to her, asking her permission. We hope to have an answer soon." He took a deep breath and hurried on. "Lady Langston assures us that she will have no objection."

The vicar looked at the older lady. He smiled. "Why don't you take Jane out into the garden while Lady Langston and I talk, Stephen?" Reluctantly, the two of them left the older couple alone.

Lady Langston played with the fringe on her reticule, waiting for the questions she knew would follow. As soon as the door closed behind the younger couple, the vicar asked, "Are you certain Mrs. Stanfield will approve of the match as much as you?"

Her face more serious than usual, Lady Langston explained. "When Jane agreed to become my companion, her mother and I had a long talk. Recognizing that keeping Jane at her side would mean that the girl would never meet anyone suitable, she encouraged her to take my offer. Of course, we knew that her very small portion would be a problem. But her mother had hopes as I did. When we parted, she entrusted Jane to me as though she were my own daughter." She sighed briefly, remembering her hopes for Jane and her own son. "I have written her several times since we arrived, telling her of Stephen's interest."

"Interest? Before this incident?"

"As soon as we arrived, he could not keep his eyes off her. I hoped it would lead to something. If only that dog had not bitten him," she said, dabbing her eyes again.

The vicar frowned. "I wish Mrs. Stanfield were closer at hand. I am not certain I approve of this hasty marriage."

"Think what it will mean for Jane. Stephen's solicitor is at hand to make all necessary arrangements in case the worst happens," she told him. "And this last year has not been an easy one for her. In society, yet not a part of it. She thinks I did not hear the gossip whenever she entered a room, but I did." She stood up. "Mr. Wickersham, if I could have my wishes, Jane would be married to my son. But that is not to be—by his choice." The vicar's eyebrows raised. "I trust you will not share that with anyone?" Lady Langston said, realizing that she had allowed her tongue to run away with her. He nodded. "Stephen Middleton cares for her. You see how he follows her with his eyes, and I think Jane will come to care for him. They are friends. That is a good beginning."

"You are a persuasive advocate, Lady Langston," the vicar said quietly.

"Then you will do what we ask?"

"Perhaps, but I wish to speak to both of them first." His voice was soft, his eyes sad. "Shall we find them?"

"Jane knows nothing of what her mother and I planned," Lady Langston reminded him, putting her hand on his arm.

"I will remember."

Walking out into the garden, the vicar watched for a moment as Stephen and Jane stood together talking quietly. He stood in front of her, one of her gloved hands in his. Stephen reached up and brushed back one of her curls. Jane turned her head slightly, letting her lips brush against his palm.

The vicar smiled. Then he breathed a prayer that Dr. Clarke was correct. "Come in, please," he called. "We need to discuss arrangements, and I would like to speak with each of you alone." Jane and Stephen exchanged rueful glances. Jane took a deep breath.

"Coming," Stephen said, taking her arm.

The vicar wasted little time on arrangements. The discussions with the engaged couple took longer. The vicar began with Jane, whom he had known all of her life.

As they walked out of the room together, leaving Stephen and Lady Langston behind with a tea tray, Stephen asked, "Does he talk with everyone who plans to marry?"

"I suppose. Do have some tea. They will return shortly." He sighed and took his seat. "She will not change her mind." Stephen stared at her, a worried frown on his face. "That is what you are worrying about, isn't it?" the older lady asked, handing him his cup. He sighed and nodded.

While Stephen waited impatiently, the vicar led Jane into his book-filled study. Moving a pile of books from one of the chairs near his desk, he offered her a seat. Then he sat behind his desk. "This is rather sudden, isn't it, my dear?" he asked. She blushed and nodded. "Are you that unhappy with Lady Langston?"

Startled, she raised her head, a line between her brows. "I'm not unhappy with Lady Langston."

"But you would not have chosen to live with her had you not had to make your way in the world. Is that correct?" the vicar asked, his face concerned.

"No," Jane admitted. She sighed. Then she quickly added, "But Stephen is not simply a chance to escape."

"Would you say that that is a consideration?"

She rose, walking around the room where she had studied during the summers because she had convinced her mother that it was unfair that her daughters would not have the same education as her sons. Hesitating, she picked up one book after another and put them back down. Finally, she admitted, "I would have to say that it played some part in my decision." She paused.

The vicar raised his eyebrows. She put the last book she had picked up back on its stack once more. "But I do care for him."

"As much as you cared for Langston?" the vicar asked, his face serious.

Jane sat back down, staring down at her blue-gloved hands. "He is very important to me," she whispered. "Maybe . . ."

"That 'maybe' is what worries me," the vicar said quietly. "Your mother is not here to advise you. I think she would want you to think about what you are doing. This is an irrevocable step."

Jane looked into the kindly face. She nodded. "I have thought about that. But Stephen needs me."

The vicar waited. When the silence grew, he cleared his throat. "I will not refuse to perform the ceremony, but I am not certain this is wise," he said, frowning. "You can change your mind. Simply let me know. I will explain to everyone."

She stared at him. Remembering the gossip the last time her wedding was called off, she was determined never to face that situation again. Firming her resolve, she straightened her back. "I do not plan to do that," she said proudly.

The vicar escorted her back to Lady Langston and took Stephen away with him. "What did he say?" Lady Langston asked. "You were so long Stephen was becoming nervous."

"He asked me a few questions," Jane told her, not wanting to explain further. "Much as he would ask anyone, I assume."

"Just what I told Stephen," the older lady said. She twitched her skirts. "I do wish I had my needlework. I had no idea that it would take so long to make the arrangements," she complained. "I do hope he hurries. This is my afternoon at home."

Stephen, too, longed for the discussion to be over. He sat in the same seat Jane had occupied, much less at ease with the vicar. When the three of them had shared informal lessons with the vicar during the summers, he had always felt the outsider. Now the vicar's eyes seemed to pierce his heart. The vicar's first question made him nervous. "What does Lord Langston think about this idea?"

Stephen twisted slightly so that he was not facing the man directly but looking over his shoulder to the filled bookcases. "I have not discussed this with him."

The vicar sat up, his face worried. "Is he not at the manor?"

"He went to London on an errand for me and stayed," Stephen said, his voice as calm as he could make it.

"He went to London, leaving you, his guest, here?" the vicar asked, appalled at Langston's manners.

"Dr. Clarke would not allow me to go, and I needed to make certain everything was in order," Stephen said in defense of his friend. "He was trying to help me."

"Yes, well . . ." The vicar stopped what he was about to say, his brow furrowed. He thought for a moment. "And what will he say when he finds out?"

That question was one that had troubled Stephen since he had first thought of asking Jane to marry him. "I do not know," he said quietly. He frowned.

"But?"

After he searched the vicar's face, Stephen said, "He probably will not like it." Before Mr. Wickersham could say anything, he added hurriedly, "He told me he planned to marry in the near future."

"Jane?" The minister's face grew more somber.

"Someone else. I cannot tell you her name. Her family is not yet ready to make an announcement. I would never have interfered between Jane and him—" He stopped himself to keep from explaining how he had left England eighteen months earlier because of Langston and Jane's engagement.

"I see." The vicar tapped his fingers as he often did when considering a difficult subject. "Did he know you were interested in Jane?"

Stephen thought of the conversation he and Langston had

had only the day before he left. "Yes." Nothing in his face revealed how angry that conversation had been.

The silence grew between them. Finally Mr. Wickersham said, "I have known Langston longer than you. He is not a good man to cross. Are you prepared for his anger?"

Stephen slumped back in his chair, his face as serious as the vicar's. Slowly, as if the words were being pulled from him, he said, "I care for Jane. Have cared for her for some time. I accepted the fact that Langston and she would marry and tried to put her out of my mind. But now . . ." He ran his hand over his face as if he could wipe away all doubts. "If we had time." He closed his eyes. "But I do not. This is the only way I can protect her and my sister," he explained.

Recognizing the pain and the hope in his voice, the vicar left his chair and stood behind Stephen. Putting his hands on the younger man's shoulders, he said, "I have told Jane that if she had no objections, neither would I. But I am afraid. Langston's temper can be fierce."

Stephen stiffened. "I will deal with Langston," he said.

The quietness of his voice reassured Wickersham. He stepped back, taking his hands from Stephen's shoulders. A smile crossed his face. "Send me word when the license arrives."

Chapter Seven

After they returned to the manor, the ladies retired to supervise the maids who were doing the sewing on Jane's clothes and to prepare for callers. Stephen wandered into the library. As usual when he was disturbed, he began to pace.

Instead of solving problems, the visit to the vicar had only increased Stephen's doubts. Although he knew that the situation would be easier if Langston stayed in London, he wanted to face him, to explain his motives. Surely, once he understood how much Stephen cared for Jane, Langston would not disapprove. Stephen laughed ruefully. Even though he could be generous to a fault if he thought of the idea, Langston was possessive. At school, he had more than once destroyed an item he no longer wanted rather than share it with someone else. And he still wanted Jane.

Reminding himself that Langston planned to marry someone else did not help. If he only had time to wait. He stopped, his face somber. If he died, Jane would be free, free to marry Langston if he were not already wed. The thought made him burn with anger. Then he calmed himself. Would he want Jane to mourn him for the rest of her life? He forced himself to think clearly, pushing as much emotion aside as he could. He sighed. He would have to be certain Abercrombie included her right to remarry in the settlements. Quickly, he made his way to the study.

"You want to do what?" the solicitor asked, his brow creased in a frown.

"Include it," Stephen said. He stared at his lawyer until the man dropped his eyes and picked up his pen again.

Stephen sat in a chair before the desk. "What else should I include to protect her interests?"

Abercrombie squirmed. "You must include a provision to nullify the nullification of the settlement should you die within a year and a day. And have you decided on who the trustees will be?" he asked, disapproval in every syllable.

"Yes." He took a deep breath. "As long as I am alive, I will serve. After I am gone, you and an officer of the bank will serve." The solicitor nodded, his face solemn. "Should I make any other provisions?"

"I believe those will be sufficient." He started to write and then a thought came to him. "What about Miss Caroline's mother?"

"What?"

"She will not be pleased that someone else will have control of her daughter's inheritance," he said dryly, remembering the tantrums the lady had had when she discovered that her husband's son and not she had been appointed guardian of her daughter and her daughter's fortune.

Stephen merely looked at him. Abercrombie lowered his eyes. "Well, yes, I understand. Have you written your family to explain what has happened?" he asked diffidently.

"Not until I know something more definite. Caroline would become ill with worry if she knew." And my stepmother would be rubbing her hands with glee, he added to himself. "There will be time enough later. When will these papers be ready to sign?" he asked, getting up and walking toward the door.

"Later today," the solicitor assured him.

"Is there anything else?" Abercrombie shook his head, bending over the document in front of him. "Let me know if you have need of me."

Still restless, he wandered about for a few minutes before he returned to his room. "I want riding clothes, Vernon." Without a word, the man pulled out the required garments.

Vernon held out Stephen's coat and smoothed it over his shoulders. He stepped back, his head cocked to one side. Taking a handkerchief, he wiped a spot from Stephen's right boot. "There."

"I will simply get them dirty again when I ride," Stephen reminded him, smiling at his valet's earnest expression.

"A spot on your boots would diminish my reputation," the valet said sternly. "The ladies would notice."

"The ladies?"

"At luncheon." Stephen frowned. "Shall I tell them not to expect you?" the valet asked.

"No. I will postpone my ride until it is over." He picked up his hat and whip and left the room, a thoughtful look on his face.

As he entered the sitting room a few moments later, he felt his heart race as he sighted Jane, her head bent over something white. "Ah, there you are, Stephen," Lady Langston said. "Come sit beside me. Jane is busy with her sewing, and I have made a hopeless mull of mine. So I put it aside."

Jane raised her head and smiled at him. Like him, she had her doubts. Had she truly said she would marry him? Letting her eyes drift over his shoulders, down his long body, she caught her breath, feeling as though she could not get enough air. She blushed as she thought of his lips on hers. Their eyes met, and hers were the first to fall. She felt the heat in her cheeks grow. Keeping her eyes on the handkerchief she was embroidering, she reminded herself that she had known Stephen for years. Stealing a glance under her long lashes, she wondered why she had never noticed him before.

Lady Langston's question brought Jane's eyes up. "Did my son give you any information about when he will return?" Stephen shook his head, his eyes on Jane. "I suppose he is dancing attendance on that girl he intends to marry." Stephen stared at her. "Yes, I know. Did he think to keep it from me forever?" She laughed bitterly. "We have known for weeks now, haven't we, Jane?" Her companion nodded, feeling once again the heaviness in her heart. "Several of my acquaintances, I will not call them friends, did not hesitate to inform me." She frowned. "I do wish my son would not try to hide things from me. It does no good."

Wishing to change the conversation, Stephen agreed.

"You are right. I still remember how you discovered that we were the ones raiding the strawberries from the forcing house."

"You naughty children. Just when I planned to serve them at a dinner party too." She patted his cheek. "You constantly surprised me." The amusement in her voice was reflected in her eyes.

"You and Langston certainly made my summers much happier than they would have been," Stephen added, remembering the despair he had felt when his father had written that his stepmother did not want him to come home.

"That woman has much to answer for. Did I tell you I saw her in London?" Lady Langston asked, a frown marring her face. She continued without waiting for him to answer. "I would speak to her about her companions, Stephen. Every rake in town was paying her attention. And she did not seem to discourage them."

His face carefully blank, although the anger he had felt when he realized the reputation his stepmother was acquiring had returned, Stephen made a noncommittal answer. Before Lady Langston could continue, luncheon was announced.

With the servants about, conversation stayed general. As soon as it was finished, Stephen made his excuses and hurried to the stables, giving orders to have his horse saddled. While he waited, he wished once more that Langston had returned.

When Stephen returned later that afternoon, the day had turned stormy. As he walked into the sitting room where they normally had tea, he was surprised by a bevy of ladies. Before he could withdraw, Lady Langston called him to her side, introducing him to one lady after another until he was surrounded. Jane, catching sight of his face, made her way to his side. She slipped her arm through his. "Did you and Mr. Abercrombie need me?" she asked.

Grasping the escape she had provided, Stephen did not hesitate. "I will not keep you from the ladies long. But we need you in the study," he said, making his apologies.

Although Lady Langston frowned as the two of them

walked from the room, they heard her say to one of the ladies sitting near her, "They make a delightful couple. I am so happy I could bring them together."

As soon as the door closed behind them, Jane breathed a sigh of relief. "And I am so happy to escape," she whispered to Stephen. "You are my hero."

"And I thought I owed you my thanks. How did you know I needed rescuing?" Stephen asked with a smile.

"The look on your face. I haven't seen anyone look so desperate since the gardener found us feasting on those strawberries."

"Not that bad?"

"Worse," she assured him.

Stephen glanced back at the room they had just left. "I suppose that was my only chance for tea," he said wistfully.

Jane smiled up at him. "You go to the library, and I will speak to Smythe." He watched her walk away before he turned to enter the other room.

"Mr. Middleton, I was just about to ask you to join me," Mr. Abercrombie said, putting his pen to one side.

"Is everything ready?"

"Almost." He handed Stephen several pages. "Does the last paragraph on page two read as you want?"

Stephen turned to the page and read the paragraph. "You are certain that my stepmother will not be able to have the settlement voided if I die within the next year?" he asked, frowning.

"There is precedent for this provision," the solicitor assured him. "And no one could say you are not in your right mind. We merely need your signature and the signatures of your witnesses. Whom did you have in mind?" Abercrombie tapped the end of the pen against the paper.

"I thought the vicar," Stephen said. "We can ask him before he marries us."

"Excellent choice. A vicar always makes a reputable witness in court. If it should come to that," the solicitor added, noting Stephen's raised eyebrows.

The door opened. The men looked up and then stood as Jane, followed by a footman with a tea tray, walked into the room. "Let me move some of these books," Abercrombie suggested, hurriedly cleaning a spot on the desk on which to put the tray. "Please take this chair, Miss Stanfield."

Jane made her way to the desk and poured the tea, handing each man his cup. She poured one for herself and sat back, allowing the footman to pass the bread and butter and biscuits. When everyone had been served, she asked, "Did you truly need to see me?" Her eyes danced.

"Not immediately," Stephen admitted. Abercrombie cleared his throat as if reminding him of their earlier discussion. "But you will need to sign the settlement." He frowned.

"Stephen, I do wish you would change your mind. I do not want you to settle anything on me." Abercrombie stared at her in surprise, his opinion of her changing dramatically.

"Whether you want it or not, I have done so." He frowned again.

"Then what is wrong?" she asked. The solicitor looked from one to the other nervously.

"I wish we could wait for your family's solicitor to read through the settlement," he admitted. Abercrombie opened his mouth to protest, but Stephen shook his head. "You have no one to protect your interests. I could be taking advantage of you."

"How? By forcing me to take money I do not want?" Jane asked. She smiled at her future husband. "I ask you, Mr. Abercrombie, is he taking advantage of me?"

"No," the lawyer said, glancing at his employer.

"I am forcing you to make decisions very quickly," Stephen reminded her, the guilt he felt at using her very strong.

She glanced at Mr. Abercrombie. Taking a last sip of tea, he put his cup in his saucer and stood up. "I think I will take a walk in the garden. If you will excuse me?"

As he watched his solicitor walk from the room, Stephen turned to Jane. "You have condemned him to a wet afternoon," he said teasingly.

She raised her eyebrows. "It is raining," he explained. "I wish I had your talent of disposing of people so easily."

"Stephen!" Jane blushed as she thought of the autocratic way in which she had dismissed Abercrombie. "I am certain he will not go walking in the rain."

"Jane!" Stephen mocked her. He walked across the room to stand by her chair. He pulled her up to face him. Looking deep into Jane's green eyes, he searched for the answer he sought. Unsuccessful, he smiled down at her. "You must sign the settlement," he told her.

She turned away from him, moving to the corner of the desk and picking up a small bust that sat there. "Why?"

Stephen moved behind her and put his hands on her shoulders. "If I am not here, you must be protected."

"Don't say that!" she cried, turning to face him. "You will be all right. You will." She blinked, surprised by her own determination.

"But we must also provide for the other eventuality," he reminded her. "You will need this to help provide for Caroline."

"Your sister." Jane paused. "Does she know what has happened?"

"No. There will be time enough to write her when we know more. I did write to tell her that we planned to marry soon." He caressed Jane's cheek with a finger. "How soon can we expect to hear from your mother?"

"A few days at least." Jane trembled and lowered her eyes, blinking rapidly to keep back the tears. She did wish her mother would be there to share the moment with her. "Don't you think we can wait?"

Stephen shook his head, sorry to make her unhappy. "I promise we will visit her," he said as he had done earlier. "And she can stay with us," he added.

Jane's eyes grew wide. "You would not mind?"

"No. I hope you will not mind having my sister with us. My stepmother will be removing to the dower house."

"Without your sister?"

"I am my sister's guardian. And where I live, she lives." He glanced at his betrothed, trying to determine her reaction.

Jane blinked once and then twice. "How big is your

home?" she asked cautiously, remembering that his step-mother had felt her peace would be disturbed by a boy.

"Larger than the manor," he assured her. "I think we have at least fifteen or twenty bedrooms."

"What?" Jane longed for a fan to cool her heated cheeks.

"Almost every generation has added to it," he explained. "I cannot tell you exactly because I have spent little time there. You will enjoy refurbishing the place."

As Jane thought of the size of the house, she felt a sinking sensation in her stomach. "So big," she whispered.

"I also have a house in London and a hunting box near Melton," he admitted. Then he snapped his fingers. "I forgot the houses my uncle left me."

"You forgot?" she asked. "How could you forget houses?" She stared at him as though she had never seen him before. She had known he had money and land but not how much.

"I have been gone," he reminded her. "Perhaps your mother would care to live in one of them."

"Instead of with us?"

"Wherever she wishes," he said hastily, sensing a disaster about to happen. "Shall we wait and ask her?" He watched as Jane sat down, his relief evident on his face.

"I do not mean to be inquisitive, Stephen," Jane said quietly. "But how much are you worth?"

He sat down near her, his eyes fixed on his boots, disappointed by her question. "I suppose I should have had you read the settlement before this," he admitted. When he told her, her eyes opened wide and then closed in horror.

"I cannot marry you," she said quietly.

"What?" Stephen sat back in his chair. A refrain ran through his head: Jane is rejecting me because I am wealthy.

Jane got up, her eyes anguished. "People will call me a fortune hunter." She clasped her hands so tightly that all color began to drain from them. Then she put them over her mouth.

"You promised," Stephen reminded her, trying to put his

arms around her. She moved away. Despite his confusion at her rejection, he was elated, too.

"You never told me." Jane turned and faced him, her green eyes blazing angrily. "How can I protect your sister if everyone thinks I am a fortune hunter?"

Stephen tried to soothe her. "No one will question you when they become acquainted with you."

"And what of all those people in London who will not choose to get to know me? What about the patronesses of Almack's? How will we ever obtain vouchers for your sister?" Jane, her nerves already lacerated by the remarks of the ladies who had come to see Lady Langston, felt ready to sink to the floor.

"You were given vouchers during your Season. I remember having to put on knee breeches just to be able to stand up with you," Stephen said indignantly. He turned her to face him once more. Putting his hand beneath her chin, he forced her to look up at him. "Jane, you are not a nobody. You have friends in the *ton*. They will not desert you. And I will be there."

"How can you promise that?" she asked. She watched his expression change and wished she could call the words back. "Oh, Stephen, I am sorry," she whispered, catching his face in her hands. "I did not mean it."

"But it is the truth." He stepped back, away from her. His face was bleak. "Jane, I wish to marry you," he said quietly. "You are the only woman I have asked to share my life, however long it is, but if you wish to change your mind . . ." He paused, staring at her, wishing that the force of his will would make her agree to the marriage.

She took a deep breath. Looking into his eyes, she tried to find an answer. Then she closed her own. "Oh, I wish you were not so wealthy," she muttered, mostly to herself.

Stephen smiled and waited. Finally, she opened her eyes again. Stephen simply stared at her, one eyebrow raised. "I suppose you could not give some of it away?" she asked with a rueful smile.

"I am trying to," he reminded her, "but you will not take it." He took a deep breath, hope beginning to fill his heart once more. "Jane, will you marry me?" he asked, his voice thick with emotion.

All at once the thought of what the world would say meant less to her than making him happy. She looked at him, the faintest smile drifting over her lips. "Yes," she murmured. Before the word was out of her mouth, Stephen had grabbed her and pulled her into his arms. His lips plundered hers hungrily, sending waves of emotion through her. Stephen's heart pounded against hers. Jane reached up to cradle his cheek. "Oh, Stephen." His name was the last thing he allowed her to say for some time.

When she realized later that she was sitting on his lap, the ribbon at her neckline undone, Jane blushed. She tried to get up, to rearrange her clothing. "What if Lady Langston comes in?" she asked, her cheeks burning. She lowered her eyelashes and then looked up. The look in Stephen's blue eyes made her catch her breath. She smoothed his hair back from his face. Catching her hand, Stephen brought it to his lips, leaving a kiss in her palm.

"We are betrothed," he reminded her. "And we will be married as soon as the license arrives." He kissed her neck and tried to kiss the tops of her breasts.

"Stephen," she said, scandalized now that she was thinking more rationally. She pulled away from him and stood up, wondering why her knees were so weak she could hardly stand. "Lady Langston will be wondering where we are."

A bell rang. Stephen looked at the mantel clock. "Is it already time to dress for dinner?"

"What? We have been in here for hours! What will Lady Langston think?"

"Nothing. Remember I told her that Abercrombie needed to talk to the both of us," Stephen said, pushing her hands away so that he could retie the ribbon at the neckline of her dress.

"That excuse will last only so long as she does not speak to Abercrombie," Jane reminded him, trying to get her hair back in place. What had he done with her pins? she wondered, searching the floor. Stephen handed her several, and she glared at him as she tried to twist her hair into some semblance of order.

"Here's your ribbon." He stepped back, wondering if he should tell her how rumpled she was. "If you take the back stairs, no one will see you."

"No one but the servants," she reminded him, wanting to be angry but unable to sustain it. She opened the door to the hallway cautiously and then shut it quickly.

"What is wrong?"

"Mr. Abercrombie is going upstairs."

Stephen walked to the door. "Wait a minute," Jane suggested.

Stephen ignored her. He waved her forward. "He is gone."

She slipped by him. Before she could leave the room, Stephen grabbed her once more. "Until dinner," he said, kissing her. Then he pushed her from the room.

For a few moments, Jane was too caught up in sensation to move. Then, glancing around, she made her way to the back staircase.

Stephen remained in the study for a few more minutes. He laughed when he thought of Jane's worry about his wealth. Then his eyes darkened to a midnight blue. "Has a messenger arrived for me?" he asked the footman who had just come into the hallway. The man shook his head. Stephen hid his disappointment. He would have to wait until tomorrow to make Jane his own. A pang of guilt tore through him. What would Langston say?

Chapter Eight

Jane, rushing upstairs, closed the door of her room behind her. She glanced in the mirror. Her eyes widened as she realized how disheveled she was. Sinking into the chair near her desk, she covered her face with her hands. Her cheeks grew red as she remembered Stephen's hands and lips on her neck and shoulders. What was happening to her?

During her engagement to Langston, they had shared some stolen kisses, but those had had little resemblance to the ones she and Stephen had shared only a few minutes before. Was she a wanton? A knock at her door startled her. "Come," she called, moving behind the screen that shielded her as she washed.

"Lady Langston asked that I help you dress," the maid told her. "I finished altering several of the dresses this afternoon. We thought this would be suitable for the evening." She placed a pomona-green dress with a gold tulle overskirt on the bed.

Jane peered around the screen at the dress. "Is that for this evening?" she asked, looking at the square cut neckline trimmed with gold lace. "Isn't it rather low cut for a simple dinner?"

Miller stared at her, her face astonished. All at once Jane remembered discussing the dress the day before and blushed. Refraining from an answer, the maid asked, "Are you ready for me to do your hair?"

When the woman had returned to Lady Langston, Jane stared at herself in the mirror. After her first Season, her mother had allowed her to dress in colors, but none of her dresses had been cut as low as Lady Langston liked them. Jane turned in front of the mirror, noting the way the gold tulle overdress swayed when she did. She stared at the deep square-cut neckline and blushed when she thought of the way Stephen's eyes would widen as he caught sight of her.

What was wrong with her? Why did the attention of one man mean so much? When she was first introduced to society, while other girls had giggled over the attentions of one man after another, she, secure in her knowledge that she and Langston would marry, had smiled and danced with many men without worrying about the effect she was having. If gentlemen sent her flowers, she acknowledged them with a note. And when their compliments grew too fulsome, she refused their invitations to dance. Within a few weeks of the beginning of the Season, her dance card was always full, usually with gentlemen who knew she would not expect them to declare for her. It had been great fun. When her mother had scolded her once or twice for discouraging one of her suitors, she had said, "I am going to marry Langston, Mama. I do not mean to change my mind. And it would be wrong of me to raise expectations when I know I will not accept."

Putting those thoughts to one side, she twirled around the room, enjoying the sway of her dress. How she missed dancing. Catching sight of herself in the mirror, she stopped. She stared at her flushed cheeks. Once only Langston had made her feel this way. Was she so desperate to marry that the persuasion of a possibly dying man would turn her head? The sadness that had been part of her for a year resurfaced. What was she doing? How could she marry Stephen?

That thought hovered in the back of her mind during dinner. Even Stephen's obvious approval of the way she looked and Lady Langston's compliments did not erase it. She longed for Langston to return. If she could see him just once more, she would know what to do. Perhaps she should send word to the vicar that she had changed her mind.

"Jane?" Stephen said, his voice soft.

Startled, she turned to him. "What?" Her voice was sharper than she had intended.

"What is wrong?"

"Nothing," she lied. He stared at her, willing her to tell the truth, but she simply smiled. A frown creased his brow. When the ladies rose to leave the men to their port, Stephen followed them into the sitting room.

Taking his seat next to Jane, he watched as she poured the tea and gave it to the footman to distribute. He waited patiently until Jane took a sip of her tea and then asked, "Jane, may we talk? Alone?"

The teacup in her hand shook dangerously. Replacing it in its saucer, she keep her eyes downcast and shook her head. "Not tonight," she whispered. Perhaps by morning these fears and doubts would have disappeared.

"Why not?"

Lady Langston glanced at them and frowned. "Jane, dear, you are not looking your best. Have you been sleeping properly?" she asked. She put her cup on the table beside her. "I do not want anyone to say that you look less than glowing at your wedding. You know how people talk."

Jane flushed. Before she could speak, Stephen said, "I think Jane looks splendid. That green dress makes her green eyes more beautiful."

Lady Langston laughed. Jane smiled briefly, wondering if he truly meant what he was saying. Her doubts, never far from the surface, overwhelmed her. What would he say if she told him she had changed her mind? "Perhaps I should retire now," Jane said quietly. Her face was carefully composed.

"An excellent idea," Lady Langston said, drowning out Stephen's protest. She turned to her son's friend. "When do you expect the license to arrive?"

Jane said good night and slipped from the room as Stephen explained, "I had hoped it would arrive this afternoon. I expect it by tomorrow afternoon at the latest."

Tomorrow, Jane thought as she walked up the stairs. I will be married to Stephen by this time tomorrow. By the time she reached her room she was shaking. Should she tell him she had changed her mind? Would Lady Langston support her decision? What if the lady refused to keep her on as companion?

She entered her room. Taking down her hair and slipping out of her gown without help was difficult. As she put the dress away, she stopped. Tomorrow. Once again the thought of her marriage frightened her. Stephen would have the right to share her room, to be present as she dressed. She glanced at the bed, now turned down for the night, and shivered. He would have the right to share her bed. Although she was trembling, she felt a tingling in her body. Was she lost to all propriety? How she wished her mother were present! Caught up in her swiftly changing emotions and vivid pictures of what her life might be like, she lay awake for hours before finally falling into a deep sleep.

The next morning came too slowly for Stephen and too fast for Jane. Dressed in a coat of his favorite blue that made his shoulders seem much wider, he waited for her in the breakfast room for almost an hour. Finally deciding that she was not coming, he frowned and walked outside. Restless, he glanced around the garden. Then he walked toward the stables.

"Here to see the dogs, Mr. Middleton?" the head groom asked, his face somber. Stephen, surprised that he had not thought of the dogs before, nodded. "Dickson, the man who looks after them, returned last night. He's with them now," the groom added.

Stephen thanked him, wondering at the man's changed attitude. He walked toward the enclosure where the dogs were penned. As he got closer, he stopped. "What are you doing in there?" he called to the man who was standing in the middle of the pack, inspecting the dogs one by one. The man simply finished his inspection and then left the enclosure, carefully closing the gate behind him.

"Those dogs may have rabies," Stephen said. "You must be more careful. Do not endanger yourself."

"Always careful," the older man said quietly. "But my

dogs dinna have rabies." He bent and rubbed the head of one of the dogs poking his nose through the fence.

"How do you know?" Stephen's voice was sharper than he had intended, his pulse racing. The man sounded so certain.

The man turned and stared at him. "Not any in these parts. Not in my lifetime. Dinna listen to the boy. He was just frightened."

"Are you certain?" Stephen's heart was beating so loudly he knew that the groom could hear it. "I am not going to die" pulsed through his brain.

"Sure enough to walk among them, sir," the groom said. Then he glanced at the small pond nearby. "Were frogs about?" he asked, his forehead wrinkling as he looked back at the dogs.

"What? A frog? How should I know?" Stephen asked, his elation subsiding for a moment. "Where are you going?"

"To speak to Jem, the boy," Dickson told him. Stephen trailed along after him, wondering if the man was right. Dr. Clarke had said that he knew of no rabies in the area. Maybe there was a chance.

"Mornin'." Dickson greeted each man as he passed. "Seen Jem?" Stephen followed him, determined to be present for the interview. Finally they found the lad cleaning out a stall.

"Jem. A minute of your time, lad," Dickson said quietly. He saw the boy's shoulders tense as if for a blow. "No, lad, not to worry. Just a question or two." He signaled Stephen to stay back. "Tell me about the day you had to kill the dogs."

The boy recounted his story and then paused. "I did just as Da told me I should. Did I do right?" His face was anxious. "Milord was not angry."

"Nor am I," Dickson assured him. "'Twas early?"

The lad nodded vigorously. "Sun had just come up."

"Good lad. Now think hard. Any frogs about?"

"Frogs?" Jem frowned as he tried to remember. Then his face cleared. "Making a frightful racket they were that morning." Stephen listened carefully, still not understanding the line of questioning.

"Any in with the dogs?" Dickson asked. He shifted from foot to foot, waiting for the boy to reply.

"I disremember. Maybe." The boy tried to think of the details of that morning, but all that came to him was the fear. "Noticed the froth and went to get the gun. That was right, wasn't it?" The young boy looked at the older man, fear once more in his face.

Dickson nodded. "The frogs?" he asked again. This time his voice was sterner.

Jem straightened his shoulders and thought about that morning as he had done often in the past few days. "Think there was," he admitted.

"Good lad," Dickson said, his face creasing into a smile. "Now get along with your work lest you get both of us in trouble." He turned and walked out of the stall. As soon as he was out of earshot, he motioned to Stephen to follow him outside.

"Well? What was that about? Frogs?" Stephen demanded.

"Just as I thought," Dickson said. He ran his hand over his face.

"What do you mean?"

"Dogs enjoy playing with frogs, chewing on them—"

"And?" Stephen interrupted him, impatient. How could frogs have anything to do with rabies?

"Then they froth at the mouth," the groom explained. He picked up a brush.

"What?" Stephen grabbed him by the arm and turned Dickson to face him.

"Just so, sir. No rabies. Just frogs," Dickson said, pulling his arm free and walking away.

"Frogs," Stephen whispered. He caught up with the groom, who was walking toward the dogs' kennel. "Are you certain?"

"Near as I can be, not being here myself," Dickson assured him. He whistled to the dogs, and they stopped their milling around to group at the gate, waiting to be released.

"You do not plan to let them out?" Stephen asked, his face set in angry lines.

"Dinna see why not," the groom told him.

"Dr. Clarke said to keep them penned," Stephen told him. "And Lord Langston agreed."

"But they dinna have rabies," the groom said, his fingers reaching through the fence once more to pet his charges.

"So you say. But you were not here," Stephen reminded him. "Better to keep them penned than to take a chance. It will only be for a few more days."

The man frowned but nodded reluctantly. "Dinna think Lord Langston would doubt my word," he muttered under his breath.

"If he wishes to change his orders once he returns home, he can do so. Until then, the dogs stay penned," Stephen said firmly. His tone made the man glance at him in surprise.

"Dinna make any sense. 'Twas frogs," the groom muttered as Stephen turned around and headed toward the house.

For the first time since the boy had killed the dogs, Stephen walked with a lighter step. "Frogs," he muttered. He laughed as he walked hurriedly toward the house, anxious to tell Jane what he had discovered. Then he paused and smiled. If Dickson were right, he and Jane would be able to wait until her mother arrived.

Jane had awakened later than usual that morning. Reluctant to see Stephen again, she asked for breakfast in her room but only drank her chocolate. Finally, realizing the time, she hurried to Lady Langston's room, certain the lady would be angry with her. When she entered, she was surprised to see the lady up and dressed. "You did not have to rush to my side this morning," Lady Langston said. "You should be spending time with your betrothed." She glanced in the mirror and frowned, unaware of Jane's stiffening behind her. "I declare I am positively hagridden," she said, noting the lines about her eyes.

The last year had taught Jane something of the vagaries of her employer's character. Realizing that the older lady needed some reassurance, Jane picked up a bottle from the dressing table as she had done before. "Nonsense. Because I have been keeping you so busy with my affairs, you have been neglecting yourself. A few minutes with the Denmark lotion should restore you." Now was not the time to tell Lady Langston about her change in plans.

"Perhaps you are right. Miller, I need you." The lady stretched out on the chaise, closing her eyes, her maid hovering nearby. Miller smiled at the younger lady. Jane handed the maid the bottle of lotion and reluctantly started toward the door, wondering how Stephen would take her change of mind. "And, Jane, would you read from where I left the ribbon to mark my place?"

Taking her seat, Jane picked up the book Lady Langston indicated, relieved to postpone her confrontation with Stephen. "One day," she began. Sometime later she was still reading, her throat becoming scratchy.

Finally, Lady Langston yawned and stretched. "I think we have left it on long enough, Miller." Jane almost confided in her then. Only the thought that she should tell Stephen first held her words back. Lady Langston allowed her maid to remove the lotion. "How delightful. Jane, I do not know what I shall do without you. I should hate Stephen for taking you away, but he is such a dear boy that it would be wrong." The lady glanced in the mirror, noting with satisfaction the improvement in her skin. "Denmark lotion, Miller. We must remember it." She smiled at her companion. "I have kept you from Stephen long enough. Go and find him."

Had Lady Langston been more observant, she would have realized how reluctantly Jane left her suite. Pausing at the door, the younger lady looked back, her eyes shadowed by worry. What would Lady Langston say when she realized that Jane had changed her mind? What would her mother think?

Stephen too was having his own doubts. Should he tell Jane about Dickson's theory? His steps toward the house slowed. She had agreed to marry him only because he might be dying. Would she change her mind once she knew that he was not? He paused. Then he turned, his steps taking him away from the house.

When Jane walked slowly down the stairs, she knew what she must do. The only problem was finding Stephen. No one knew where he had gone, not even Mr. Abercrombie, who was fidgeting restlessly. "I do not understand him, Miss Stanfield. First he insisted that I rush. Now when the documents are prepared and waiting, he disappears." His eyes grew wide with horror. "Suppose something has happened to him! We must go look for him." He hurried toward the door of the study.

"Mr. Abercrombie," Jane said, her voice firm although inside she was trembling. He stopped and looked back at her. "He had breakfast this morning as he usually does. Had he been ill someone would have told me. Perhaps he simply needs some time to himself." She took a deep breath, hoping she was right.

The solicitor walked back across the room, his eyes noting her pallor. "I do wish we knew when he would return."

"I will tell the footman to let you know as soon as he comes in." With Abercrombie's thank-you's echoing behind her, she made her way to the library. What if he had become ill while he was alone? What would happen to him? Wishing that Dr. Clarke were nearby to give her more information, Jane walked slowly around the library before she finally picked up a book and tried to read. Instead of the words on the page, she saw Stephen's face and hurt eyes as she explained she had changed her mind. She shut her eyes and shivered. She did not want to hurt him.

Last night her decision had seemed so reasonable. Now she was not sure. He would let her go. She was certain of that. Stephen would never force her to do something she did not want to do. He never had. The last few days had stirred memories she thought she had forgotten.

Putting her book to one side, she got up and began to walk about the room once more. She was so deep in thought that when the door opened she jumped. Smythe frowned. "A letter just arrived for you by special messenger. I thought you should have it at once," he explained, wondering at the despairing look she wore.

"Thank you, Smythe," she said quietly as she took the letter. Recognizing the handwriting as her mother's, she hesitated a moment before breaking the seal. A sense of calm seized her as she began to read. Her uncle, younger sister, and mother were all well. As her mother described the activities in the neighborhood, Jane smiled. Her mother did so enjoy society. She paused. If she married Stephen, her mother would have the resources to live as she had before. She could even return home if she wished. Jane knew that Stephen would offer to help with the mortgages if she asked. She sighed.

As she continued to read, the question of what she was to do was never far from her mind. The last paragraph, a postscript obviously written hastily, made her sit upright.

Dearest Jane, what wonderful news! I am very happy for you and yet, at the same time, sad. What Stephen must be going through. How wonderful that you can be there at his side. Trust Dr. Clarke. If he says he doubts that Stephen has rabies, I am certain he knows best. I wish that I could be there for your marriage and to explain the duties of a wife. For that I must trust Lady Langston. Stephen has promised me that you would be here as soon as the problem is resolved. I wait with impatience to see you. Stephen is a fine man, my dear. Now I may tell you the truth. I always wondered why you preferred Langston when Stephen was nearby. Such wonderful manners. You should read the letter he sent me. Your uncle is pleased too. He asked me to send you his best wishes. Now, my darling daughter, I must finish this so that I can write to Stephen. Remember you are always in my thoughts and prayers. Your loving mother.

Jane stared at the paper in her hands for a few more minutes. Then she closed her eyes. Her mother approved of what she was doing. What would she say if Jane changed her mind? Refolding the letter carefully so that she could read it later, Jane held it close to her heart, knowing that there was no way out. She must marry Stephen. To do otherwise would break her mother's heart.

She stood up, her head held high, her back straight. She closed her eyes for a moment and then walked from the room and up the stairs to her room.

When Stephen returned to the house, Smythe handed him the letter from Mrs. Stanfield. "The groom just returned with this, Mr. Middleton," he said.

"So soon? He must be exhausted. I hope you saw to his comfort. And give him this for me." Stephen handed the butler some coins. Smythe bowed and left, knowing that when Stephen finally left his own vale would be substantial. Even as a boy, Stephen had remembered the servants.

Like Jane, Stephen found the library the most comfortable room in the house. He sat down and opened Mrs. Stanfield's letter. Like the one she had written to Jane, she expressed her sorrow at what had happened and then her confidence in Dr. Clarke's opinion. Then she gave her permission for them to marry. Stephen closed his eyes for a moment. This letter would certainly relieve Mr. Wickersham. Jane would be his wife by nightfall. The thought made his heart beat faster. Jane would be his! Her mother's approval drove the last thought of explaining Dickson's theory from his mind.

At luncheon Lady Langston, who had also had a letter from Mrs. Stanfield, was in the alt. Careful not to reveal that she too had written Mrs. Stanfield, Lady Langston questioned Jane carefully about her letter. "Of course, she is delighted. What mother would not be?" She smiled at Stephen. "He is so handsome."

And you will no longer have to support me, Jane added to herself cynically. Then ashamed of what she was thinking, she said aloud, "Mama sends you her fond regard."

"How kind!" Lady Langston said with a smile. Her letter had been much more effusive. The footman removed her soup plate and then presented the next dishes. She refused the filet of sole she was offered, accepting instead a mushroom omelette dressed with French greens. She glanced at the other members of her party and nodded as she noted the way Stephen's appetite had improved. "Try some of the sole, dear boy. I remembered that you and Langston always enjoyed it when you were younger."

Stephen smiled at her and accepted the fish. He glanced at Jane. Although her mother had given her approval to their marriage, Jane was not responding as he had expected. Whenever she thought no one was watching, she was biting her lower lip, a sure sign that something was worrying her. And her responses to him were subdued. Determining to seek her out after luncheon, Stephen maintained a pleasant conversation.

His plans, however, were interrupted. As the footmen passed the desserts—strawberries (for Jane and Stephen, Lady Langston had announced with a laugh), a syllabub, and some sweetmeats, Smythe entered the room bearing a letter on a silver tray.

"This has just arrived, Mr. Middleton. I thought you should have it at once," he said. He handed him the letter and waited expectantly.

Stephen stared at it for a moment, not recognizing the handwriting. Then he broke the seal. "It is the license," he exclaimed. "We can be married immediately." He smiled at Jane, who trembled inwardly.

"Then we have much to do. Send word to Mr. Wickersham and the others," Lady Langston ordered. "The messages have already been written. Smythe, have grooms deliver them immediately and ask them to meet us at the church at four. And send the two maids I selected to decorate the church. Come, people, we have only two hours to prepare." Like a field marshal gathering her troops about her, she stood up and prepared to go to work. "Jane, come. We have much to do! Stephen, we will meet you at the church."

Now that the moment had come, Jane hesitated. She turned to look back at Stephen. He smiled at her. Turning around, she closed her eyes and took a deep breath. Then she followed Lady Langston from the room, hoping for a moment of peace so that she could compose her thoughts.

That hope was not to be. As they walked up the stairs together, Lady Langston continued to give directions. "You go to your room. I will send Miller to you to help with your bath and to dress your hair. As soon as she finishes, send her back to me. When I am dressed, I will come to you."

"I do not need your maid, Lady Langston. One of the other girls can help me," Jane protested.

"Nonsense. She has an extraordinary talent for hair. I want you to look your best today. You did say your mother put you in my care. I am sure she would agree with me."

The argument silenced Jane. Helplessly, she gave herself over to the skilled hands of the maid. Only when her hair was curled and pinned into a charming knot with a few wispy curls did she have her time alone. She sat where Miller had left her, in front of the mirror at her dressing table, and stared at herself in dismay. Her hair had never looked better. The loose robe she wore over her chemise and stays was one of her own, sadly out of style, she was certain, but still becoming. The soft pink sprigged muslin fell open, and she stared at her bosom, rising above her stays. Stephen would see her like this, she thought, her cheeks flaming red.

The thought made her too nervous to stay seated although Miller had ordered her not to move. Why had she agreed to visit the manor with Lady Langston? If she had expressed a desire to visit her family, her employer would have agreed. But she had wanted to see Langston again. Langston! She closed her eyes and stood still, wondering what he would say when he found out.

The silence of her thoughts was broken as her door swung open. Hastily, she turned around. "I was told to remove the tub," a small voice said. Jane turned around. A young girl stood there, twisting her hands nervously.

"Did they send you alone?" Jane asked, noting how small the girl was.

"No, miss. There are two footmen outside. May they come in?" The young maid glanced at Jane's state of undress, her eyes wide.

"Help me move the screen back where it usually goes.

And when I am behind it, you can call them in. What is your name?"

"Annie Miller, miss."

"Miller? Any relation to Lady Langston's maid?"

"She's my aunt." The girl was speaking in almost a whisper. "She persuaded Lady Langston to give me a chance. I want to be a lady's maid just like her." The girl's eyes were wide. "But there are no other ladies in the house." She sighed wistfully. "But it is an opportunity," she said as if quoting someone else.

Almost without realizing what she was saying, Jane told her, "As soon as the tub is empty, return to me. I shall need a maid." Then she heard what she had said. Well, Stephen would not begrudge her a maid, she was certain.

The girl's face lit up. Then she paused. "Just for today?" she asked. Jane shook her head. A bright smile lit the girl's face. "You will not be disappointed, miss. I am a hard worker. And my aunt has been teaching me how to care for a lady's clothing. You have only to tell me if you dislike the way I am doing something and I will change—"

Wondering if she had done the right thing, Jane broke into her comments. "Take the tub away. Then return. We will discuss your duties later."

By the time the girl returned, full of her own importance, both Lady Langston and Miller were with Jane. Catching sight of her niece, the maid frowned. "What are you doing here, Annie?" she asked quietly, pulling her into a corner.

"Miss Stanfield said I could be her maid," the girl said proudly.

The maid glanced at Jane, who could not help overhearing the conversation. She nodded. Miller turned back to her niece. "Then you must watch what I do carefully." Nodding, the girl stayed out of the way and observed, moving only when her aunt requested.

Although Jane protested that she could put them on herself, the maid helped her into her silk stockings and tied the garters above her knees. Next she helped her with her slippers and tied the ribbons around her ankles. A fine muslin petticoat trimmed with lace followed. "This is not mine," Jane protested.

"It is a gift from me," Lady Langston told her. She glanced in the mirror and smoothed her eyebrow. "Lucinda had me order a dozen new petticoats for her when I was in London. She can be happy with fewer." She inspected Jane, nodding in satisfaction. "Now the dress. Miller and another maid—was that you, Annie?" The girl nodded, her face glowing with pride. Lady Langston did not stop. "Finished the dress for your wedding yesterday. Fortunate the license took so long to arrive."

"My dress?" Jane asked, trying to look over her shoulder. "I thought we agreed that I would wear your green walking dress."

"I changed my mind. You needed a new dress for a wedding. And Miller agreed. The material is not as elegant as we would have found in London, but I think you will be pleased. Miller," she directed.

The maid pulled the muslin from around the dress. Jane walked closer and put out a hand to touch the fine muslin. "You found this in the village?"

"Rather a surprise," Lady Langston agreed. "Probably ordered to please someone, and she did not like it. Now do not dawdle, girl. Stephen will be waiting."

The dress, though simply cut with a deep square neckline, was white embroidered with small yellow flowers on green stems. Around the neckline and waist was a matching green ribbon. On the bed beside it lay a green spencer, also cut simply.

As Miller pulled the dress into place, she apologized. "There was no time to add lace or other decoration. I have saved the extra material should you need it. Also Annie embroiders beautifully. She can add any decoration you choose." She finished hooking Jane into the dress and picked up the spencer.

Looking into the mirror a few minutes later, Jane smiled. "I do not believe I shall want any changes. I like the way this looks." Miller and her niece exchanged pleased smiles.

"Now for the bonnet. Here we had to work with what we

had, but Miller added new ribbons," Lady Langston explained, handing Jane the capote bonnet with green ribbons. "The yellow straw is just the thing." As Jane stared at herself in the mirror, at the dress made just for her, she realized how much she had resented losing her place in the world.

Lady Langston said, "Now we must go or we will be late." Jane froze. Then she took a deep breath. She glanced at herself in the mirror once more. At least Stephen would not think of her as a dowd.

Stephen, although pleased by the thought that Jane would soon be his wife, still felt guilty. He knew he should have told Jane the truth. Perhaps he would have a chance before the ceremony. Impatient to explain, he hurried Vernon, refusing to allow him to try another neckcloth when the sixth one did not crease as the valet expected. He allowed Vernon to smooth his dark green coat over his shoulders until not a crease showed. Then he glanced in the mirror. His buff pantaloons and pale gold waistcoat completed his costume. "Should I wear a fob?" he asked.

"You are dressed just as you should be," Vernon assured him. Stephen picked up his hat, cane, and gloves and started to leave the room. "Haven't you forgotten something?" the valet asked, his face puzzled.

Stephen stopped. "A handkerchief. Give me a handkerchief."

His valet handed him one and watched as he tucked it in his sleeve. When Stephen opened the door, he asked, "Do you have the ring?"

"Ring? What ring?" Stephen asked in a panic.

"Miss Stanfield's wedding ring," the valet explained.

Stephen cursed, using words that Vernon had not heard since Stephen had discovered how his stepmother had wasted his sister's inheritance. Stephen started to run his hand through his hair, but Vernon stopped him, using the same tone of voice he had used since he was in Cambridge. "Do not do that. You do not want people to think I have no knowledge of good grooming."

"But what am I to do?"

"Perhaps one of your own rings will serve until another can be procured," Vernon suggested. Stephen nodded and waited impatiently until Vernon displayed three for his choice. "The emerald. Perhaps it will not fall off."

"It is the smallest one you have." The ring was one that Stephen never wore although he refused to travel without it.

"It was my mother's," Stephen explained, closing his eyes briefly, wondering what his mother would have thought of Jane. Remembering the way Jane held up to adversity, he was certain she would have liked her.

As he walked down the stairs, he frowned. "Have the ladies come down yet?" he asked Smythe.

"Not yet. But Mr. Abercrombie has asked if you will join him in the study."

When Stephen walked in a few moments later, he saw Abercrombie put a piece of paper into a satchel. "What are you doing?"

"I thought as soon as the wedding is over I will be on my way to London," the solicitor explained. "It does not grow dark until late in the evening. And even though I will need to stop for the night, I will be in London before the close of day tomorrow. Then I will be file the settlements and your will."

"Do you have enough to cover your expenses? Shall I give you another draft?"

"The one you gave me will be sufficient," the man assured him. "If you do not mind, I will ride with you to the church. The vicar and doctor will meet us there and have agreed to witness your signature. Then when Miss Stanfield arrives, she can sign. I have arranged for a coach from the local inn and will leave immediately after the ceremony," the solicitor explained.

Stephen merely nodded. The solicitor picked up his satchel and held the door. Stephen walked from the room, glancing up the staircase once more in hopes of seeing Jane.

Chapter Nine

The next time Stephen saw Jane that day was when the door at the back of the church opened and she entered on the arm of the squire, a friend of her father. As he stared at her, he felt a surge of joy run through him.

For Jane the walk down the aisle of the small church she had attended as she was growing up seemed endless. She grasped the squire's arm so tightly that he patted her hand as gently as he knew how. When he placed her hand in Stephen's, she jerked as though she planned to take it away. Then she grew calm.

The vicar looked from one to the other, concerned because they were avoiding each other's eyes. He began the service, hoping he was not making a mistake. Then Stephen looked at Jane, and the vicar smiled at the emotion in his eyes. Although neither of them could have repeated the exact words of the ceremony, their responses were quiet and calm. Not one of the small group attending the wedding realized the turmoil in their hearts. One or two of the ladies brushed tears from their eyes as they thought of the gallant way Stephen and Jane faced his possible death.

While the two of them were signing their marriage lines, Lady Langston beamed and then added her signature as witness. "I have told the servants to arrange a wedding supper," she said. "Our friends will join us. Oh, Jane, your mother will be so pleased."

Jane smiled politely and then allowed herself to be placed within a carriage. When Stephen got in and closed the door, she looked up, startled. "But Lady Langston?" she asked as she felt the coach begin to move.

"She is following in her own carriage," Stephen explained.

"Oh." The two of them sat there for a moment. "Did you know—" Jane began.

"Did you expect?" Stephen asked at the same time. Both fell silent.

"You go first."

"No, you," he insisted.

Jane laughed nervously. "We sound as though we have just met."

"I suppose you could say we had. Good afternoon, Mrs. Middleton," Stephen said, his voice not quite steady.

"Mrs. Middleton? Oh, you mean me." Jane blushed and looked at her hands, still gloveless. "This is a lovely ring," she said breathlessly. She touched the emerald lightly.

"It belonged to my mother. My father gave it to her on her wedding day. She had green eyes like you," Stephen told her, seizing her hand in his.

"Your mother? You have never said much about her. Do you remember her?"

"Yes, she did not die until after I went away to school." His eyes darkened as he remembered the messenger who had come to take him home for her funeral. And as soon has his father was out of mourning, he had found a new, much younger wife who did not care to have a stepson only four years younger than she about to remind her she was a second wife.

"Oh." Jane searched for other topics of conversation but could think of none.

Before the silence had grown oppressive, they arrived at the manor. The footmen and Smythe greeted them as Stephen handed Jane from the carriage. "May I say how happy we are for you, Mrs. Middleton," Smythe said, standing aside.

"Thank you," Jane murmured, feeling as though he were talking to someone else. Stephen too added his thanks.

"Lady Langston suggested that everyone meet in the sitting room," Smythe added, taking Jane's bonnet and Stephen's cane and hat.

Stephen nodded his head, trying to remember what was happening next. "Why?" he whispered as he walked beside his wife.

She glanced up at him, a puzzled look on her face. "The wedding supper," she whispered back.

"What?"

"Lady Langston invited the vicar and some of our friends back to the manor for a wedding supper," she said somewhat louder. "She was talking about it at the church."

Not wanting to admit that the only thing he had paid attention to at the church was Jane, Stephen said, "Oh. How nice of her."

"She has been most kind," Jane added. "Without her, I would have come to you with no bride's clothes."

"Did I tell you how lovely you look?" he asked, smiling at her.

"Not until now." Jane smiled at him. She stepped back, took a look at him, and then looked down at her own dress. "Everyone must think we planned this."

"What?"

"Stephen, we are dressed in the same colors—or almost the same colors," Jane said, laughing.

"Well, I simply put on the clothes Vernon picked out," he explained.

Jane laughed again. "And Miller chose this for me. I wonder if they knew." Stephen and she exchanged a smile.

Before they could say more, the door to the sitting room opened, and Lady Langston entered. "My dears, that went off most splendidly. Our guests will be here shortly. Did Mr. Abercrombie get off?"

Stephen, who had given no thought to his solicitor since he had signed the settlements, nodded.

Before he could say anything, Lady Langston continued, "I hope you gave him the announcement to run in the gazettes." When Stephen nodded once more, she added, "Then it will appear by the end of the week. Although some people have already left town, word will spread. Come, Jane, stand beside me, and you stand beside her, Stephen.

We must greet your guests." She twitched her pale gold silk skirts into place once more and smiled.

As the people who had known Jane for most of her life walked into the room and greeted them, Stephen wondered what she was thinking. Jane smiled at the guests, greeting the squire and his wife warmly. "Your father would be so proud of you," the squire told her, patting her hand as he had done earlier. He turned to Stephen. "You have won the hand of a wonderful girl." His wife simply smiled, allowing him to do all the talking. Her arch look at Jane told the younger lady she wondered how Jane had been so lucky.

Before long, they took their places in the dining room. The cook had provided an elegant repast, beginning with a light chicken soup with wine and mushrooms, which both Jane and Stephen accepted. Smythe personally filled their glasses with wine. Jane drank hers quickly while Stephen sipped his.

While the party was in the dining room, another coach rolled up to the door. A footman came in and whispered something in Smythe's ear. Noting the footmen were in place and capable of carrying on without him, Smythe hurried from the room.

When he arrived in the entrance hall, Langston had just entered, escorting a lady past the first blush of youth but definitely still beautiful. "Smythe," Langston said, thankful that he could turn his guest over to his butler, "show Mrs. Middleton to her room."

Smythe sent a maid for the housekeeper and then nodded. "Shall I assign Mrs. Middleton a maid, sir?" he asked, his face not revealing his emotions.

"No, her maid and my valet follow with the luggage." Neither Langston's voice nor face revealed any emotion. After hours alone with Stephen's stepmother in a coach, he longed for quiet. Why had he ever given in to the impulse to strike back at Stephen?

"This way, please." The housekeeper led the way up the stairs, mentally reviewing the empty bedchambers that would be suitable.

As soon as she was out of sight, Langston turned to his butler. "I suppose you had better send up a tea tray."

"Yes, sir." The butler, his face impassive, waited.

"Where's my mother?" Langston asked, smothering a yawn. The lady had chattered so much he had not been able to sleep on the journey to the manor although he had tried.

"With her guests in the dining room."

"Guests? Well, I am in no condition to receive them like this. I suppose I must change. Tell her I will join her shortly," he said as he ran up the stairs.

Smythe, who had no illusions about his master's temper, watched him, his eyes narrowed. Maybe I should have said something, he thought. Then he shrugged his shoulders. It was not my place. He hurried back to the dining room to instruct the servants to lay more places.

As he took off his neckcloth and shirt, Langston cursed. If only I had not gone to that cursed ball the evening before, he thought. Bored as he often was, he had inspected his invitations and chosen the ones that offered the most excitement. Lady Dinsmore might not be accepted by the highest rung of society, but her entertainments offered a chance for the bachelors of the *ton* to encounter the faster ladies, mostly widows and bored wives also looking for amusement. It was there he had met Stephen's stepmother, although she bristled every time he called her that. Her name was Arabella, he reminded himself as she had reminded him all day.

A spirit of mischief had led him to tell her what had happened to Stephen. Her first response was a look of joy that she had hid quickly under a look of concern. He was not certain he had truly seen it. Then she had insisted that he escort her to her stepson's side or she would go alone. Realizing what his mother would have said when she arrived unescorted and uninvited on the steps of the manor, Langston reluctantly agreed. And he had paid for his mischief, he told himself, as he dunked his head in the water in the bowl. At least the trip to London had been worthwhile. He had signed his marriage settlement, and the notice would appear in the papers this week. He grimaced as he thought of the anger in his fiancée's face when she realized that he was returning to the country. Fortunately, when she discovered Stephen's plight, she sent him on his errand of mercy with her best wishes.

Langston picked up another neckcloth and put it around his neck. Creasing it carefully, he smoothed it into place. Realizing he could not get into his jacket without help, he yanked the bellpull. While he waited, he combed his hair into the windswept style he preferred. Glancing in his mirror, he grimaced. He was going to have to tell his mother about his engagement now. And Jane. He paused, surprised that he had not dwelled on his former betrothed since he had left for London. In fact, had it not been for Stephen's betrayal he would not have thought of her at all. He smiled bitterly. If his present betrothed knew about her, he would be in trouble. Lydia regarded him as her possession, bought and paid for. Only the thought of the money that her father had already settled on him and of her extraordinary beauty made him willing to step into the parson's mousetrap.

With the footman's help, Langston was finally ready. He took a deep breath and walked down the stairs. Pausing in the doorway of the dining room, he glanced around the room, frowning slightly. "Langston," his mother called. "How fortunate you arrived. Now you can lead the toasts." She smiled at him over the heads of her guests, wishing that he had arrived just a half an hour later.

"Toasts?"

"The wedding toasts," his mother replied. Maybe telling him about Stephen and Jane's marriage in public would prevent the explosion she expected. "Stephen and Jane were married today."

The smile on Langston's face froze for a moment. He blinked. Realizing that everyone in the room had their eyes on him, watching his reaction, he forced himself to smile. He walked to the head of the table and took his seat, taking up his wineglass, which the footman quickly filled. "May I wish you every happiness," he said quietly, a smile on his face though Stephen could read the anger in his eyes. Then his eyes narrowed. "But I have invited a guest who should be part of this celebration. Let me ask her to join us." Calling a footman to his side, he sent him off with the message. Jane and Stephen looked at each other and then away. From long experience, they knew when Langston was up to mischief.

Lady Langston simply smiled. Directing the servants to refill her guests' glasses, she lifted her own. "To the happy couple," she said. Other guests followed her suit. Langston downed each glass as though he were trying to wash a bad taste from his mouth.

Finally, the squire raised his glass. "Since your papa is not here, I will take his place. You, sir," speaking to Stephen, "are entrusted with a great gift this day. I hope you will care for her."

"I will," Stephen promised, turning to smile at Jane. Langston tightened his hand around his wineglass. He started to say something else, but the door opened.

"Ah, here is my guest now," Langston said, standing up. "May I introduce Mrs. Middleton, Stephen's stepmama?"

Jane's eyes opened wide as they took in the vision before her. A petite lady of the type called a pocket Venus, her dark hair in short curls that framed a pixie face, dressed in a gown of apricot silk with deep bands of blond lace, stood framed in the doorway. She gasped. Stephen frowned. "Surely he is mistaken?" she asked her husband in a whisper.

He shook his head. "No." The one word told Jane that Stephen was not happy. She grasped his hand tightly. He looked at her and smiled ruefully. "I suppose I should have expected something like this."

As the ripples of surprise moved around the room, Arabella Middleton moved toward the table, taking the seat next to Langston. Lady Langston frowned at her son. He smiled back, but the smile did not reach his eyes. "Langston asked me to join the celebration. I do so love a party. What are we celebrating?" She smiled at him, her dark lashes dropping over her eyes coquettishly.

His eyes dancing with mischief, Langston said, "I knew

you would want to join us as we celebrated Stephen and Jane's wedding."

The smile on her face froze. She turned slowly to face her stepson. "Wedding?" she asked softly. "Wedding? Wedding? How dare you?" By the time she spoke the last word she was shouting. She got up and moved toward the couple, her hands curved into claws. Most of the guests froze.

Moving quickly, Lady Langston rose, too. Before Arabella could reach her target, Lady Langston grabbed her by the arm. "I know you wish to give them your blessings," she said, giving Arabella a shake that was evident to most of the guests.

"My blessing?" Arabella asked. Her eyes flashed, and she glared first at her stepson and then at his new wife. "I think not!" She jerked her arm free from Lady Langston's grasp. "Langston, I wish to leave immediately." Without waiting for his answer, she spun around and left the room, leaving the guests stunned.

"Well, I never," the squire's wife whispered to the lady across the table.

"Perhaps journeys to the country do not agree with her," the squire suggested. His wife and her friend turned to stare at him, and he reached for his wineglass.

Lady Langston gathered her composure. "Shall we retire to the sitting room, ladies?" she asked. The gentlemen left behind exchanged nervous glances, wanting to discuss what had happened but not willing to further embarrass Stephen.

Glancing at his friend at the head of the table, Stephen downed one glass of port and then excused himself. "I think I will join my wife."

Langston frowned at him and then held up his glass to be refilled once more. "As you wish," he said, through clenched teeth. The other men looked from Stephen to their host and made their own excuses.

Before long, all the guests had departed. Lady Langston, Jane, and Stephen saw them on their way. Then Lady Langston said, "I am exhausted. I will see you tomorrow." She smiled at them and walked up the stairs.

Jane and Stephen stood there awkwardly. "Now I understand why the wedding couple usually takes a wedding journey," Stephen finally said. He ran his hand through his hair, pushing it back from his forehead.

"What do you mean?" Jane asked. She longed to find a quiet place to sit down and think. She kept her eyes down as if to hide her confusion.

"They want to get away." He sighed. "Jane, I apologize for the way my stepmother acted." He turned to look at her and grabbed her hands.

Startled, she just stood there for a moment, wondering at the look on his face. "You did nothing."

"That is right. I just sat there and let her make a fool of herself." Stephen dropped her hands and turned around. His shoulders sagged.

"What could you have done?" Jane asked, stepping closer to him. "Did you know she was expected?"

"Expected? She was the last person I expected to see. I deliberately did not tell her what has been happening." He turned around just in time to see the maid and footman glance around the open door. "Shall we find a more private place to discuss this?" he suggested.

"Where?"

"If we go to the library, someone is certain to interrupt us," Stephen said. He looked as though searching for an escape.

"The garden?"

When they opened the door, it had started to rain. "Blast!" Stephen said. He shut the door. Then he looked at Jane again. The look on his face puzzled her. He took a deep breath. "We could go to our rooms."

Jane stepped back. "Our rooms?" Her voice was shaky.

"I suppose I should say our new rooms. Vernon said he would move my things as soon as I left for the church and that he would get someone to move your things while we were at the ceremony."

"Move my things?" Jane repeated, taking a few more steps backward. Her hand was at her throat. Although she had grown up with servants, this last year she had become accustomed to waiting on herself, on having at least a room that was all hers. "Why did we have to move?"

Stephen looked at her, one eyebrow raised. "Did you expect me to move into your room?" he asked, confused by her reaction.

"I—I—" Jane began. Then she stopped. Taking a deep breath, she squared her shoulders and looked into his deep blue eyes. "I had not thought about it at all," she admitted. Sharing a room with Stephen—the thought sent shivers through her.

"Come upstairs. Lady Langston had us moved into one of the suites. We can talk there," he said, taking her hand and leading her to the stairs. "I will have Vernon send up a tea tray."

"Annie can do it," Jane told him, smiling to herself.

"Who is Annie?" Stephen asked, drawing her hand through his arm.

"My maid. I hired her this morning. That was all right, wasn't it?" Jane asked, her green eyes wide.

"You may have all the maids you wish," he assured her. "But what made you decide on her?"

As Jane explained, she forgot to be nervous. At the top of the stairs, she stumbled. Stephen lifted her lightly and kept her from falling. He turned toward their new rooms.

A door closed behind them. "Stephen!" He froze as he recognized the voice. Slowly the two of them turned around. "How dare you embarrass me like that!" Arabella Middleton said, throwing her golden brown cloak about her shoulders. Her dark eyes flashed with anger.

"Embarrass you?" Stephen asked. His hand tightened protectively over Jane's. His voice was quiet but cold.

"I am certain no one intended anyone be embarrassed," Jane said, trying to smooth over the situation.

Arabella glared at her. "I did not ask for your opinion," she said bitingly.

"You will treat my wife with respect!" Stephen told her, the controlled anger in his tone evident to Jane.

"Stephen," she pleaded, looking up at him, her hands on his upper arms. He glanced at her and dampened his anger.

"Wife? This wedding happened very quickly. I saw no engagement announcement in the paper." Arabella tossed her head, her dark curls dancing. She inspected him, looking for illness.

"Jane has been in mourning until recently," Stephen explained.

"For my father," Jane added, exchanging a brief smile with her new husband. Arabella tightened her mouth, making her look like a shrew.

"How convenient." Pausing before a mirror, Arabella took a moment to smooth her curls and rearrange her face so that her lines did not show.

"And why are you here?" Stephen asked, certain he knew the answer. Jane tensed and waited for the reply.

"Langston invited me." Arabella turned to face him. "He told me some tale about you having rabies." She paused and smiled insincerely. "Of course, I hurried to your side only to find he was wrong. You look perfectly healthy to me."

"I am." Stephen felt Jane's hand tighten on his arm. He smiled down at her. Her eyes wide, she smiled back, hoping he was right. Then they both looked at Arabella.

"Then I am *de trop* here," she said. "Where is Langston? I am ready to leave."

Jane bit her lip to keep from suggesting that it was too late to leave that day. Stephen told her, "I last saw Langston in the dining hall. Shall I send someone to inquire if he is still there?"

"No!" His stepmother remembered her manners. "I will seek him there myself." She took a few steps toward the staircase. Stephen relaxed a trifle but stiffened immediately when she turned back, her smile positively venomous. "I suppose you know that your hasty marriage will have people counting. I shall enjoy the speculation."

"Not everyone wins a husband on her back," Stephen said. Jane stiffened, surprised. Arabella flushed an angry red. "Let me know where you will be for the next few weeks, Arabella. My solicitor has some items to review with you." She glared at him and hurried down the stairs.

Stephen ran his hand over his face. "I'm sorry you had to be present for that, Jane. She is usually more circumspect."

"Has she always disliked you so much?" she asked as they turned down the corridor once more. Stephen opened their door and waited for her to enter. Nervously, she glanced around. Feeling his arm urging her forward, she crossed the threshold. When the door closed behind them, she stiffened. Stephen put his hands on her shoulders and felt her tense again. Taking her arm once more, he led her to the settee.

When she was seated, he yanked the bellpull and took the chair nearby. Jane's spine was as straight as a ferule. But when she realized that he planned to sit opposite her, she relaxed a trifle. "Poor Stephen," she whispered, the thought of his peril never far from her mind.

Stephen smiled ruefully at her almost unintelligible words. "Rather, poor Jane. You must be regretting your decision to marry me." Jane looked up, her brow creased with a frown. The emotional ups and downs of the last few hours had exhausted her. She yawned and covered her mouth hastily. Stephen laughed bitterly, the sound grating on her already overwrought nerves.

"Excuse me. I did not sleep very well last night." She blushed as she realized what she had revealed. "I will be all right when I have some tea."

As though her words were magic, Vernon scratched on the door and entered. Quickly, Stephen gave their request for tea and, remembering that Jane had eaten little except the soup, asked that Cook send up a light supper. "And send up Mrs. Middleton's maid." Jane's face flamed again at the realization that he had the right to order the details of her life, and she ducked her head, staring at her hands.

Stephen heard rather than watched Vernon leave. His eyes were on his wife. His wife, the words rang in his mind. "Would you be more comfortable without your spencer?" he asked. "The room seems rather warm to me." Jane stiffened once more.

"I am fine," she said quietly, staring at her hands. Then

her head came up. "Stephen, why does that woman"—she refused to call her his stepmother—"hate you?"

He leaned back in his chair, looking everywhere but at her. Finally, he got up and began to pace. "She should not have insulted you," he said, his teeth clenched.

"Me?" Jane twisted around on the settee until she could face him once more. "She insulted you."

"And you."

"She hates you."

Stephen took his seat again and put his head in his hands. "I thought this would all be settled before she knew anything about it."

"There is nothing she can do to dissolve the marriage, is there?" Jane asked, not sure what she wanted his answer to be.

"Nothing. If she knew Abercrombie had been here, she would have been more upset. She doesn't like him."

"Why?"

This time Stephen raised his head, his smile broad. "He does not let her have her way. She is the reason I came home from Canada early. Abercrombie suggested it."

"She was?" Although he had mentioned his stepmother once or twice and said she was a bad influence on her daughter, Jane knew few details. She leaned forward, knowing that if Stephen died she would have the responsibility for dealing with this woman.

"After Father died, she was incensed by his will." Stephen ran his hand through his hair, pushing back the lock of hair on his forehead.

"Why? Was her jointure less than she expected?" That had happened to her mother.

"No. But she expected Father to leave her some property instead of just a life interest in the dower house. And she didn't like the fact that I was Caroline's guardian and in charge of her inheritance."

"You mentioned that before. Did she truly expect to be left in charge?" Jane remembered the confusion that followed her father's death and wondered how they would have managed if her mother and she had had to make the decisions alone. They had gotten the advice of the agent who had served the family for years and had still had problems. But most of their difficulties had stemmed from lack of money. Surely Stephen's stepmother didn't have to worry about that.

"No. But she expected her trustees, men she had known all her life and could control, to be in sole charge." Stephen laughed ruefully. "Maybe I should have let her go her own way."

"You couldn't do that. Everyone would have blamed you. What did she do to make you return from Canada?" Before Stephen could answer, Vernon had returned with a footman and Annie. Leaving the men arranging the tea things, Jane walked into the bedroom with her maid.

"Should you like to change, Mrs. Middleton?" Annie had been practicing her mistress's new title all afternoon. "I moved your things earlier."

"What?" Jane paused, trying to remember just what she had that would be appropriate.

"My aunt suggested this." Annie held out a simple blue dress, its lace-lined neckline caught with ribbons. "Or you could be more informal." She held up a light gold dressing gown that Jane remembered Lady Langston buying just before they left London.

"That is not mine," she protested, running her hand over the soft silk, enjoying how it felt against her skin.

"Lady Langston insists. My aunt says it is not as becoming as she thought it would be. But it will look very nice on you," Annie said, tempting her mistress as she had been coached to do. Jane glanced at it wistfully. "I could remove your stays so that you would be more comfortable."

Her mistress stiffened. "Mr. Middleton is waiting tea for me," she said hesitantly, longing for the comfort of the dressing gown yet shy about appearing in front of Stephen in such an informal dress.

"You are married," Annie reminded her. Though the maid was young, she was aware of the relationships between men and women.

Jane flushed again. The girl was right. And Stephen

might succumb to the disease at any time. She glanced at the dressing gown once more. "I will wear it," she said in a voice so low that Annie strained to hear it. The maid smiled.

Waiting for his wife to reenter the room, Stephen paced nervously. He had already given Vernon his instructions, and Vernon would instruct his wife's maid. Neither of the servants was to enter this suite until they were called for. His heart beating so loudly that he was sure Jane could hear it, he turned when the bedroom door opened and Jane walked in. The gold lights in her hair caught the color of the dressing gown and glowed. He gasped, feeling his heart in his throat.

Annie slipped through the door behind Jane and left the room. "He is so much in love with her," she told her aunt when she reached the servants' hall where the staff were celebrating the wedding. Vernon, not far away, nodded.

Stephen crossed to where Jane was standing just inside the door. He took her hand in his and carried it to his lips. Jane felt a flutter of excitement. Her heart began beating faster. Her eyes were huge. "Come." She allowed him to lead her to the settee once more. "Shall I fix your tea?" he asked, a mischievous look in his eyes.

"No. I will do it," she replied. Happy to have something to occupy her and to avoid his gaze, she kept her eyes on what she was doing.

"I'm glad. Any tea I make is usually undrinkable, or so the men I traveled with told me. Vernon usually took over that chore," he explained. He reached up and pushed back a curl that had fallen over her ear. She shivered and caught her breath.

"With practice you might improve," she said softly. Handing him his cup, her hand touched his. Both quivered as though they had been struck. As soon as he had the teacup in his grasp, she pulled back and poured her own cup.

"Have something to eat," he suggested, his voice husky. He wanted to sweep her in his arms and crush her against him but was afraid of her reaction.

She glanced at the plates of cakes and other tasty morsels and felt her throat close. She could barely swallow her tea, and he wanted her to eat. She shook her head. Then she picked up her cup and took another sip.

The silence was deafening. Stephen cleared his throat. Jane jumped, splashing tea on the table. Grabbing a serviette, she wiped it up quickly. Holding the cloth, she looked around as though she did not know what to do with it. "Put it on the tray, and the servants will take care of it later," Stephen suggested. As if reluctant to follow his advice, she held it for a moment and then put it down. Once again the silence stretched between them. Stephen put his cup on the tray and turned to Jane, noticing the way her hand trembled as she took another sip of tea. He cleared his throat again. Once again she jumped. "Jane, you don't have to be afraid of me," he said. Knowing being alone with him in her dressing gown was new to her, he tried to be patient. But her behavior was not what he expected. He frowned as she clasped her hands tighter and whispered something. "What?"

"I said I am not afraid of you," she said more loudly.

"Then why do you jump every time I touch you or start to talk?"

"Why? Today has not been particularly easy for me. How would you like everyone staring at you while your new husband's stepmother causes a scene because you just married her stepson?" His question had been the spark that renewed her anger.

"Staring at you? How do you think I felt when Langston walked in and then introduced her?"

"Langston? What has he to do with this?" Her green eyes flashed with fire.

"He's the one who bears the responsibility for what happened today," Stephen said. "My stepmother would not even be here if he had not brought her."

"All he did was introduce her." Jane defended her former betrothed even though she had to admit at least to herself that he had helped to cause the scene.

"And tell her we had just wed."

"Did you plan to keep it a secret? Are you ashamed of me?" Jane stood up, squaring her shoulders and facing him. Stephen also stood up. He reached for her hands, but she pulled back.

"Of course, I am not ashamed of you. I simply hoped to protect you from her tongue." He glanced at her, but Jane was looking over his shoulder instead of at him. "She can have all the temper tantrums she wants if she does not disturb you."

"Me?" Jane shook her head. She glanced at him through her thick eyelashes, surprised to realize how pleased she was that he was worried about her. "Has she always been like this?" She sat down again on the settee. Stephen started to sit down beside her but thought better of it. He took the chair across from her once more.

"I understand she can be very pleasant if she likes you," he said. He reached up and untied his cravat. Jane's eyes widened. "However, I can't speak from personal experience." He twisted his neck, glad to be free from the starched neckcloth. He tried to stretch his arms to release the tension in his back, but his coat was too tight. Jane watched him, her nerves tense. He started to pull his jacket off.

"What are you doing?" she asked, her voice breathless.

"Trying to get out of this thing. I should have had Vernon help me off with it before he left."

"I will send for him." Jane started to get up.

"No, just grab a sleeve and pull." She sat there for a moment, trying to decide what to do. "Jane, come here. You have seen me in my shirtsleeves before."

Realizing he was right, she got up to stand at his right side. Pulling on the sleeve, she helped him get one arm free and then watched as he pulled the coat off completely. His shoulders seemed much broader without the coat. Then he unbuttoned his waistcoat. She gasped.

"Jane, what is wrong? You were never missish in your life," Stephen asked, throwing his garments over the back of his chair.

"And how would you know? Since your father died, I

have seen you a total of . . ." She began to count the days on her fingers.

"What difference does that make? I haven't changed."

"Some people do." Her voice was sharp.

"Do not accuse me of Langston's follies." He glared at her.

"What do you mean?"

"I mean had you been engaged to me I would never have deserted you." The words left his mouth before he could stop them. "Jane, I am sorry. I did not intend to say that. I would never hurt you."

"The truth never hurt anyone," she said softly, blinking hard to keep her tears from falling.

Stephen made a rude noise. She looked up, startled, tears pooling at the corners of her eyes. "Who told you that?" he demanded. "Some 'kind' friend?" He left his chair and took a seat beside her. "Jane, don't lie to me. I hurt you, my stepmother ruined our wedding breakfast, and Langston did not help."

She let a few tears run down her cheeks and brushed them away angrily. "Does that mean you do not plan to be truthful with me?" she asked.

"No. Of course, not." He took a deep breath. Now was the time to tell her about the frogs. He hesitated, not wanting to cause any more turmoil, and the opportunity slipped away.

"Then explain to me the animosity between you and your stepmother."

Stephen picked up her hand and held it. Jane didn't pull away. "I was the heir," he began, "and she was a second wife." Patiently, he answered her questions until they both began to yawn. "Come to bed," he suggested.

Chapter Ten

As Jane allowed Stephen to usher her into the bedroom, her mind raced. She glanced at her husband again, her eyes hidden under her lashes. Over and over again, she reminded herself that this was Stephen, her friend, a man who cared for her. However, the thought of what would happen when they were in bed together sent shivers through her. She glanced at the drapery-hung bed across the room and then blushed.

Stephen, too, looked toward the bed. Then he turned his head away. Taking a deep breath and putting thoughts of Jane and him together in it behind him, he said, "You take the bed. I will sleep on the cot in the dressing room."

"What?" Jane swung around until she stood in front of him. The sense of relief she felt at first disappeared, and doubts filled her mind.

"I will sleep in there," he said once more, avoiding her eyes. "Good night."

Realizing that he intended to leave her alone, Jane said, "Stephen." He stopped but did not turn around. "You do not have to do that." She was shocked as she realized what she had said but did not withdraw her words. She trembled.

He turned around and came back to stand in front of her. "You are sweet," he whispered as he bent his head and kissed her. Then he stepped back before he lost control of his emotions. "But I must."

Her senses reeled with his kiss. His words, however, chilled her. She backed away from him until her back was against the bed. Her dressing gown fell open slightly, giving him a tantalizing glimpse of her breasts barely contained by her chemise. She searched his face, not at all certain what she was looking for. Then she turned her back, her head bowed.

Stephen took a step or two forward; then he stopped. "Jane," he whispered, emotion making his voice shake.

"No. You do not have to explain," she said, gaining control of her voice so that she did not reveal her hurt. "We can talk in the morning."

"But I want you to know why . . ."

She turned to look at him, her face expressionless. Never would he know how much it had cost her to make the offer. Stephen winced as he realized how much he had hurt her. "No explanation is necessary."

"Yes, it is." He crossed the space separating them. She stiffened. "Jane, you do not understand."

"What is it that I do not understand? That you do not want to spend our wedding night with me? I think you made that perfectly clear," she said, shaking with anger and some other undefined feeling.

"Not want! Jane, you cannot believe that?"

"Why not? You are sleeping in the dressing room, aren't you?"

"I thought you would understand. I've rushed you so that I wanted to give you some time." He reached out and cupped her face with his hand. As she realized what he had said, she smiled, warmed by his care for her. Jane relaxed and moved her head so that her lips caressed his palm. He took a deep breath and stepped back once more. She frowned. "And . . ."

Jane turned her back on him, biting her lip. The confidence she had worked so hard to restore during the last year began to crumble. And her hopes died unborn. "Go to bed," she whispered, fighting the urge to throw herself on the bed and weep loudly.

"No. Not until I've explained." His voice was soft and pleading.

Jane hardened her heart. "You did. You want to give me more time."

"Partly." Stephen let out the breath he was holding in a rush. "Damn it, Jane. This is so hard for me."

She turned around once more. "What is so hard about getting in bed?"

"You don't understand."

"Then explain it to me," she demanded. Her eyes flashed, and just for a moment Stephen saw the adventuresome girl she had once been, a girl who would not take no for an answer.

He ran his hand through his hair. "I can't . . ." Stephen hesitated, not wanting to shock her.

"Stephen, first you tell me you want to explain, and then you say you can't? This is not like you. What is wrong? Are you ill?"

"No. It's Langston," he blurted out.

Jane stared at him for a moment and then shook her head. "What did you say?"

"I wish we had left as soon as the ceremony was over."

"Because we would have avoided that woman?" Jane leaned against the edge of the bed.

"No. Yes. For that reason too." He ran his hand through his hair again and began to pace. Jane frowned. "If we were anywhere else, you and I would share that bed tonight," he said softly.

"Anywhere else?" As she realized what he had said, Jane felt as if a heavy load had been lifted from her. "Are you doing this because we are at the manor?" She took a few steps towards him.

Stephen looked at her, not trying to hide his emotions. What she saw in his eyes made her catch her breath. "Of course. This is Langston's home."

"But I am your wife," she reminded him, wondering how the words that had seemed so frightening earlier that day now seemed so right.

"I know," he said with a groan. "But I am going to sleep in the dressing room." He turned and walked across the room, afraid to turn and look at her for fear he would lose his resolution.

"Stephen." He stopped, his shoulders stiff. "The ser-

vants?" The coldness that had been part of her voice early
in their discussion had disappeared, and his name was a caress.

"They won't come until we ring for them." He opened
the door and walked through, closing it after him. Because
he did not turn around, he did not see the smile that played
across her lips.

Jane slipped out of the dressing gown, her petticoat, and
chemise and into the nightgown Annie had laid out for her.
She yawned and climbed into bed, pulling the pillows into
her arms. "Mrs. Stephen Middleton," she whispered as she
drifted off to sleep almost immediately, thinking how honorable her husband was. Stephen, however, lay awake for
hours, fighting the urge to open the door and join her.

Stephen was not the only one who had a disturbed night.
By the time Arabella Middleton found Langston, he had
consumed several bottles of port but was not completely
castaway. He raised his head as she walked in the door of
the library where he had moved on Smythe's suggestion.
"Still here?" he asked, noting the cloak that she wore.

"Where else would I be? I have no carriage. Surely you
remember that. I am dependent on you." She flashed her
dark eyes at him, trying to gauge his reaction. Seeing his
face harden, she changed her tactics. Crossing the room,
she paused beside the chair in which he had remained even
though good manners required him to stand. Running her
fingers down the side of his face, she said, "I am so unhappy." She smiled sadly. "I am certain you will do your
best to correct the situation." She bent and kissed him
lightly, running her fingers down his thigh. "If you take me
back to London now, I will be forever grateful." The look
on her face promised what form her gratitude would take.

"Frankly, my dear, as delightful as your offer is, I cannot
accept," he drawled, standing up at last. He held on to the
back of the chair. Her face lost its cajoling look. "It is too
late, and I am in no shape for a long drive. Perhaps I can interest you in more delightful entertainment here?"

"How can you expect me to stay under such unpleasant
conditions?" Her eyes filled with tears, and she let one

teardrop roll down her cheek. "You should have heard what Stephen and that woman said to me." She sank down in the chair he had just vacated and buried her head in her hands.

"When?" Langston looked around for another chair. He took the few steps to reach it and sat down heavily, sighing loudly.

She raised her head. "Just a few minutes ago, in the hall." Her voice quivered dramatically. Once again she let a tear roll down her cheek.

Oblivious to her machinations, Langston sat up straighter. "They are still here?"

Arabella bit down on her lip to keep from giving him a sharp answer. "It is just like Stephen. He is too much of a clutchpurse to take her on a wedding journey, I imagine. You cannot believe the number of economies he has insisted I make. His father would be horrified to know how his heir was treating me." She dabbed her eyes with her handkerchief, always keeping her eyes on her host.

No matter how much he had had to drink, Langston recognized her tricks. Remembering how Stephen's father had left his estate, he was certain the older man had known exactly what his young wife would do and had taken steps to prevent her outrunning her budget. No wonder she disliked Stephen. Stephen. Stephen and Jane. Stephen and Jane upstairs together. Langston's expression hardened.

"I do not know why he has never liked me. I have tried so hard to be a good stepmother. You cannot know how much his actions hurt me," Arabella added. "Oh, Langston. I am so very alone." Before he had time to stop her, she had crossed the few steps that separated them and thrown herself on his lap, crying softly into his shoulder. "You do understand? I know you do. I simply can no longer stay here."

His arms closed tightly around her, his hand coming up her side to rest under her breast. Langston took a breath. She pressed against him more tightly, one of her hands moving back to his thigh. He took a deep breath, reveling in the exotic fragrance she wore. Bending his head, he kissed her. Her lips opened, and he deepened the kiss. Arabella denied him nothing, slipping her tongue into his

mouth. When he pulled back a few minutes later, he was
flushed. Arabella once again ran her hand down his face.
"You will take me to London, won't you?" she asked, her
eyes wide and pleading.

His eyes narrowed. "Perhaps. Now I think we should
continue this discussion elsewhere," he said, trying to decide whether his rooms or hers were closer.

"Elsewhere?" she asked. For Arabella, the "perhaps" was
as good as a promise. She smiled up at him.

"One of the footmen could come in at any time," Langston
told her, knowing that he had given orders that he not be disturbed until he rang. "Think of the gossip if he found us in
here alone."

Arabella looked at him, not certain if he was protecting
her reputation or his own. "But—"

He helped her to her feet and stood up beside her. "I am
certain we can find someplace much more private and comfortable." He watched as she rearranged her bodice. "There
you can tell me exactly what we should do." Arabella could
not keep a glint of satisfaction from crossing her face as
they walked out the door.

When they reached the door to her room, he persuaded
her to dismiss her maid until they had worked out the details and waited nearby until the woman left. Slipping
through the door a few minutes later, he pulled her into his
arms. Before she could explain her plan, he captured her
lips. Wrapping her arms around him, she returned the kiss,
never loath to use her wiles to get her way. "But we must
make plans," she protested when he picked her up and carried her to the bed.

"Later." When Langston left her room during the early
hours of the morning, Arabella was asleep, a satisfied expression on her face. As he crept down the corridor to his
own room, he passed the room Stephen usually occupied,
and he paused, clenched his teeth, and walked thoughtfully
down the corridor.

When he woke the next morning, Stephen smoothed the
bed on which he had slept. Entering the bedroom, he
crossed to the large bed, his eyes softening as he watched

Jane curl up on her side. He put out a hand to smooth her hair away from her face and then drew it back, afraid he would wake her. The faint shadows that had ringed her eyes were still there. Longing to slide into bed with her, instead he went into the sitting room and yanked the bellpull. When Vernon and Annie appeared a short time later, he sent Annie for a breakfast tray and allowed Vernon to shave him. By the time she returned, he was dressed in his favorite blue riding coat, buff pantaloons, and glossy Hessians.

Sending the servants away once more, he walked into the bedroom and started to take a seat where he could watch Jane. As he was moving a chair, he hit the small table beside the bed. Before he could grab it, a heavy candlestick hit the floor with a thud. Trying to catch himself from sliding to the floor, he grabbed the side of the bed, pulling the covers off his wife.

Jane, more dozing than asleep, opened her eyes when she heard the thud. When the bedcovers were pulled from her grasp, she sat up, pushing her nightgown down around her legs. "What—" she began.

Stephen pulled himself up and rearranged the covers around her. "I was trying not to wake you," he explained. He smiled at her ruefully.

Jane drew her restored covers up to her neck and looked at him with wide eyes. "Hmmm."

"Shall I call Annie for you?" he asked, reminding himself that they were still in Langston's home. He crossed to the widow and pulled back the drapes. "It is a beautiful day."

Jane, who preferred to spend a few minutes by herself when she first woke up, merely looked at him, disconcerted. As the light filled the room, the shock of waking up and finding a man in her room disappeared as she remembered the events of the previous day. "What?" she asked again, her voice sleep roughened.

"Do you want me to send for Annie? She brought up some breakfast earlier, but I decided to wait for you."

Stephen made his voice light, but it took effort to stay near the window.

"Chocolate?" Jane brightened.

"She brought a pot. Shall I get you some?" Stephen walked through the door into the sitting room, leaving the door open. "It does not appear to be too hot."

Pouring her a cup, he brought it to her, carrying it carefully so that he did not spill any. Jane reached for it eagerly. Their fingers met as they had the previous evening. Both jumped back, dropping the cup. Chocolate flew all over the bed. "Oh, no," Jane moaned, looking at the mess in the center of the bed.

"Blast! It was my fault. Come, get out of there. Are you all right? Did it burn you?" Stephen lifted her from the bed and put her on the floor. He held her hands and inspected them for burns.

"I'm fine. A trifle wet and sticky." Jane held her wet nightgown away from her body. She glanced up at her husband. Seeing the way he was staring at her, she blushed. "Send for Annie, please," she whispered as she turned away to pick up the dressing gown and hold it in front of her.

Reluctantly, Stephen did as she asked. Jane glanced at the dressing room and then back at Stephen. Longing for a moment alone to slip out of the wet garment and to complete her morning routine, she shifted from foot to foot. As the silence grew between them, Stephen finally left the room.

Sometime later, she joined him the sitting room. "I sent for a fresh pot of chocolate," he said, pouring her a cup. "This time I promise not to spill it."

"You? I did it." Jane sat down and let him put the cup in front of her on the low table. The soft blue morning gown fell around her feet.

"That is a pretty dress. I always have liked you in blue."

"Thank Lady Langston. Without her kindness and her maid, I would still be in gray," she told him.

"When we get to London, you will order a whole new wardrobe."

The tone of his voice made Jane bristle. Except for the year she had spent as a companion, she had enjoyed the freedom of being able to make up her own mind. "Perhaps I do not want one," she said, her eyes flashing. "Besides, I thought we were going to see my mother."

Stephen recognized the tone that appeared in her voice whenever she resented something she was being told to do. "Listen to me, married one day and acting as a tyrant already," he said, trying to placate her. "I merely thought you would enjoy shopping. You can order your mother and sister new clothes, too. But if you would prefer not?"

Jane eyed him warily. "Do not try to cut me up sweet, Stephen. I know your tricks." She sipped her chocolate. "Mama and Louise will love new clothes, and so will I, as I am sure you already realize. You already know how limited my wardrobe is."

Stephen relaxed. Jane had a wicked temper, but she was usually reasonable. He sat up, an idea forming in his mind. "You can order new gowns in the village. Why didn't I think of that before?"

"Nonsense. Thanks to Lady Langston's generosity I have enough dresses for now. Any that I ordered here would have to be replaced later. And I am not as wasteful as that."

"You don't need to practice false economies, my dear," Stephen reminded her. He took a bite of muffin. Pleased at the excuse to spend more time with his wife, Stephen had not wanted to brave the breakfast room that morning.

"I am not. She is the one who made my gray dresses before I went to work for Lady Langston. Mama said it wouldn't be proper for me to continue in black and accept Lady Langston's offer of a position."

"Those things came from this village?" Disgust was evident in every word. "Then I positively forbid you to visit her shop," Stephen said firmly. He watched Jane stiffen. "Now do not tell me you have changed your mind and would like a dress from her hands just because I have said you couldn't. I know you too well."

Jane laughed ruefully. "I don't know what has come over

me, reverting to old habits that way. I assure you I have come to be the most biddable creature imaginable."

"You may have had to make yourself agreeable to suit Lady Langston. But I like you just the way you are." His face and voice were serious as he thought of her listless attitude the evening she and Lady Langston had arrived. "At least the way you are when you are with me."

Jane flushed. She poured herself another cup of chocolate she did not want and sipped it, giving herself a excuse for not answering. Stephen took another bite of muffin but could barely swallow. He crumbled the rest on his plate before setting it to one side. As each wondered what the other was thinking, silence stretched between them.

Stephen finally stood up and began to walk about the room. He cleared his throat. Jane looked up, but he merely looked at the floor. For the first time that day, she stared at his broad shoulders and dark hair. He glanced at her, and she lowered her eyes. As soon as he looked away, she continued her inspection. That tall, handsome man was her husband. He had the right to enter her bedroom as he had done that morning.

Finally she put her cup back on the tray and stood up. "Will we join Langston and his mother for luncheon?" she asked, her hand smoothing a wrinkle from her frock.

"We must. To do less would be an insult."

"What will you say to him?"

Stephen froze, his hand on the back of the settee. Jane did not see the way his fingers grew whiter as his grip tightened. "Who?" His voice was as calm as he could make it.

"Langston. Stephen, we must talk to him." Jane stood up and crossed to his side. She reached out and put her hand on his sleeve. He covered her hand with his own.

"No." She gasped and stepped back. He smiled and shook his head. "That is a duty I will take on myself," he explained. "I am the one who insisted that you marry me."

"I agreed," she said quietly. "Let us go together."

"No. It will be better if I go alone." He walked to the door, wishing that the interview with his friend were over. He opened the door and stepped into the hallway.

"Check on the dogs while you are out, Stephen," Jane called as the door swung closed behind him. Stephen jumped. He stared at the heavy wooden door that stood between him and his wife. The dogs. He should go back in there and explain. As he stood there staring at the panels, a door farther down the hallway opened. Not wanting to encounter his stepmother, he turned away and hurried down the staircase.

Jane reentered the bedroom and inspected herself in the mirror. She glanced at the bed, already stripped of the chocolate-soiled sheets, and smiled as she remembered how reluctant Stephen had been to leave her the previous evening. She grimaced as she thought of the way she had demanded an explanation. He was so honorable. Picking up a handkerchief and her reticule, she hurried from the room.

Seeing Miller in the hallway, she asked, "Has Lady Langston already gone down?"

"She is in her room," the maid replied. Jane nodded and walked slowly to the room her former employer occupied. As she had for the last year, she knocked on the door and entered.

"Jane, my dear. I did not expect to see you here this morning," Lady Langston said, sitting upright in bed. "Has your husband deserted you?"

"He has gone to talk to Langston." Jane twisted her handkerchief nervously in her fingers.

"Langston. That will not do. Call Miller for me. I must finish dressing immediately," the older lady said as she moved to the edge of the bed.

"I suggested it," Jane admitted, wondering if Lady Langston were right to be so upset.

"You did what?" Seeing Jane's face and the way she was still twisting her handkerchief, Lady Langston hurried to her side. "Jane, you must go after Stephen. It is always better to let Langston have some time to adjust before confronting him. I thought that boy had more sense. And you, too. Go! Quickly now!" She practically pushed Jane from her room.

After asking for Langston in the house, Stephen headed

toward the stables. He was only halfway there when he met him. Langston, usually a late riser, had not been able to sleep for long after he had returned to his room. As soon as it was light enough to see, he had dressed and gone for a ride.

Although he traveled fields he knew well, he did not see them. Only long familiarity with the land kept the horse from stumbling once or twice. Finally, he pulled his horse to a stop, near the boundary to Jane's home. The morning mist was just beginning to burn off, and the green grass stretched around him when he slid off his horse and climbed the rock that had served as sentry post for many of their games. As the day wore on, he sat there, thinking of his actions when he learned of the marriage. "Stephen should have told me," he muttered to himself. Without really knowing what he was doing, he picked up a rock and threw it into the field. A short time later he laughed bitterly as he remembered the way he had reacted to Stephen's merely talking to Jane. "She is mine," he whispered again, trying to believe his words. This time his words mocked him, reminding him of the petty way he had acted. "His stepmother. Blast! If Stephen ever finds out." He paused. "Or Jane." For the first time, Langston admitted to himself that his life had changed. He had not wanted it to. He had wanted to keep it the same, keep Jane tied to him although he was not tied to her. He laughed loudly and bitterly, startling his horse grazing only a few feet away. "Jane and Stephen," he whispered. He closed his eyes as if to shut out the memory of them together. In spite of his anger, he could not imagine his life without them. If they found out what he had done, if he did not mend his fences with them soon, they would be lost to him. The thought brought him to his feet and on his horse.

By the time he returned to the stables, he had rehearsed his apology. And with luck, he would be able to send Arabella off with his coachman before she could create any more trouble.

Throwing his reins to the waiting groom, Langston did not notice the man until he called out. "My lord."

Impatient to face Stephen, Langston paused. He squared his shoulders and turned around. "Yes? Dickson, is that you?"

"Yes, my lord."

"What did you want?"

"What am I to do about the dogs?"

"The dogs?"

"They've not had a good run in days," the man reminded him.

"Of course, they haven't. They are penned until we are sure they don't have rabies."

"They don't. I told Mr. Middleton yesterday."

Langston froze. "Told him what?" he asked, his voice very quiet.

"About the frogs. Can't I let them out?" He tightened the reins he was holding, and the horse snorted. Dickson reached up and patted the animal.

"Frogs?" Langston asked, wondering if the man had had an accident to disorder his mind while he was away. In as few words as possible, Dickson told him the story. "And Mr. Middleton knows this?" Langston asked when he had finished.

"Yes. I told him yesterd'y mornin'." His master's eyes narrowed, and he began walking toward the house. "But what about the dogs?" Dickson called. Langston did not answer him. His strides lengthened until he was almost running. His groom shook his head and led the horse back into the stables.

When Langston met Stephen a few minutes later, he had forgotten his determination to make peace with him. "Well, look at the bridegroom. I thought you would be still abed," he said too heartily. His eyes narrowed.

Stephen gritted his teeth and kept a pleasant look on his face. "I was just looking for you."

"For me? If I were you, I would be with my wife."

"Jane and I don't want any unpleasantness between the three of us—" Stephen stopped and smiled at his friend.

"Jane and I? You've been talking about me. Rather

strange thing to do when you've just been wed. I imagine I will keep my wife too busy to think of former fiancées."

Every word that Langston said sent arrows into Stephen's already lacerated emotions. He squared his shoulders and took a deep breath, reminding himself that he had known the interview would not be pleasant. His own guilt at the way he had manipulated Jane into marrying him cut at him even worse than the words. "Langston."

Before he could finish what he was saying, Jane ran up, breathless. "Stephen. Langston."

"What are you doing here?"

"Can't stay away from the man you married?"

"Lady Langston sent me," Jane explained, looking from one to the other. She didn't like what she saw. Both men's jaws were set and their shoulders squared. When this had happened when they were boys, they would throw punches at each other until one or the other had a bloody nose. She didn't want to think what they would do to one another now.

"My mother. She will be so pleased with our news," Langston said, looking at Stephen and smiling wickedly. Stephen took a deep breath as if to brace himself for something unpleasant.

"What news?" Jane asked, her eyes moving from one face to another.

"You mean Stephen didn't tell you?" Langston paused. Stephen took a step forward, one hand up as if to ward off a blow, not at all certain what Langston was about to say.

"What?" Jane turned to stare at her husband, waiting for him to speak.

Before Stephen had said more than her name, Langston hurried on. "It's wonderful news." His smile mocked his words. "Yesterday, before you were wed, Stephen discovered that he didn't have rabies."

Chapter Eleven

Jane froze. Her eyes narrowed. Slowly she turned to face her husband of just one day. "You knew this yesterday?" she asked, her voice cold and crisp. Langston smiled wickedly. He looked from one to the other in anticipation, much as he had done when they were children and he had stirred up some trouble.

Stephen cleared his throat. His eyes dropped. He shifted nervously. Then he squared his shoulders and raised his head. Looking into her eyes, he whispered, "Jane."

"Stephen, did you know?" she asked again. Her eyes flashed with green fire much as they had done when he and Langston had done something she didn't like when they were growing up. "Did you?"

"It was only one man's opinion," Stephen finally got out.

"And that man is the one in charge of my dogs," Langston reminded him. "He knows them well."

"You knew." Stephen looked into Jane's face and saw the shock there. "You knew and did not tell me." Her voice shook with rage.

"I couldn't. His story was so unbelievable. He said frogs caused the dogs to foam at the mouth," Stephen explained.

"Frogs?" Jane looked from one to the other as if expecting them to explain further. She almost laughed. "Frogs?"

Stephen nodded and continued. "Isn't it ridiculous?" he asked when he had finished, encouraged by her reaction.

Once again she froze. Forgetting that Langston was present, she stepped closer to her husband. "Have you forgotten what you promised me last night?" she asked, staring at him.

"Of course not!" he said as he tried to remember specifically what they had talked about. Working to control his emotions had taken most of his concentration.

"Then how could you lie to me?"

"Lie? I didn't lie." The accusation stung him. Already suffering from guilt because he had "stolen" her from Langston and because he felt he had taken advantage of her, he was not ready to accept any more.

"Ha!" Jane turned her back and walked toward the house. Stephen followed. Langston, enjoying the contretemps he had created, hurried after them.

Stephen caught up to his wife and grabbed her by the arm. She stared up at him and then down at his hand on her arm. This time her stare did nothing but harden his resolve. "Don't walk away from me."

"I have nothing more to say to you," she said. "Let me go." She twisted in his grasp, but he maintained his hold.

"Not until we discuss this," Stephen said, trying to keep his anger under control.

"You lied to me," she said once again. As usual, she could not maintain the white heat of her anger for long. Tears began to well up in her eyes, and her voice shook.

"I didn't." Seeing her distress tore at his heart. "Jane, I'm sorry."

"Sorry." The word sent steel down her spine. Any softening she had felt for him disappeared. "And I suppose you are going to say that you didn't tell me because I didn't need to know."

"No, I won't say that. I did it because I was frightened." His low words and grave face gave her pause. He let go of her arm, and she stepped back, not sure of her next move.

Langston, a silent observer until now, laughed. "You have the coolest nerves of anyone I know. You were frightened?" Once more he laughed mockingly.

Stephen and Jane had forgotten he was present. They turned to glare at him. "What are you still doing here?" Stephen asked angrily.

"It is too delicious to leave. Are you certain you were only married yesterday? You sound as though you have been married for years," Langston said maliciously. "And this is my home. Or had you forgotten?"

Remembering the way he had tossed and turned in the small bed in the dressing room the evening before, Stephen said through clenched teeth, "I haven't forgotten."

Jane tossed her head. She glared at both men. "Nor have I. Stephen, we will talk later. Now I must return to Lady Langston."

"Running away, Jane?" Langston called after her. He saw her take a deep breath and waited for her angry reply. She just kept walking. "Jane?" He turned back to Stephen, his face surprised.

"If Dr. Clarke agrees, we will leave after luncheon," Stephen said quietly. "I do not want to stretch your hospitality needlessly." Like his wife, he walked quickly away.

Langston was left alone. He glanced around. Seeing a gardener working nearby, he glared at him. The man ducked his head. Muttering curses under his breath, Langston also walked toward the house.

By the time Jane reached the sitting room, Stephen was close behind her. "Jane, we need to talk."

"Not now, Stephen."

"Come upstairs so that I can explain."

"No."

He took a deep breath to keep himself from saying something he would regret. "Prepare to leave this afternoon." He turned and walked away.

"What?" Jane ran after him until she caught his sleeve, pulling him to a halt. "What do you mean?"

"If Dr. Clarke agrees with Dickson, we will leave the manor today. I will not spend another night under Langston's roof."

"Today?" she whispered. He turned to look at her, the passion he felt evident. Her eyes fell before the look in his, and she took a deep breath and started to speak.

He cut her off. "Do you want to stay and be insulted?" he asked angrily.

"Insulted? What are you talking about?"

"Langston." A door opened. A footman walked into the

hallway and looked at them curiously. They stepped apart. "Shall I give the orders to have your maid pack your possessions or shall you?"

"Tell Vernon to tell her," she murmured. He nodded and headed up the stairs. She stood where she was for a moment, staring after him. They would leave here today. And where would Stephen spend that night? The anger that had filled her only a short time earlier faded before the tingling in her veins. She blushed and covered her cheeks with her hands. How could she think of that when he had lied to her? She glanced at the stairs again, but he had disappeared. She turned back toward the sitting room.

"Did you find them?" Lady Langston called, hurrying down the stairs toward her.

"Who?"

"Stephen and Langston. They are all right? They haven't done anything foolish, have they? I have been thinking of those fights they used to have when they were boys. Have they bloodied each other's noses?" She paused on the doorsill of the sitting room. "How pretty you look, my dear. I hope that husband of yours told you." Jane blushed. "If he did not, you will have to remind him. Men are sometimes so thoughtless. Now tell me what happened. Quickly before everyone comes down for luncheon. Come; sit beside me." She settled her light lavender skirts around her and patted the place on the settee beside her.

Jane hesitated. Then she walked slowly toward her hostess. She took her seat and twisted her handkerchief in her hands.

"Well, what happened? Did they fight?"

"No. They are fine." *If you can call angry looks and words fine,* she said to herself.

"Good. I knew you could do it. A lady's job is always to keep the peace."

Jane shifted nervously and twisted her handkerchief tighter. "I did nothing," she said quietly. "They are still angry at each other."

"Still? Jane, I depended on you."

"Everything will be more comfortable soon. Stephen and I may be leaving shortly."

"Leaving. That will not do at all. We must force those two to settle their differences. They have been friends too long to let their anger fester." Lady Langston turned abruptly to face Jane. "And I refuse to allow you to leave before that woman does!"

"Who?"

"Stephen's stepmother. I will not have her here a moment longer."

"She did not leave last night?"

"Last night?"

"When Stephen and I saw her, she was demanding that Langston send her back to London immediately," Jane explained.

"Well, according to Miller, she is still here insisting that she be waited on. What can Langston have been thinking to invite her here?"

The door opened, and Arabella Middleton walked in dressed in a vivid bittersweet-red dress cut much lower than was fashionable for day wear. Her skin glowed, and her dark eyes sparkled. Immediately, Jane wished she were wearing something brighter, something that would make her stand out instead of the blue she had been so happy with only a short time before.

"Oh, Langston is not here," Arabella said after she had looked around the room.

"The last time I saw him he was between the house and the stables," Jane told her, determined not to cause additional difficulties with a woman she knew she would have to deal with for some time to come. Arabella glared at her.

"But I am certain he will join us for luncheon," his mother said, not pleased to see the woman but unwilling to exclude her. "Come. Join us."

Never happy in the company of women, Arabella frowned slightly and took her seat. "And where is my stepson?" she asked, casting a coy look at the young woman beside her hostess.

"He also will join us shortly," Jane said, hoping she was right.

"Oh." Arabella narrowed her eyes, the pleasant look she maintained when men were present disappearing. "You must tell me how you trapped him, my dear."

Both Lady Langston and Jane stared at her. "Excuse me?" Jane asked. She was certain she had not heard her correctly.

"My stepson. You moved so quickly to capture him. Are you increasing?" she asked. She inspected Jane carefully, insultingly.

"I will thank you to keep those ill-mannered comments to yourself, Mrs. Middleton. Or are you judging her by your standards?" Lady Langston said, her back stiff and her eyes glaring. Arabella returned her stare and took a deep breath. Before she could answer, the door opened, and Stephen walked in.

"Vernon and Annie assure me they can be finished packing very shortly," he said, seeing only his wife and Lady Langston.

"Leaving?" Arabella drawled out the words. Stephen stiffened. He deliberately kept his eyes on his wife. "So soon? I hope it is something I have done."

"And Smythe has sent for Dr. Clarke," he added. He smiled at Jane but ignored Arabella, an act that made her bristle.

"Why? Has something happened? Are the dogs ill?" Lady Langston asked, glancing from Stephen to Jane.

"You didn't tell her?" Stephen asked.

"I didn't have time," Jane said defensively. "I thought either you or Langston should give her the good news."

"Tell me what?" Lady Langston asked. She looked from Stephen to Jane.

"What good news?" Arabella asked sharply. She had never wasted her charm on her stepson or other women unless they could do something for her.

"The man who takes care of the dogs thinks that they were playing with frogs. That is what caused them to froth at the mouth."

"Frogs?" Lady Langston and Arabella said the word together. "How wonderful!" Lady Langston added. "What a relief it must be to the two of you." She smiled at Jane and Stephen. "You can begin your lives together; Langston can return to London, and I can go to Scotland. Delightful."

"Frogs." Arabella laughed mockingly. "You thought you were dying because of some silly frogs." She laughed again. Caught up in her own amusement, she did not hear the door open. Langston walked in. "Frogs. How delicious. Can you imagine what the *ton* will say? Frogs!"

Lady Langston opened her mouth, but before she could say a word, her son shook his head. "Still here?" he asked, looking at Arabella. "I told my coachman to be ready to take you to London early this morning."

She smiled at him sensuously. Lady Langston caught her breath and narrowed her eyes, looking from her son to Arabella, not pleased by her suspicions. "I was just too exhausted. Besides, I could not go without bidding you farewell." The charm practically oozed from Arabella. You wicked cat, Lady Langston muttered under her breath and began to search for ways to show her guest her displeasure. She glared at her son.

"You should not have stood on ceremony. We would have understood," Langston said coldly. Although she was a beauty and a delight to tumble, he wanted Arabella gone before anyone discovered what he had done. The guilt he had felt earlier that day had returned in full force.

Arabella flinched as though from a hit. She glared at him. She gathered herself and opened her mouth.

"Dr. Clarke has arrived," Smythe announced, showing the man into the room.

"Thank you for coming so quickly," Stephen said, getting up to shake the doctor's hand.

"Is something wrong? Who is my patient?" The doctor glanced around the room. When he saw the beautiful woman who had disrupted the supper the evening before, he frowned.

"Dr. Clarke, you must stay for luncheon. It will be announced in a few moments. Smythe, lay a place for the doctor," Lady Langston said, taking the opportunity to make her table even. Startled, the doctor nodded.

"Have you ever heard of dogs frothing at the mouth because of frogs?" Stephen asked. Jane leaned forward to listen to the reply.

"Frogs?"

"Dickson, the man who cares for my dogs, thinks they were playing with or chewing on a frog instead of having rabies," Langston explained. He kept his eyes fixed on the doctor, ignoring the sultry looks that Arabella was sending him.

"Hmmm." Smythe opened the door once more and announced luncheon.

"Stephen, take your wife in. Doctor, if you will escort the dowager Mrs. Middleton, and Langston, give me your arm," Lady Langston directed them. Arabella stiffened at Lady Langston's words but took the doctor's arm, smiling at him coquettishly. "I suppose I shall be called a dowager before long. Won't I, Langston?" his mother asked as they walked into the dining room. "When will your engagement announcement be in the paper?" She pitched her voice loud enough to be heard by everyone. He pulled her to a stop. "Look, Jane, he had no idea that we knew what he was planning. Come along, dear, you can give us all the details at luncheon."

As she had done earlier, Lady Langston arranged them as she wished, disregarding society's rules. Langston and she were at the head and foot with Stephen and Arabella on one side and the doctor and Jane on the other. While the servants were serving the first course, a rich chicken soup, she chattered about nothing. As soon as they were gone, she resumed her questioning. "Well, Langston, when are we going to meet the girl?"

Arabella, who had allowed herself to make a few plans that morning, listened angrily. Jane, her eyes wide, glanced at Stephen. He shrugged his shoulders. The doctor simply looked from one to the other.

"Soon. Before I left London, I suggested that she and her companion might visit so that she could meet you. If her grandfather agrees, they will arrive shortly." He glared at his mother but refused to meet Jane's or Stephen's eyes.

"Do you mean you invited her without telling me?" his mother asked.

"Are you saying you are engaged?" Arabella asked, her eyes snapping and her voice petulant.

"We can discuss this later," Langston said with a bite in his voice. "We are boring my guests."

Lady Langston glanced at the doctor and withheld the next question she was going to ask. She sipped her soup.

"Tell me more about this frog idea," the doctor suggested, talking to Stephen across the table in an effort to change the conversation. "Is this man to be trusted?"

"Definitely," Langston assured him, taking a deep breath. "As soon as luncheon is over, I will send for him."

"Be better if we try his idea and see if it works," the doctor said, sipping the last of his soup. He smiled at the two men.

Stephen leaned across the table. "Then you think he might be right?"

"He might." As the servants removed the first course and served the second, a fish course accompanied by vegetables, conversation once again became general. Arabella allowed the footman to put a small serving of everything on her plate and then played with her food, her eyes fixed on her host. After a few moments her eyes narrowed.

As the men discussed how they might test the frog theory, the ladies were discussing clothes. "Stephen insists that I have a new wardrobe," Jane confided to Lady Langston.

Arabella stared at her stepson. "I pity you," she said with a forced smile.

Both Lady Langston and Jane stared at her. They waited for her to elaborate. When she did not, Lady Langston asked, "Why?"

"He is the most cheeseparing man I have ever met," Arabella said. She put her fork on her plate. Then she inspected Jane carefully. "I suppose that will not matter to you, my dear. You do not seem to have very good taste in clothes now. I'm sure you will be able to make do."

Jane gasped. She shut her mouth and bit her tongue, realizing that Arabella was waiting to pounce on anything she said. Lady Langston turned an unbecoming shade of puce. She glared at Arabella. "I will have you know that I chose Jane's gowns," she said through clenched teeth.

"I thought they were too old for her. Were you just being kind when you agreed to wear them, Mrs. Middleton, or is your taste similar?" Arabella asked, enjoying the turmoil she was creating.

"Lady Langston has been very kind to me," Jane said. "She is a true lady." She smiled at the older lady to soothe her wounded feelings as well as indicate her opinion of her stepmother-in-law. Her own emotions were raw. Although Jane longed to claw Arabella's eyes out, she decided the best way to deal with her was to pretend she did not exist. Quietly, she addressed a question to Lady Langston, effectively shutting Arabella out of the conversation as they began discussing people they had visited in the last days.

Arabella glared at them and then turned her attention to the other end of the table. "Langston," she called, ignoring the doctor at her side. Her host stiffened but ignored her. Stephen stared at her. "Langston," she said again. Everyone at the table paused. Then they all began speaking quickly. "I will not be ignored," Arabella said, her anger gaining control over her common sense. "After last night I expected—"

"Last night?" both Lady Langston and Stephen asked. Lady Langston knew she would not like the answer.

"You should have expected nothing," Langston said, biting off his words, horrified that she would dare to discuss such a subject with his mother present. His eyes were as cold as his voice. The footmen entered to remove the fish course.

"But you said—"

Once again he cut her off. "That I would send you to London," he reminded her. "I thought you would leave as soon as you rose." His face told her to expect nothing from him.

Arabella pushed back her chair. "How dare you treat me

this way! You are nothing but a spoiled little boy!" She stood, and her chair toppled over, almost hitting a footman carrying a full platter. He jumped out of her way. "Last night I thought you were a man." Everyone stared at her.

"And I thought you were a lady," Langston said, standing up. She rushed at him, her hands like claws. "I think we had better conclude this conversation somewhere else." He grabbed her hands and pulled her from the room. "If you will excuse us."

"Stephen, go after them," Jane whispered a few moments later when she could speak. He nodded. No one wanted to look at anyone else.

When the door closed behind him, Lady Langston took a deep breath. "I always knew she was not good *ton*." She motioned to the servants to continue serving. "Doctor, I must apologize for my guest. I am certain you must be wishing yourself at Jericho. Shall we talk about something more pleasant? Tell me about what has been happening in my absence." She smiled at him and breathed a mental sigh of relief that her son was not tangled in that woman's web. Perhaps she should write some letters that afternoon to a few of her closest friends telling them how upset she was by Arabella's actions. She nodded in response to one of the doctor's comments and smiled.

Jane longed to be a mouse watching whatever was happening between Langston and Stephen and that woman. Instead she listened to the doctor's comments and asked a few questions.

As soon as he had pulled Arabella into the hallway, Langston stopped. "What were you about, madame?" he asked, his hands still holding hers tightly. "Are you trying to destroy your reputation and mine?"

She twisted and tried to pull away. "What kind of game are you playing, Langston?" she asked. "Did last night mean nothing to you?" Neither she nor the man who held her were aware that Stephen had stepped into the hall behind them. He quickly pulled the door to the dining room shut to keep their words from the others.

"No more than it meant to you. A quick tumble. And do

not tell me it was more. You used your body to get what you wanted from me." The sneer on Langston's face was like acid on her skin.

"And what about you? Did you use me? What did you want?" she asked, trying to twist away once more. When she saw his eyes glance down the deep neckline of her dress, she smiled sensuously. Instead of trying to pull away, she stepped closer, rubbing against him. Langston stepped back, but he kept hold of her hands.

Stephen clenched his teeth tightly to hold back his angry words. Langston and his stepmother? A few moments later he was glad of his silence. Langston stared at the woman he was holding away from him, contempt written in every line of his face. "A way to punish Stephen. But do you know, madame, it wasn't worth it. All these years I thought he exaggerated his problems with you. What a piece of work you are! Thank God, you are not a member of my family." She struggled in his hands, trying to reach his face. "Did you think last night meant something? That I would choose you?" He laughed bitterly. "I may have done something stupid last night, but I would not ruin my life by having anything more to do with you."

Arabella paused in her struggles to free herself. She smiled wickedly. "I am certain my stepson will enjoy hearing about our adventure. I can hardly wait to tell him and that little wife of his." Her voice was a wicked purr.

"And will he believe you?"

"I will make him. I can tell him details only a woman who had seen you nude would know." She kicked out at him but could not reach him.

"And if I tell him first, how would you look then?"

"You would tell him?"

"I think I must." Langston surprised even himself. Stephen took a deep breath. He stepped forward.

"No need," he said quietly, clapping his friend on his shoulder. "Perhaps you should let her go now. Smythe," he called, having seen the butler hovering in a doorway down the hall.

"Yes, sir." The butler's face was impassive.

"I believe the dowager Mrs. Middleton wishes to leave immediately." He had noticed earlier how much the title had upset her. "Don't you agree, Langston?"

"Do not call me that," Arabella said twisting away from Langston as he released her hands.

"What?" Stephen asked with a smile, enjoying the reaction she was showing.

"Dowager. I am not a dowager."

Langston smiled, his lips barely turning up. "But you are. For the rest of your life you will be the dowager Mrs. Middleton." He laughed, throwing his head back and letting out one peal of laughter after another. "How delicious. The dowager Mrs. Middleton." He turned to his friend. "How marvelous. It must be a positive advantage to your marriage, Stephen."

"I am happy that our wedding brought you so much amusement." His dry remark brought Langston back to reality. Stephen turned to his stepmother. "What brought you to London? I thought you had retired to the country."

"You are hateful. Both of you. I hate the country." She stomped her foot. "There is nothing to do."

"No gambling? Is that what you mean?"

Langston looked from one to the other, his eyes narrowed. A note in Stephen's voice made him wary.

"There is no one there."

"You could take a house in Brighton or Bath," Stephen suggested.

Arabella brightened. "They are so expensive. Stephen, I don't suppose you would be willing to lend me—"

"Nothing. I told you that when we met in London. If you cannot live on your jointure, then you must retire to the country. The dower house is ready for you."

"The dower house? But Caroline lives at the priory."

"And Caroline will remain there. With my wife and me." Stephen waited a moment and smiled. Langston let out the breath he had been holding and nodded his head, pleased to see that Stephen had his stepmother's measure.

"I won't! I refuse to be buried!"

"Then go to your parents. I believe your mother spends

her summers in Bath. I had heard she left London early this year. Something about gossip."

"Bath?" There is no one there but—"

"Dowagers?" Langston asked, his voice light. He smiled mockingly. She glared at him.

"You said you would send me back to London today. Did you mean that?" Arabella asked, controlling her fury.

"Certainly. The sooner the better," Langston told her. "You may have to spend a night on the road. The coachman knows the best posting inns."

"I want to leave now!" She stomped her foot once more.

"Remember, Arabella, I will pay no more of your bills," Stephen said quietly. She glared at him and hurried up the stairs. A few minutes later she was downstairs with her maid, cloaked and ready to go.

When the door of the carriage closed behind her and the coachman started the horses, the two men breathed sighs of relief. They walked back into the house. "How did you ever manage? Being around her, I mean?" Langston asked.

"I wasn't home often. You remember I spent most of my time away from school here," his friend told him. "How did you get caught in her snares?"

"It wasn't my finest hour," Langston admitted. Once he had had time to think about what he had done he was appalled. "At first in London I simply wanted to make you uncomfortable, to pay you back for flirting with Jane. Then I was in shock when I learned that you and Jane were married. You could have waited until I returned."

"And have you stand up in church and say there was some impediment?" Stephen asked.

"I wouldn't have done that." Stephen just looked at him. "Well, maybe I would have," he admitted. "But you and Jane?"

"I know I should have talked to you." Stephen took a deep breath and exhaled. "But I thought I was a dead man."

"I suppose. And when you discovered that you weren't dying, you decided to go ahead instead of letting Jane slip back into her role as my mother's companion. Just like you to rescue her." Stephen said nothing, unwilling to admit that rescue had not been on his mind and uncertain that Langston's changed attitude was a lasting one. "Well, I suppose her life will be better with you as a husband instead of with my mother as an employer." He slapped Stephen on the back. "Shall we tell her you have my blessings?"

Stephen stared at him. He was used to Langston's changeable moods, but he had not expected this one. "Why have you changed your mind?"

"About the marriage?" Stephen nodded. Langston stood in front of the mirror in the hall and straightened his cravat. He didn't look at his friend. "I had some time to think. You were right about Jane and me," he said, without looking at Stephen. His voice was very low.

"How?"

"I had not thought about what it would be like with a wife and with Jane whenever my mother visited. Much better this way. Shall we finish our luncheon?" He turned around and started down the hall. Not even to himself could he explain his rapid turnaround. All he knew was that he wanted to keep Stephen's and Jane's friendship.

"Everything will be cold," Stephen reminded him, not certain that Langston's capitulation was a lasting one but hesitant to ask more questions.

"No matter. Now I am hungry. That woman spoiled my appetite before." Langston opened the door to the dining room and walked in.

Lady Langston let the two of them be seated before she began her questioning. "Well, what happened? Is she gone? What were you thinking of to invite that woman here? Where did you meet her anyway? I am certain she is not received in the best homes. She was only on the fringes this spring. By next she may have disappeared completely."

Langston let his mother talk for a few moments. When she paused to take a breath, he said, "She is gone. I invited her merely to make Stephen uncomfortable. As usual, my plans turned back on me, and it was I who was embarrassed."

"Well, I should think so. Stephen, I apologize for my son."

"He has already apologized himself." He smiled at Jane and nodded slightly. In spite of the resentment she still felt, she smiled back and picked up her spoon to eat her syllabub. She glanced at Langston, who smiled at her wryly.

"Is there anything left besides this?" Langston asked, looking at the sweet on his plate. "Stephen and I did not finish our meal."

"I will have them bring you something." Lady Langston reached for the bell, but before she could ring it, Smythe opened the door for two footmen carrying platters of sliced sirloin, roasted capon, and vegetables.

"Good." Langston and Stephen filled their plates. Stephen gazed fondly at his wife, enjoying the faint flush that colored her cheeks when she realized that he was staring at her. Langston looked at the two of them and raised his eyebrow. "Now, Doctor, tell me what we are going to do with the dogs."

Chapter Twelve

Before the afternoon was much older, Langston had his answer. Sending Dickson to find a frog, the two ladies and gentlemen and the doctor had gone down to where the dogs were penned. "What are you going to do with the frog when you have it?" Jane asked, looking at the dogs milling around inside the pen. She and Lady Langston had been talking when the doctor had explained earlier.

"We'll select a couple of dogs and give it to them," Dr. Clarke said patiently.

Jane took a step back. "They will kill it!" Both Stephen and Langston exchanged glances. Jane had accompanied them on all their adventures but usually not hunting. Even when she fished, she wanted someone else to put the worm on her line. She could do it, but she didn't like it.

"That is the only way," Stephen said, taking her arm. "You and Lady Langston can go back to the house." Although she longed to agree, Jane looked at her hostess and shook her head.

"We will stay."

"You don't have to look," Langston told her. "Go see the horses. We will tell you when it is over." He didn't want her turning green and losing her lunch as she had done more than once when they had discovered a rabbit caught in a trap. He willed her to agree.

Stubbornly, she shook her head. "If Lady Langston can manage, so shall I." She frowned. "I just wish there were some other way."

Before long, the experiment was over. "Amazing, simply amazing. I may write a paper about this phenomenon. As soon as it started chewing on the frog, the dog started froth-ing at the mouth," Dr. Clarke said, smiling broadly. "I told you that I doubted that you would succumb to rabies, Mr. Middleton. And I was right. I wish I had known about this possibility sooner. And fortunately the dog reacted just as the boy described. Dickson was right!" He was loquacious in his excitement. "I must return home immediately." A groom found his gig and harnessed his horse.

"And I am very happy to have been wrong," Stephen ad-mitted, taking a deep breath. A smile lit his face. Jane held on to his arm tightly, as excited as he. He glanced down at her. Nervously, he cleared his throat. "I suppose this means, ah, maybe you want to, ah . . ."

"To what?" she asked. She tried to read the expression in his eyes, but he refused to look at her.

"Let us celebrate," Lady Langston said. "Since that woman is gone, maybe this time no one will interrupt us." She glared at her son. He ducked his head to avoid meeting her eyes. "I will send for tea—although I suppose you men will want something stronger. Langston, do you have any champagne, or have you drunk it all this last year?"

"There is champagne, Mama. Why?" He looked at Stephen and Jane walking together and felt a sense of loss.

"To toast the marriage. That woman interrupted us last evening. I was never so mortified. How could you bring her here?"

"Enough, Mama. I have already apologized."

"Not to me."

"Well, I am now. Remember, she is Stephen's step-mother." Langston would have said anything at that mo-ment to get his mother to hush.

"As if I could forget it. I can quite understand why he does not wish that woman to have the care of his sister. What was his father thinking of to marry her in the first place? I have no doubt he was not thinking with his head." As his mother prattled on, Langston thought of the way the widow had responded to him and felt his heart begin to beat more rapidly. At least he had had the good sense to send her away.

As they walked through the side door, Stephen pulled Jane aside. "Vernon and Annie should have everything packed. As soon as we have said our good-byes, we can be on our way."

She stared at him, remembering how he had promised to tell her the truth while he was keeping something from her. Her eyes narrowed.

He recognized the look and stiffened. Just as Stephen started to explain to his host and hostess that they were leaving in a little while, they heard the unmistakable sounds of a coach pulling to a stop. "If that is that woman again," Lady Langston began, "you will have to entertain her. I will not. Come, Jane."

More out of habit than because she wanted to, Jane walked into the sitting room after her hostess. When she realized what she had done, she looked back at Stephen. He shrugged his shoulders and smiled as if to say it was all right. He and Langston walked toward the study. Before the door closed behind the gentlemen, the front door opened, and they could hear Smythe speaking to someone.

"Please tell Lord Langston that Miss Lydia Thackeray and Mrs. Hendrickson are here. Miss Thackeray's maid and the luggage will arrive shortly," a footman announced.

Knowing that Smythe had had no instructions about these visitors, Langston stood up. "Come with me," he told Stephen. "I have someone I want you and Jane to meet."

As they walked into the hallway, Smythe stood back to let two ladies enter. As she noticed them, Stephen wondered at the look of relief that crossed the older woman's face. "Lord Langston," she said, smiling at her host.

"Mrs. Hendrickson, Lydia, you made good time. I was not certain I would see you until tomorrow," Langston said, taking his fiancée's hand and drawing her farther into the hall. "Do you insist on going upstairs to freshen up, or may I introduce you to my mother and some friends immediately?"

The older woman looked at the younger. Lydia took off her bonnet and laid it on the table under the mirror and handed her cloak to the waiting butler. She had insisted that they stop at an inn not many miles distant so that she could refresh herself for such an eventuality. "Please make the introductions." She smiled up at him, her one dimple evident. Like Langston, she too was a blond who stood only as tall as his chin. Her eyes were a pale blue. Dressed in a traveling robe of a medium blue, she was stylishly but not elaborately dressed.

"This is Stephen. I will make formal introductions in a moment," Langston said as he offered her his arm and led her into the sitting room where his mother and Jane waited. Stephen and her companion followed. "Mama, I want you to meet someone important to me."

The older lady sat up straight, her face set in severe lines at first. Jane leaned forward, not certain that she wanted to meet anyone new. When she realized who the young girl who walked into the room on Langston's arm must be, she was not sure how she felt about this girl who had usurped her place. When she had first heard rumors about her, she had been devastated. Both ladies were pleasantly surprised by the ladylike appearance of both women who entered the sitting room. "This is Miss Lydia Thackeray, who has done me the honor of accepting my hand in marriage, and her companion, Mrs. Hendrickson." He kept his eyes on his mother, remembering how he and Jane had made a similar announcement several years ago. He refused to meet Jane's eyes. "And this is my mother, Lady Langston."

To her surprise, Jane felt only a momentary pang. She looked across the room at her husband, who quickly made his way to her side.

"I am happy to meet you at last," Lady Langston said, pleased that the rumors she had heard about the girl were untrue. Granddaughter of a cit though she might be, the girl was lovely, dressed in the latest fashion, and seemed to have a pleasant manner. "Please, be seated. Refreshments will arrive shortly. How was your journey? Did you have any difficulty?"

Lydia took her seat near her hostess. "None. Grandfather insisted on sending outriders with us although I told him it was not necessary. You are so kind to welcome me so warmly." Accustomed to snubs from those more well-born than she, Lydia had dreaded meeting Langston's mother.

Stephen cleared his throat. Langston quickly said, "And may I present two of my closest friends, Jane and Stephen, Mr. and Mrs. Middleton, who are visiting us?"

As soon as the initial pleasantries were exchanged and the ladies were seated, Lydia asked Jane, "Have you known Langston long?"

"All my life," Jane said with a pleasant look. "I lived on an estate nearby."

"Then you know all his secrets. I shall insist that you reveal them all to me." She glanced at her fiancé under her lashes to see his reaction.

"And I will beg you not to, Jane," Langston said, not certain he wanted his future wife and his former fiancée to be confidantes. He and Jane exchanged a knowing glance and then laughed ruefully. "Or you either, Stephen. He was with me at school."

Before the situation could be uncomfortable, Smythe entered with the champagne.

"Champagne?" Mrs. Hendrickson asked. "Lydia, my dear, I don't think you should."

"You must. Jane and Stephen were recently married, and we must toast their life together. And our engagement," Langston said, picking up a glass and handing it to Lydia.

"One glass will not harm the girl," Lady Langston assured the companion. She smiled at the girl seated near her.

Jane and Stephen picked up their own glasses and said nothing. "Well, if Lady Langston approves, who am I to disapprove," Mrs. Hendrickson twittered nervously. "I am certain your grandfather, were he present, would say you might. One glass though. That is all."

Lady Langston took her glass. "Is her grandfather very strict?" she asked.

"Oh, my, yes," Mrs. Hendrickson assured her, frowning at the way Lydia and Langston were carrying on a quiet conversation between the two of them. "He almost refused her permission to come to the manor because Langston had not stayed in London to accompany her."

"Hmmm." Once more Lady Langston inspected her future daughter-in-law. "Langston" she called. When he didn't answer, she said more loudly, "Langston, my dear."

Changing his focus, he looked at his mother. "Yes?"

"Shouldn't you make the toast?"

"Certainly. To my bride." Jane and Stephen looked at each other, well accustomed to his self-absorption. They took a sip of the wine.

"Langston!" his mother said again. Her impatience was evident in her tone. He looked at her, puzzled. She nodded at Stephen and Jane.

He held up his glass again. "And to my dear friends. May their life together be as long and as happy as I hope mine will be with Miss Thackeray." Mrs. Hendrickson giggled quietly and sipped her champagne.

As the door opened again, everyone in the room but Miss Thackeray and her companion stiffened, not certain what would happen next. They breathed a sigh of relief when Smythe entered and crossed to Stephen, who listened for a moment and then turned to Jane. "Everything is ready so that we can leave."

"Leave? Nonsense. It is too late in the day to think of leaving now. I shall insist that you spend at least one more night with us," Lady Langston said, putting her glass down. "You will only be able to cover a few miles before it will be time to stop for the night. And, my dears, the inns on the road to your mother are not what I would recommend. And you've made no provision for the horses. At least give us time to send a groom ahead and make the arrangements. And what will Miss Thackeray and Mrs. Hendrickson think when you desert us so soon after they arrive?"

"Please, do stay. I have so many questions about Langston that I wish to ask you," the younger woman said. "He even refuses to tell me his given name. He says he had it changed when he inherited the title." She giggled, and the dimple in her cheek deepened. She glanced at Lady Langston, who smiled at her, and then back at Jane.

"I'm afraid he made us promise never to reveal it. Even before he inherited his title, he never used it," Stephen said with a laugh. He smiled at his wife and raised an eyebrow as if asking for her collaboration. She nodded solemnly but spoiled her reaction by glancing at Langston with laughing eyes.

"For shame! You asked Miss Thackeray to marry you without revealing that deep, dark secret," she said.

"I will never know how I allowed myself to be persuaded to bestow it on my boy. What was I thinking about? Of course, we did it because we thought his grand-uncle, who had the original name, would provide for him. He did leave him a few pounds but nothing like he should have. I have regretted my mistake since he died," Lady Langston said. "But enough about that. Your wedding is soon enough to learn."

"My wedding?" Langston asked.

"You have to give your full name when you marry," Stephen explained, looking fondly at his wife and remembering his own ceremony only the day before. "We really should be on our way, my dear."

"One more night," Lady Langston pleaded. The events of the last two days had been exhausting, and she was not looking forward to entertaining two strangers by herself.

"Mama is right. You might as well wait until tomorrow. One night will not make that much difference," Langston added.

Jane looked at her husband. Stephen, who had been looking forward to a night not spent under his friend's roof, shrugged. "I suppose you are right," he said grudgingly. Jane relaxed a little.

"Of course, I am," Lady Langston said. "Now, my dear"— she turned to Lydia—"I am certain you are dying for a chance to freshen up. You look lovely as you are, of course, but I am certain you want to see where you will be staying. Perhaps tomorrow Jane can . . ." she paused before she finished her sentence, realizing that to ask her former companion to show the house to Langston's new fiancée would be unwise. "I can show you about the house. And, Langston, you will need to send an express to your sister in Scotland."

"Why?" he asked.

"We will talk about it later," she said, glaring at him, unwilling to let Lydia know how her arrival had altered her plans.

"I think I should tell my maid that we are not leaving until tomorrow. We can talk together later," Jane said, standing up.

"And I need to talk to my valet," Stephen added. "We are pleased to meet you, Miss Thackeray." Both Jane and Stephen ignored Langston's pleading looks and walked from the room. Neither said anything as they climbed the stairs to their rooms.

As soon as the door of their chambers had closed behind them, Jane let out a sigh of relief. She sank onto the settee while Stephen crossed to the bellpull and pulled it. He then walked to the table where the decanters were and poured himself a glass of wine. "Would you like some?" he asked Jane, his back still turned toward her.

She shook her head, then realizing that he could not see the movement said, "No. What I really want is tea."

"Send Annie for some as soon as she gets here." He took his glass and sat down across from her. For a few moments, they remained silent. Before it became too uncomfortable, the door opened, and Vernon and Annie walked in.

"Shall I have the luggage taken down?" Vernon asked, although he had already heard rumors that they were not leaving that day.

"We are staying one more night," Stephen told him. "But we will leave without fail tomorrow morning. I suppose we won't be able to have dinner up here?" he asked Jane.

"Lady Langston will certainly expect to see us at her table," she said. "And with Miss Thackeray here, Langston will, too." She rubbed her eyes.

"I think you need a nap instead of tea, my dear." He inspected Jane's pale cheeks and the lack of emotion in her eyes, wondering not for the first time how the appearance of Langston's fiancée had affected her. She had not seemed unduly upset, but he was the first to admit that she could successfully hide her emotions from him.

"I would think you would be the one to need a nap. After spending the night in that—" Stephen stopped what she was about to say with a glare. "Oh," she whispered, looking at the two servants. She blushed.

He yawned and stretched. The two servants exchanged knowing glances and quickly unpacked what would be needed that evening and the next morning, taking the garments away to be pressed. When the door closed behind them, Stephen suggested, "Get some rest."

"Are you trying to avoid talking to me?"

"About what?"

Jane got up and crossed to stand in front of him. "You are avoiding it again," she said, her eyes flashing.

"What?"

"Stephen, you know we must discuss the fact that you lied to me."

"I did not!" Although his words were forceful, he could not meet her eyes.

"Oh, you may not have actually said the words, Stephen, but you deliberately did not tell me everything. To me, that is the same as lying." She glared at him.

"And when did you expect me to talk to you?"

"You could have found the time," she said, her voice sounding harsh even to herself. She sighed and yawned once more.

"I tried to. I was going to talk to you before the ceremony, but I didn't have the chance," he admitted.

She yawned again. "You had hours last evening." She blinked rapidly, trying to stay awake.

"Look at you. You can hardly keep your eyes open. Take a nap," Stephen suggested, exhausted himself. "After what has happened today, I need one, too. I promise you that we will not go to bed this evening until we have talked." The emotions of the day had left him drained. He walked toward the dressing room. "I can't think clearly now."

Jane watched him go, her eyes only half open, too weary to force the issue. "Don't think that because I am doing as you suggest now that I will forget," she said in a voice that though level was very determined.

"I don't," he promised her.

Chapter Thirteen

The calm that rest brought lasted only a short time that evening. From the moment they gathered in the salon before dinner, both Stephen and Jane recognized that something had upset Langston's fiancée. Although she was as cordial to Lady Langston and to Stephen as she had been that afternoon, she barely spoke to Langston, and Jane might well have been absent from the way that Lydia ignored her.

"Jane, Stephen"—Lady Langston's greeting was tinged with relief—"I was just telling Miss Thackeray how pleased I am to have her visit. Jane can tell you about the ladies of the neighborhood, especially those more of your own age. I am certain you will enjoy meeting them." She cast imploring eyes at Jane, begging her to help.

"And they will enjoy meeting you," Jane agreed. She took the seat Lady Langston had indicated. "We are quite lively here, visiting back and forth. And someone is always giving a party, especially during hunting season and in the winter."

"How delightful. My dear Lydia, I told you that you had nothing to fear. The dear girl was afraid there would be nothing to do here," Mrs. Hendrickson explained. "She has been so accustomed to being busy. She orders her grandfather's household, has done so since she was merely a girl." Her companion cast Lydia an arch look.

"You exaggerate, Mrs. Hendrickson," Lydia said quietly, frowning slightly. "My grandfather's housekeeper has been with him for years and knows just what he likes. I have very little to do." In the guise of straightening the skirt of the simple but very fashionable blue dress that she wore, she faced Lady Langston, turning her back on Jane.

"Nonsense, my dear. I am certain Lady Langston and Mrs. Middleton appreciate the difficulties of running a household," her companion continued.

"As indeed I do," Lady Langston said. "Jane, whom do you recommend to receive our first visits?"

As the ladies discussed their neighbors, the two gentlemen drifted to the end of the room. Stephen, noticing Jane's puzzled expressions and the way Lydia avoided looking at Jane, asked Langston, "What has happened?"

"I don't know. Since Lydia entered this room, she has made it very clear that something upset her," he admitted. "She has done little but glare at me. I suppose Mama said something she shouldn't, trying to get me to change my mind."

"Nonsense. Your mother has more sense than that. Unless"—Stephen paused—"has your engagement been announced?"

"In the gazettes as we speak. Took care of it when I was in London." Langston glanced toward his fiancée, who shifted in her chair and settled her blue gauze skirts about her once more.

"Then she would not try to interfere. Knows there's no way of backing out."

"Unless the lady agrees," Langston reminded him, looking at Jane.

"You're right. But would Miss Thackeray have come all this way to tell you good-bye?" Stephen asked.

"No, she wouldn't have come to met my mother if she were thinking of crying off. Would she?" Langston turned and looked at the young woman who had agreed to marry him. She noticed his look but kept her eyes fixed on his mother. "I suppose I shall find out what is wrong soon enough. Have you ever noticed how much simpler life was when we were younger?" Stephen and he laughed. The ladies turned to look at them and then began their conversations again.

When Smythe announced dinner, everyone relaxed slightly,

knowing that at least at the table they could concentrate on one person at a time. "I hope you do not mind country hours. After being in London, they always seem strange to me. I amaze most of the neighborhood because I refuse to eat as early as most of my neighbors do," Lady Langston said as she led them into the dining room. Remembering the last meal they had shared there, Stephen, Jane, and Langston reluctantly followed. "Had I known"—Lady Langston paused, realizing that what she intended to say would be impolite, and changed her words—"when you would arrive, I would have invited guests to meet you. Now the gentlemen and ladies are uneven. I suppose I could have asked the vicar to dine with us."

Mrs. Hendrickson begged her not to think about that. "Lydia never knows who will be invited for dinner. Her grandfather never worries about the numbers. If his friends are about when it is time for a meal, he invites them home. Isn't that right, my dear?" Lydia nodded as she took her place beside Stephen and at Langston's right hand, turning her head toward Stephen so that she would not have to talk to her fiancé.

The expression on her face puzzled Stephen. Had he not known better he would have said she pitied him. "Tell me about your grandfather's business, Miss Thackeray," he urged as the footman presented the soup plate.

Lydia put down her spoon. "You will have to ask my grandfather about that. He refuses to allow me to have anything to do with his business. The only time he is not so strict is when we have guests for dinner." She glanced across the table at Jane, who was talking with her hostess. Her face hardened. "You and your wife seem to have a very unusual relationship."

"What?" Without knowing why, Stephen felt a frisson of fear curl up his spine. He shivered. Quickly he said, "Perhaps it is because we have known each other much longer than most married couples."

"Perhaps that explains it." For a few minutes conversation between them lapsed as each sipped the soup. Finally Lydia put her spoon beside her soup plate. She sat back in her chair, her eyes fixed on Stephen's face. Out of the corner of her eye, she noticed Langston looking her way but ignored him. Stephen asked her a few questions, some of which she answered briefly but most of which she ignored.

Having exhausted all ordinary topics of discussion, he glanced at Lady Langston hoping she would rescue him from an uncomfortable situation. The older lady merely continued her conversation with his wife.

"You and your wife are obviously part of the *ton*. Is your marriage what they call *marriage à la mode?*" Lydia asked, drawing his attention back to her, and then she stared at him as though willing him to answer. Her once sympathetic voice seemed to accuse him of some crime. Stephen glanced at Langston, wondering if Lydia were less presentable than he had earlier thought. Too uncertain in his recent marriage to be willing to discuss it, he sought unsuccessfully for some way to alter her conversation. Then he breathed a sigh of relief when Lady Langston gave orders for the servants to remove the first course and present the barons of beef with vegetables and roast pheasants. He faced his hostess with a smile.

"You will enjoy Jane's mother. I know that you didn't have a chance to get to know her well when you were growing up, but she is a delightful person," Lady Langston told him. As they continued their conversation and Mrs. Hendrickson spoke to Jane, they were aware that something was amiss at the other end of the table. Nervously covering the silence of that pair, the others chatted about inconsequential things.

"Do not speak to me; I have nothing to say to you now," Lydia said quietly when good manners would have dictated that she speak to Langston. She kept her eyes on her plate. Langston bit his lip, wondering not for the first time what had happened to change her behavior. Lydia cut her meat into small bites and pushed them around her plate. Remembering his guest the evening before who had done much the same thing, Langston braced for another explosion.

Fortunately, Lydia was much better behaved than Arabella had been. Although she ignored Langston for the rest of the meal and avoided looking directly at Jane, when it was time to change dinner partners again, she encouraged Stephen to talk about himself, filling the quiet moments with pleasing prattle. Stephen relaxed a trifle, but Langston and Jane grew more tense.

When the ladies withdrew, both Stephen and Langston breathed a sigh of relief. "Something is very wrong," Stephen told his friend.

"And how did you reach that conclusion?" Langston asked sarcastically. "Did you study women's behavior when you went to the university?"

"What did you do to that girl? When we went upstairs this afternoon, she was pleasant. Now it is difficult to get a sensible word out of her. She sounds just like those pattern cards of courtesy who never care about your answer but only about their own questions." Stephen frowned. "You must have done something."

"Me?" Langston stepped back, his hand on his chest as though shocked by Stephen's question.

"She wouldn't talk to you," Stephen reminded him. "Asked me stupid questions. It was as though she had never been at a dinner party before."

"Not quite. She knew how to keep me quiet."

"What did she say?"

"That she had nothing to say to me."

Stephen shook his head and patted his friend on the shoulder. "At least she didn't demand that you send her back to London." The two men exchanged a rueful glance.

"But what am I to do?" Langston complained.

"What do you usually do when a woman acts this way?"

"Send her a new trinket. But there's not a jeweler around here," Langston said, throwing up his hands. "I should never have gotten involved with a cit's granddaughter. She doesn't have any idea how to behave."

"I wouldn't be so quick to judge her. She behaved properly this afternoon. Did you frighten her when you were alone? She has obviously been sheltered."

"Alone? Her companion and my mother saw to that. The closest I got to her was a brief kiss on the cheek. And the few times we have been alone she has not been hesitant about returning my kisses," Langston said, pouring himself another glass of port. "Do you want another glass?"

"One more," Stephen said. He pushed his hair back from his forehead. "Then I don't understand it."

"I don't think I understand anything about women. Even Jane confuses me at times."

"Only at times? She keeps me in a state of confusion."

"That's natural. You're her husband."

"And you'll be Miss Thackeray's husband. Maybe we aren't supposed to understand anything about women," Stephen said as he sipped his wine.

Langston grinned. "Think Jane will accept that explanation?" he asked. He took a drink of his wine, thankful that for the first time in many days he and Stephen could enjoy the easy relationship they had always shared.

"Not for a moment," Stephen assured him. "Maybe you'll have better luck with your fiancée."

"Gad, I hope so. I have had all the emotion I can stand today." he closed his eyes and sighed. Then he sat bolt upright. "What if your stepmother had stayed?"

"Count your blessings that she is on her way to London. In the mood she was in, she would have ripped Miss Thackeray to shreds," Stephen told him with a shudder.

"Only after she tried to destroy Jane," Langston reminded him. "How could your father stand to be married to her?"

"I doubt she treated him to the same scenes she made with us. He wouldn't have stood for them. And had she made him too uncomfortable he would have left her in the country. Besides, she flattered him, I suppose, and made him feel young." Stephen paused, surprised by his own words. "That must have been it," he muttered to himself.

Silence, the comfortable kind between friends who understand each other, fell. As they finished their port, Langston sat up. "Have to talk to Jane."

"To Jane? Maybe she can help you with Miss Thackeray, but I doubt it. Did you notice how your fiancée was ignoring her?"

"No more than she ignored me. At least she didn't tell

Jane she didn't want to talk to her." He walked toward the door.

"Just remember Jane is my wife now," Stephen told him. Langston stopped and stared at him. "You must admit you have a convenient memory, Langston. You sold Roxbury your black hunter and then took it out the next afternoon."

"You are not Roxbury, and Jane is no horse. Need her advice, that's all. Told you I gave you my blessing."

"No, you didn't."

"Must have slipped my mind."

Deciding to ask the question that had been teasing him all day, Stephen put out a hand and stopped Langston. "If we have your blessing, why have you been acting this way?"

His friend slowly turned to face him. At first his face showed no emotion. Then he sighed and smiled ruefully. "Not going to let me off without an explanation, are you?" he asked.

"No."

"Thought not." Langston sat down once more and Stephen followed. "You know what I used to be like."

"Used to be?" Stephen asked, his eyebrows rising.

"Gad, Stephen, we're not boys anymore. Of course, I have changed." His friend looked skeptical. Langston laughed bitterly. "Of course, you have seen no inkling of that these last few days, have you? As soon as I saw Jane, it was as though the last year had never happened, as though you would appear and capture her attention, and she would forget about me once again." He laughed. "And she did."

"What are you talking about?" Stephen asked. He picked up his wineglass to take a drink, but it was empty.

"The most surprising day of my life was the day Jane said she would marry me," Langston said, his eyes downcast. Stephen stared at him.

"What?"

"Thought she would accept you."

"But, I—I never said anything."

"But I knew. And if you had, she might have accepted

you." Langston looked up, his face serious. "Might have been better if she had."

Stephen put down the glass he had been holding very carefully. "Why?" he asked.

"Then I would still have both of you for my friends."

"You do."

Langston just looked at Stephen. Then he sighed again. "Don't know how you can say that after the way I have acted. I was like a little boy with a toy he is not willing to share with anyone. How can you stand me?"

Stephen took a deep breath, wondering at a maturity that had not been evident in his friend before this. "You are my friend," he said quietly, more at peace with his friend and with himself than he had been for some time.

"Forgot that." Langston got up and walked toward the door, bringing their talk to an end. Walking much more quickly than his friend, Langston strode down the hall and opened the door to the salon where the women were waiting.

"And what else have you forgotten?" Stephen asked. Langston ignored him and walked into the salon.

He was in time to hear Langston say, "Jane, I need to talk to you."

Before Jane had a chance to answer, Lydia burst into tears. "I can't," she cried. "I simply can't."

"Can't do what?" both Lady Langston and Mrs. Hendrickson asked, disturbed. They rushed to her side. Jane, who had been the focus of Lydia's disdain all evening, simply stared at her. The two gentlemen stopped where they were, more upset by her tears than they would admit.

"I thought I could," Lydia said through her sobs. "Grandfather explained it all to me, but I can't!" She buried her head in her hands.

Lady Langston and Mrs. Hendrickson looked at each other, puzzled. "This is not like her," her companion assured Lady Langston. "She has never done this before."

"Well, something is wrong," the older lady declared. She pulled up a chair next to her future daughter-in-law and said, "Tell me about it." Langston started toward them, and she waved him back.

"Grandfather said that Langston would have a mistress; that all men of his rank did. I was to ignore it. But I can't. I can't!" Her sobs began anew.

Lady Langston stared at her son, wondering who had told this young girl about his opera dancer. Even *she* was not certain exactly who the woman was. How had this girl found out? "My dear, are you certain?" she asked as she pressed a handkerchief into Lydia's hand.

"Yes, the servants here were talking, and my maid overheard."

"Here?" Lady Langston raised her head and glared at her son. Jane and Stephen exchanged troubled glances. Mrs. Hendrickson stared at her charge, wondering at her behavior.

Lydia raised her head and controlled her sobs with an effort. "How do you do it?" she asked Stephen.

"Me? What are you talking about?"

"How can you sit through dinner when you know what the two of them have been doing? The servants said you knew," Lydia said. She struggled to speak without sobbing.

"Knew what?" Stephen stared at her without understanding.

"About your wife and Langston." She burst into tears again, leaning against Lady Langston's shoulder, burying her head as though she were a child.

Langston, who had wanted to take his mother's place for some time, started forward, but his mother frowned and refused to give way for him. "Jane and I?"

"They were talking about you and Mrs. Middleton," Lydia whispered. Mrs. Hendrickson stared at the two of them. Jane stared right back.

"I am afraid your maid misunderstood," Stephen said in a quiet voice, realizing what must have happened. Remembering Smythe's presence in the hall earlier that day, he was not surprised. He took a seat beside Jane and took her hand in his. "Since she is in a strange house, she doesn't know anyone. And I am certain that the servants at the manor didn't explain. They must have been discussing my stepmother."

"Your stepmother?" Lydia sat up and stared at him, a look of disbelief on her face. Mrs. Hendrickson sat back down, her eyes fixed on him also.

"He is right, I am afraid. When Langston was in London making the final arrangements with you, he saw her somewhere and invited her to visit the manor and help celebrate Stephen and Jane's marriage," Lady Langston said. During the afternoon when everyone else had retired, she and her son had had a very interesting discussion. She reached up and smoothed back the girl's hair as she had done her son's when he was smaller.

"Marriage?" Mrs. Hendrickson focused on the word. "Were your nupituals recent then?" she asked, looking from Jane to Stephen.

Stephen tightened his hand on Jane's; he looked at her, waiting for her to respond. She simply blushed, a rosy color giving her pale cheeks a warm tint. "We were wed yesterday," he admitted.

"Yesterday?" Both Lydia and Mrs. Hendrickson looked at the two of them, astonished. "But why? What?" Lydia stumbled over the words, her face flushing.

"I think my fiancée and I need to discuss this," Langston said, taking her hand and pulling her to her feet. "If you will excuse us." His face was set in hard lines.

Lydia took one look at his face and decided not to argue. "But if it wasn't this Mrs. Middleton, I must apologize."

"We both agree on that," he told her, pulling her from the room. "But you can do that later." His own guilt over his behavior with Arabella made his voice harsher than he intended. Lydia took another look at him and made no protest.

The door closed behind them. "Please, do not think she acts like this most of the time," Mrs. Hendrickson said, wringing her hands. "I don't understand what happened. She is usually the most amiable creature. Please do not judge her too harshly. She has been rather anxious since she accepted Lord Langston. Her grandfather has such high expectations."

"If Mrs. and Mrs. Middleton can forget, I am certain I can, too," Lady Langston said. She frowned slightly. "I wonder which of our servants caused this?"

"With the disturbance my stepmother made before she left today, it could have been any of them," Stephen told her. "And to expect them to be silent about such a commotion would be too much. Much better to lay the blame where it belongs—on my stepmother."

"You are being too kind," Lady Langston told him. "Some of the blame must be laid at Langston's door. He knew what that woman was like when he asked her to visit us."

"I think he misjudged her," Jane said quietly. Stephen frowned. Why did she have to take Langston's part? "I know I did. Stephen never talked about his difficulties with her, and neither of us imagined that she could be so unprincipled."

Ever avid for gossip, Mrs. Hendrickson leaned forward. "Is she a member of the *ton*?"

In spite of her own decision to share at least some of the incident with her friends, Lady Langston was not about to share her disgust with a member of a lower class. "She is," she said blightingly and turned to Jane. "Do you still plan to leave tomorrow? I do wish you would stay longer."

Although he was aware that the statement was merely a chance to change the conversation, Stephen looked at her gratefully. "Jane is anxious to see her mother. And I look forward to seeing her again."

"Did you ever dream when you were children that the two of you would be married?" Lady Langston asked, looking from one to the other.

Remembering his own dreams, Stephen shook his head. "I was too busy trying to keep up with the two of them to worry about anything," Jane said. She smiled at her husband as though to soften her words. "It was years before I thought about marriage. Only old people were married." She laughed softly and looked up at Stephen, inviting him to share her laughter. His face was grave. Jane stared into his eyes, her slight smile fading.

"You sound as though you had known your husband and Lord Langston a very long time. How comfortable you must be with him," Mrs. Hendrickson said, leaning forward slightly.

Before anyone could reply, the door opened. Everyone turned. Langston stood back and let his fiancée enter the room before he did. "Lydia has something she wants to say to you."

Lydia looked at him and then back at the four seated across the room. She blinked rapidly to keep the tears from spilling from her eyes. "I wish to apologize to everyone," she said in a whisper, appearing more like a child than a young woman about to be married. She cleared her throat.

"And?" Langston prompted her.

"I am sorry I embarrassed you. Mrs. Middleton, I especially regret the accusation I leveled at you. Langston explained everything. I hope you can forgive me." She hung her head much like a puppy that has been spanked for chewing on its master's boots.

"Everything?" Stephen asked, drawling the word out. He raised an eyebrow. Jane opened her eyes very wide.

"She knows that we have been friends for years, and when we were young and foolish, Jane and I were engaged but decided that we would not suit," Langston said hurriedly.

Stephen looked at his wife, trying to read her emotions, but she kept them hidden behind a mask of calm. "You must think I have no manners," Lydia added. "My grandfather would have banished me to my room. I am so sorry."

Jane had her doubts about the sincerity of the girl's apology, but before she could say anything, Stephen said, "Consider it forgotten." He had his eyes fixed on his friend. "Had we grown angry every time someone said something we didn't like, we would no longer be friends. Isn't that right, Jane?"

A little less ready to accept Lydia's apology, Jane merely

nodded. Then, she relented. "I must admit that situation has been a confusing one. Ever since that boy killed the dogs."

"Dogs, what dogs?" Lydia and Mrs. Hendrickson asked. Stephen and Langston looked at each other and laughed. Jane glanced at the two of them and smiled. Even Lady Langston relaxed enough to laugh softly.

"My dear, you would have been amazed. For the last few days, we have never known whether we were on our heads or on our heels," Lady Langston said, looking at her son, Jane, and Stephen. "Have we, my dears? First . . ."

Chapter Fourteen

When Stephen and Jane entered their rooms sometime later, both were silent. Annie, who had been sewing in the sitting room, stood up. "You shouldn't have waited up for me," Jane said, stripping off her gloves and handing them and her reticule to her.

"Why not let her help you get ready for bed?" Stephen suggested.

Jane blushed. "But we need—"

"To talk. Yes, I know. But we can be more comfortable if we get ready for bed. Is Vernon here?"

"In the dressing room, sir," Annie assured him, her eyes wide.

"Good." Stephen walked through the bedroom while Jane followed. "I will rejoin you in a few minutes."

Her heart racing, Jane allowed Annie to remove her gown, petticoat, stays, and chemise. "Hurry, Annie," she whispered as the girl took off her stockings and garter. When her maid gave her a knowing look, she blushed but did not say another word. What would she think if she knew that Jane would probably spend another night alone?

As she slipped her dressing gown over her nightgown, she heard a knock at the dressing room door. "Come," she called. "Annie, go to bed. We are leaving as soon as we get up tomorrow." She picked up a brush, ignoring her husband's valet as he walked through the room. She glanced up and found her husband watching her run her brush through her hair, his face serious.

"Come into the sitting room," he said and held out his

hand. Without thinking, she placed her own in his and allowed him to lead her into the next room.

"You and Langston seemed much friendlier after dinner," she said, taking her seat and arranging the skirts of the
dressing gown so that no portion of her nightgown showed.

"At least we talked." Stephen sat beside her and stared
into the small fire that burned in the fireplace. "He says he
has changed."

She laughed wryly. "I have heard that before," she said
quietly. She smoothed a wrinkle from the skirt under her
hand. "You remember how often he used to say that."

"You're right, but I believe him this time. He seems different, older. And he said . . ." Stephen paused, his face serious.

"That he would never do it again. He has said that many
times before, Stephen. You know he has." Jane's tone of
voice was cynical. In the last few days, she had been reminded once again how heedless and uncaring of others'
feelings Langston was. How had she forgotten how infuri-
ating he could be?

"I know. But maybe this time . . ."

"Will be different? How many times have you said that?
You always look for the best in him." Jane said accusingly.
"And how many times have you been disappointed?"

Stephen turned to look at her, more hopeful than he had
been for hours. "What about you? You agreed to marry
him." He smiled at her, trying to relieve the seriousness of
the moment.

His ploy didn't work. "Well, I also agreed to marry you.
And the only marriage ceremony I went through was with
you," she reminded him. She stared at her clasped hands,
trying to explore her own emotions. Why had she agreed to
marry him? Had anyone else in such a situation asked her,
she would have refused.

"Yes, I haven't forgotten. You were a beautiful bride."
He reached out to take her hand, but she pulled it back.
"Jane, what is wrong?"

"Wrong?" She turned to face him, her eyes flashing.

"Think of the last day and a half and ask me that again. You lie to me to get me to marry you; your mother—"

"Stepmother."

She changed the word and continued her list. "Your step-mother insults me repeatedly; Langston's betrothed insults me; and when the sweet little thing flutters her eyelashes and sheds a few tears before she makes an apology, you answer for me. And you ask me what is wrong?" She got up and stood over him, "Shall I go on?"

"What do you mean I answered for you? You weren't saying anything." He stood up too, moving closer to her. She stepped back, hitting the back of her legs on a low table, almost falling. Stephen grabbed her and pulled her closer to him. As soon as she had regained her balance, she pushed him away, moving closer to the fireplace.

"She was talking to me. You should have waited to see what I would do," she told him angrily. The emotions she had been repressing for the last two days threatened to overwhelm her.

"And what would you have done? Ignore her forever?" As willing as he was to accept blame for what he knew he had done wrong, he was not going to accept more guilt than he deserved. He crossed to the opposite side of the fireplace and faced her.

"That was my choice." Her voice was low but full of emotion. "You took it away from me. Just as you took my choice from me when you didn't tell me about the possibility of the frogs."

"I was afraid."

"Of what? Stephen, I have known you for years. You aren't frightened of anything."

He lowered his eyes and turned toward the table where the decanter of wine and glasses sat. He picked up the decanter, his fingers white as his grip tightened. "You don't know me as well as you think," he said, pouring himself a glass of wine.

"That is obvious." She stared at his back, noting once again the width of his shoulders, now covered with a dark blue dressing gown only a shade darker than his eyes. She shivered. Suddenly, her legs felt weak, and she sank into a nearby chair. "Stephen, talk to me," she whispered, her voice pleading.

"About what? My fears?" He turned to face her once again, his eyes automatically turning to where she had been only moments before. Then he found her seated across the room, her eyes fixed on him. "I was afraid I was going to die. No, that is not strong enough. I knew I was going to die."

"But after you spoke with Dickson?" She longed to go to him, to smooth those wrinkles from his forehead, to erase the pain she could see in his eyes.

"I didn't know him. And the idea was so preposterous." He laughed bitterly. "What would you have said had I told you such a story?"

"You should have given me that chance," she said firmly. To herself she admitted that she might have laughed when she heard it. "We could have waited, given my mother a chance to come."

"Given you a chance to cry off once you met my stepmother." And saw Langston again, he added to himself.

Remembering her own feelings yesterday before she received her mother's letter, she blushed and hung her head. Stephen, his legs now as weak as hers had been a few minutes earlier, sat down in a chair across the room, staring at her, the fear that he had claimed holding him tight in its grasp. She had planned to cry off. Jane kept her eyes on her skirts, smoothing them with her hands. "Look at me," he demanded. Her head came up, a look of embarrassment in her eyes. Her eyes met his for a moment. Then she blushed again and lowered them quickly. "You were going to cry off, weren't you?" he demanded. "What happened? Did you decide that having your own home, even if it included me, was better than being a companion all your life?" His hurt and anger were like whips against her skin.

"Stephen, everything was happening so quickly. My mother . . ." She paused to gain control of her shaking voice, wondering if he would always look at her with those accusing eyes.

"What about your mother?"

"I longed to talk to her. Everything was so confusing. I was frightened. Had we had more time . . ."

"Time for what? And what were you frightened of? Me?" His voice reflected his astonishment.

"No," she began, her voice low. Then she raised her head, a militant look on her face. "Yes." She stared at him, willing him to contradict her.

"Me? You were afraid of me? But I would never, could never—"

Jane hastened to reassure him. "Oh, I know you would never willingly hurt me. But think of this from my side. Here I was alone, my family miles away, being encouraged to marry a man I had just seen after months and months of separation. You seemed more concerned with providing your sister protection than me. I thought I was merely a convenient bride."

"Convenient? Jane, let me explain." His heart was pounding so hard that he could hardly breathe.

His wife ignored him and continued. "And Lady Langston? I know she meant all for the best, but whose best? Her first consideration is her son, smoothing his path." She paused, gathering her facts. When he would have spoken, she hurried on. "No, let me finish."

She took a deep breath. "All she cared about was getting me out of Langston's life before he married Miss Thackeray."

"I think you wrong her as well as me," Stephen said quietly. But her words had struck a chord within him.

"Oh, I do not doubt she likes me, wishes me the best, but it is Langston whom she truly loves. And for the last year, I have kept her from him."

"I think you are assuming too much responsibility. I am certain Langston was pleased when his mother moved to Bath," her husband said dryly.

"I am sure he was. But it was because of me that he decided to spend Christmas with friends instead of his mother. And because of me, he avoided her all during the Season."

"Jane, listen to you. We both know Langston. He does what he wants. Had he wanted his mother for something, he wouldn't have hesitated to call on her even if you were present. I am certain he was only too happy to pursue Miss Thackeray without his mother's supervision."

"I am only reporting what she thought. And how do you think that made me feel?" Once more her voice was angry and accusing. "Almost as bad as I felt when you explained the reason you wanted to marry me so quickly."

Stephen walked to the table that held the wine decanter and poured himself another glass. "Would you care for some?" he asked her, ignoring her last statement until he could think it through. She shook her head, sending her hair flying about. Pulling it over her shoulder, she began braiding it. Stephen stared at her, fascinated. He blinked and said in a quiet voice, "Jane, you must have known what your life would be like with Lady Langston. And I did need a wife in case I died. But I wouldn't have asked just anyone to marry me. Are you blaming me for thinking I was going to die?"

"Blaming you? I am not blaming anyone. I am simply trying to explain." She paused as she remembered what had started her on this line of thought.

"Explain why you thought of crying off," Stephen said, taking his seat once more. She was his wife, he reminded himself. She had willingly signed their marriage lines.

"You were rushing me so. I hardly knew where to turn, and Lady Langston was so excited, planning my clothes, my life." She looked at the man who had been her husband for little more than twenty-four hours and sighed. "I simply wanted to be sure—"

"Of what?"

"That what we were doing was right. That I wasn't taking advantage of you."

"Of me? Jane, it was I who had all the advantages." He leaned forward, his forehead creased.

She shook her head. "You had someone to care for your sister. But I, I would have my own home, someplace where I would be in charge. Earlier you accused me of agreeing to marry you simply because I wanted to escape being Lady

Langston's companion. I feared you were right." She sat back, her head down, her gaze on her hands.

Her husband stood up slowly, gazing at his wife. He crossed the room and knelt beside her chair, taking her hands in his. "Jane, look at me," he begged. Her revelations had reaffirmed his suspicions.

She looked into his blue eyes. He smiled at her. "I relied on your wanting to change your life," he admitted. "Would you have accepted me if you were still living with your mother at your home?"

"Had I been living there she would have accepted you for me," she said, pulling back slightly, remembering her mother's letter. He refused to let go of her hands.

"Jane, listen to yourself."

"I know. But I am trying to explain how I felt. I don't know what I would have done." She pulled her hands free and clasped them tightly before her. He sat down in front of her, his eyes still on her face.

"Go on." Nothing of the turmoil he felt within showed on his face or in his voice.

She got up, carefully stepping around him, and walked toward the fireplace. Leaning against it, she stared into the fire. Stephen turned to watch her, for the moment willing to allow the silence between them to grow. A minute or two went by. She turned back to face him, surprised to see him still on the floor. "Stephen, you cannot imagine the turmoil in my life for the last year."

He said nothing, merely watched her. She turned back to stare at the fire once more, more comfortable when she didn't have to face him. "Even before my father died, I knew something was wrong—both with him and with Langston," she admitted. She turned back to look at him. "I had already begun to suspect that we would never marry. He and Father always had some excuse for not sending the announcement to the papers. My friends had even stopped asking when we were to be wed. And, to be honest, I had begun to wonder why I had accepted him."

"But—you seemed so happy." Stephen almost stuttered in his haste to get the words out. Jane had been thinking about not marrying Langston. The words echoed in his mind.

"And how was I supposed to appear? The world already pitied me. Can you imagine what the *ton* would have said had I announced that I was no longer in love with him? I can hear them now. 'Poor girl. She is trying so hard but convincing no one.' And think how his mother would have felt."

"But when you first arrived here, you stared at him whenever you believed no one was watching you. I thought—"

"And so did I. Even though I had considered breaking my engagement, I had not. After my father died, I offered to let him go simply because that was the thing to do. I never dreamed that he would agree, that money was more important to him than I was." Once again her voice was bitter and sharp. Stephen, realizing the delicacy of the moment, was silent, waiting for her to continue. She crossed to the chair beside him and sank down. She looked in his face as if worried about what she would see there. The affection in his eyes made her lower her own. "This is so hard."

"What is?"

"Admitting this to you, to myself."

"Admitting what?"

She looked up and stared into his face. She took a deep breath that caused Stephen to look lower than her eyes. "That for a year I have been deceiving myself, that I had convinced myself that I loved him." She looked up once more. "But I didn't. I know that now."

"That is all I need to hear." He reached for her, but she pulled back.

"No, Stephen." She softened her words with a shy smile. "Don't you see. Nothing has changed."

He slowly got to his feet. "Are you telling me that you want to annul our marriage?" He looked down at her, his eyes almost black with emotion.

"No, Stephen. No." She got up and stood in front of him. "I am just saying what I said before. Everything is moving too fast. I don't know what I want." Her eyes begged him to understand.

"Are you telling me you don't want to leave with me tomorrow?" He turned his back, walking behind the settee as though putting a barrier between her words and him.

"No." She shook her head and came to kneel on the settee facing him. "I am simply asking you to give me a little time."

"But last night?"

Jane stood up, her eyes flashing. "Think about last night, Stephen. Langston, staring at me with that look of betrayal in his eyes; your stepmother insulting me. And Lady Langston so careful to explain my duty to me."

"Your duty?" Stephen had given little thought to anyone but Jane the evening before.

"To provide you an heir, if possible, before you died."

He sagged against the piece of furniture that was holding him up. "She told you *that*?

"Don't you see why I was angry? Everyone was telling me what to do, leaving me with no choice. And then you rejected me," Jane said.

"Jane, you must know—"

"What I know now and what I felt last night are two different things. Can you understand how I felt earlier today when Langston told me about the frogs?" She sank down on the settee, curling up in a corner, her face hidden on her knees.

Quickly, Stephen came around and sat beside her, once more taking her hands in his. "Jane, Jane," he begged. "I would rather injure myself than injure you. I started to tell you last night. I wish I had."

"I wish you had, too. Why didn't you?" She looked into his eyes, wishing that she knew more of his as well as her own feelings.

This time it was he who pulled away, turning so that she could only see his profile. "I told you I was frightened," he said quietly.

"But I don't understand. I know you thought you were dying. But was that all?" He shook his head. "Then what?"

"I was frightened of losing you," he said, so quietly that she almost didn't hear him.

"Losing me? But we were already married."

He faced her once again. "But you can change your mind. We could get an annulment. We could still do it."

"An annulment. You mentioned that earlier. I never thought about it. What made you bring it up?" Jane reached out and pushed back the lock of hair that hung in his face.

He captured her hand, his fingers tightening around hers. Then slowly he bought her hand to his lips, kissing it so softly that had she not been watching she might not have realized what he was doing. He held her hand against his cheek. When he spoke, his voice was so soft she had to strain to hear. He took a deep breath, and his words rushed out like water breaking through a dam. "I was afraid you accepted me only because you felt sorry for me." He brought her hand to his lips again, turning it over to place a kiss in her palm. Her fingers touched his lips.

A shiver went through her as it had every time he had caressed her. "Stephen," she whispered.

"Yes?" The warmth of his breath against her hand sent another shiver though her. He tugged on her hand to pull her closer, but she resisted. He sat back, his face reflecting his disappointment. "What is wrong?"

"We still need to talk," she reminded him.

"About what?"

She pulled her hand free and stood up. He stood up beside her, longing to gather her into his arms. Reading the emotion on his face, she stepped back, careful this time to avoid the table. "About everything that happened today."

"You cannot hold me responsible for my stepmother," he protested, unwilling to expose all of his emotions until he was more certain of her.

"I don't. But I wasn't referring to her. I was talking about the way you responded to that little, little . . ." The more she thought about the way Lydia had treated her, the angrier she became.

"Child," he supplied, trying to defuse her anger.

"She is no child."

"She is not very old and so inexperienced."

"Inexperienced? Did you see the way she brought

Langston to heel? It is evident who will rule that household."

"What do you care about Langston?" Stephen's eyes narrowed dangerously.

"I don't care about him except as a friend. Do you wish me to forget the years we shared? That would include you, you know." Her eyes flashed at him, and the color in her cheeks was pure anger.

"Then why are you concerned about him?"

"About him? You didn't see the way you reacted to her. Smiling and agreeing as though she had not spent hours insulting me."

"Me?"

"Yes, you. So anxious to soothe the 'child' that you were not paying any attention to me. You scarcely looked at me before you accepted her apology."

"What did you want me to do? Ignore her as you were doing?" Although his words were angry, his mind was filled with joy. She was jealous.

"I wanted you to let me answer for myself. Is this what our married life will be? My having no say in anything?" Jane's voice quivered in spite of herself. She fought back her tears, refusing to let him see how upset she was.

"What are you talking about?" Somehow Stephen had lost the focus of the conversation.

"Are you going to make all the decisions for me?"

"What decisions?" he asked, confused and dismayed by the direction their conversation was taking.

"Like today. Accepting her apology without asking me."

"Asking you? How could I have asked you?"

She continued, ignoring him. "Telling me we were leaving as soon as the servants could pack. Is this the way it will always be?" She turned to stare at him, her green eyes as hard as emeralds.

"What? Are you angry because I said I was leaving? What did you expect me to do with Langston acting as he was? Stay forever?"

"You could have asked me. It would have taken only a moment. But no, you announced it to the world first." The anger that had disappeared earlier returned in full force as she convinced herself that she had been ill used.

Stephen took a deep breath and moved closer to her. "And if I promise I will never do such a thing again, will that satisfy you?" he asked, his voice low. Thinking about the way he had acted toward her today, he had to admit that she had reason for anger. Jane had never enjoyed following; she had always wanted to have a voice in what they did.

She stared at him, trying to decide if his words were sincere or only designed to soothe her. She searched his face for her answer, but it was her memory that provided it. It had been Stephen who had listened to her and who had convinced Langston that her ideas were good. If he had listened then, she thought. "I suppose."

"Since I never had a wife before, you will have to teach me how I must proceed," Stephen said with a laugh, pleased that her eyes had softened toward him. He stepped forward and put his arms around her. "Am I doing this right?"

Her eyes wide, she nodded. He bent his head and kissed her. Her arms wrapped around his neck, and he pulled her closer. "Stephen," she whispered against his lips. He slid his hand up her side to touch her breast. He felt her freeze and put it back around her waist. Leaning against him, she breathed a sigh of regret that he took for a sigh of relief. He kissed her deeply once more and then stepped back.

"Time for bed," he said in a voice still hoarse with emotion. Her eyes widened. "I'll see you in the morning."

"Stephen." Her voice too was husky.

"What?" He paused, his hand on the door to the bedroom. Slowly, as though he was not certain what he was doing, he turned to face her. His face was set in determined lines.

"Good night." She watched as his face softened.

"Good night," he murmured, watching her wistfully. Then he turned and walked from the room.

She stood staring after him for a moment. Then she carefully banked the few remaining embers of the fire and blew out all but one of the candles. She wiggled her shoulders, releasing the tension there. Then she too walked into the bedroom, to the empty bed that waited there for her.

As she lay in bed staring at the canopy above her, she thought about the way she had acted and wondered at herself. What kind of marriage would they have? As she waited for sleep to come, almost too exhausted to relax, she thought again about Stephen's suggestion of an annulment and the resulting talk it would generate. Not for anyone was she willing to face another storm of gossip. But what about Stephen? Did he want to be free? The question haunted her until she slept.

Stephen too lay awake in his narrow bed for some time. Jane had said she didn't love Langston. Was she only saying that because she thought he expected it, because she was his wife? What if she regretted the marriage? Could he let her go? Thinking of her warm lips under his, he groaned. And what about her idea that he had only asked her to marry him because she was convenient. Convenient? He laughed bitterly. Then his laughter died. He would have to be careful. He knew he would have to convince her that life with him was preferable to any other. Lady Langston certainly would never take her back. Jane had been right in her assessment of that lady's motives. And Langston too was claimed. He smiled as he remembered Jane's reading of Lydia's character. His friend had better watch what he was doing or his wife would run his life. In spite of the turmoil still in his life, with a smile on his lips, he too drifted off to sleep.

Chapter Fifteen

Stephen and Jane left the manor the next morning. Although Jane had begged her not to do so, even Lady Langston appeared hours before she normally left her room just to say good-bye to them. She clasped Jane in her arms and patted her gently. "Tell your mother I shall write her soon, my dear."

"I shall. And you must send me all the news of Scotland," Jane told her, kissing her cheek.

"The children will miss you so."

"And I them." From a distance of a hundred miles or more, even the most naughty child of the family seemed an angel. "Please give them my kind regards."

Langston stood near his mother, his eyes moving back and forth between his friends as if seeking some answer he could not find. "Shall I see you again soon?" he asked Stephen, just the hint of nervousness in his voice.

"I'm not certain. We haven't discussed any plans other than visiting Jane's family and seeing Caroline." He glanced at his wife, hoping that she had overheard his remarks and had realized that he was not making decisions without consulting her. He was hoping for just a smile, but she was still talking to Lady Langston and missed his remarks. "When do you plan to wed? We will certainly want to be there for that."

"Sometime in the spring. I will expect you to stand up with me." Langston hesitated as if expecting Stephen's refusal.

Determined to accept any olive branch that Langston was willing to offer, Stephen stepped forward and shook his hand. "Simply send me word. Will you be married here?"

"Gad, no. I'm certain Lydia's grandfather has already chosen a church in London." He smiled. "Forgive me?" he whispered, once again consumed by guilt.

"Certainly," Stephen told him, much as he had done for years. Maybe this time his friend meant it. "And you must visit us when we decide where we will live."

"Maybe later," Langston said, looking at his betrothed, who was not hiding her anxiety very well. Although he had done most of the talking the evening before, she had not been shy about expressing her opinion of his behavior. "Lydia, come here," he said, motioning her to take her place by his side. She flushed and hurried toward him. "Now take your leave of the Middletons," he directed as though she were the child that Stephen had called her. She shot him a hard glance from under her long lashes but did as he asked.

"I do hope you will pay us another visit as soon as we return from our wedding journey," she said, looking up at Stephen with bright eyes.

Jane walked to Stephen's side and put her hand on his arm. Almost unconsciously, he put that arm around her and pulled her closer to him. "We will be happy to be members of your first house party," Jane replied. Even though Stephen had said he would ask her before making decisions, she intended to remind him that she had a voice in their marriage. She did not want to be in the same situation that her mother had been in, being consulted only when her husband couldn't avoid it. The moment the idea crossed her mind, Jane admitted that her mother had been content to let her father make all of the decisions except those that had concerned her children. But she didn't intend to live like that.

Lydia's face lit up like a child's on Christmas. "A house party?" She looked up at her betrothed. "How grand that sounds."

"A house party? I will be happy to help you plan it," Lady Langston offered, visions of a restored manor filling her head with pleasure.

"After we are married, Mama," Langston said quickly,

before she had planned an entire fortnight. "Jane and Stephen promised to return for it."

"But that is so far away," the older lady complained.

"After your son's wedding, you will have something else to look forward to," Mrs. Hendrickson said, trying to enter the conversation. Lady Langston stared at her for a long moment, and she fell silent.

As the horses on the chaise began to shift restlessly, Steven helped Jane up the steps of the carriage. She paused at the door and looked back, almost as though she were saying a final good-bye to the place where she had been so happy and so miserable. Stephen said good-bye to the ladies and clasped Langston's hand one last time. Then he joined his wife, her maid, and his valet in the carriage.

As they traveled to the inn where Langston had assured him he would be able to hire a carriage for the servants, neither Stephen nor Jane said more than a word or two, both somewhat relieved that the servants were present to inhibit conversation. Stephen, who had not slept much the night before, pulled his hat over his eyes and leaned back in a corner, trying to calm his mind enough to doze off.

His wife, her own night restless, glanced at him and wished that she could follow his example. Instead, she smiled at the servants and pulled out her book, turning the pages regularly although she could not have told anyone what she had read. Interposed over the pages was Stephen's face when he had told her he had been frightened of having her change her mind. Then followed Langston's as he had told her good-bye once more. Stephen and Langston? Closing her eyes as if trying to escape their faces, she wondered what was wrong with her. How could she have changed her mind so readily? She shivered as she remembered Stephen's hands and lips caressing her and the brief touch of Langston's hand on hers, almost like that of a brother.

Like his wife, Stephen sat with his eyes closed, reliving the last evening. Jane had said that she no longer loved Langston. But it didn't mean that she loved her husband, he reminded himself. She cared for him. He was certain of that, but love? As he thought of what their life might be, he in love with her, she merely friends with him, bleakness engulfed him.

When the chaise pulled into the inn where they planned to hire a carriage, both husband and wife gave a sigh of relief. The two servants followed them from the coach and into the inn, exchanging worried glances. While Stephen entered the private parlor he had requested, Annie followed her mistress to the best bedchamber to help her freshen up.

"I never had the chance to see the inside of a bedchamber at an inn on our trip out from London," Annie said, handing Jane a towel to dry her hands on.

"But you had to stop somewhere."

"We did. But the common room was good enough for the likes of the groom and me," Annie told her. She dipped her fingers into the water. "Hot and everything."

Jane finished straightening her hair and put her hat back on. "When you stop, I will tell Vernon that he is to engage a room so that you can rest."

"And what call would there be for that? He'll just think I'm getting above myself. I shall do quite well as it is. Just think; Mr. Middleton is hiring a coach just for Mr. Vernon and me." The girl was practically bubbling with excitement. Jane smiled, pleased to have something besides her husband to think about for the moment.

When Jane returned to the chaise, Stephen handed her in once more, his groom standing nearby with his saddled horse. "Would you object if I ride for a while? I want to blow some cobwebs out," he asked, his blue eyes serious. He tried to read her face, but during the last year she had grown accustomed to hiding her feelings.

Only the tiniest quiver in her voice revealed her dismay when she said, "No. Enjoy your ride."

"Enjoy your ride," she said to herself in a wistful voice after he had closed the door. "He will think you want to avoid him." The honesty that was part of her nature made her admit that in a way she did, at least until she knew her own mind. "And what I will do when I know it is a mystery to me. I am married to the man." She pulled her bonnet off and put in on the seat in front of her. Propping herself in the corner, she stared out the window at the changing country-side. Finally her eyelids began to droop.

By the time they stopped to change horses, Jane was awake once more. Stephen, who had hurried ahead, handed her from the carriage and escorted her into a private parlor where he had arranged for a meal to be served.

"Did you have a pleasant ride?" she asked in her brightest voice.

Stephen stared at her, recognizing that tone. He wondered what had upset her. "Just what I needed. I wish I had brought two horses so that you could ride with me. Or have you lost your fondness for riding?" Remembering the way she had thrown her heart over the fences as she was growing up, he doubted she had.

"I would enjoy a ride." Jane smiled, her entire face glowing. "But I haven't a saddle."

"We can have you fitted for a new one, and we'll find you a mount as soon as we return to the priory. One of my"—he paused and changed his word—"our neighbors has a breeding farm. I am sure he will be able to provide something. His horses are very good. Should I buy you a hunter, too?"

"Not at first," Jane said, still smiling. "It's been too long since I've been on horseback. Besides, I would rather the fox went free." She laughed and allowed him to seat her.

"You were the one who protested when we set snares, weren't you?" her husband said as he sat across from her and nodded at the serving woman. "I hope you will be able to eat the venison the landlord has promised us for luncheon."

"You wretch. You ordered it just to make me cringe," she complained.

"Cringe with every bite you take, you mean?"

"It is unfair to remind me how foolish I am. I cannot help it if I prefer not to see my food killed. At least I don't enjoy killing things." She let her eyelashes sweep her cheeks and then glanced at him again. He smiled at her.

"But you enjoy eating them," he reminded her. He watched as she put a slice of venison on her plate.

The serving maid hovered nearby to refill their glasses or offer them another slice of meat. She disappeared at one point to return with a roasted capon and mushroom fritters. Jane took only one fritter, but Stephen accepted some of everything.

"Do you think you have enough?" his wife asked, looking at his full plate.

"I am hungry from my ride."

"Hmmph!" She glared at him.

"And what does that mean?" he asked, putting his knife and fork beside his plate. One look at his wife's face told him that the pleasant conversation they had been enjoying was at an end. "Jane, tell me what that sound meant."

She glanced around and saw the servant waiting near the door. "Not now," she said firmly.

Stephen followed her gaze. Quickly he sent the woman from the room. "Now?" he asked. She simply looked at him. "Am I supposed to guess?"

Already slightly ashamed of her reaction, Jane shook her head. She cleared her throat nervously and took another sip of wine. "It was nothing."

"Jane, I have known you for years. That sound meant something."

She fixed her eyes on a spot on the wall behind him. "If you must know, I didn't want you to ride. I wanted you in the coach with me." Her words came out of her mouth so fast that Stephen had to concentrate to decipher them. She lowered her head and peeked up under her lashes.

He stared at her. "You wanted me to accompany you in the coach?" he asked, not certain that he had heard her correctly.

"Yes," she whispered.

"Then why didn't you tell me when I asked? I cannot read your mind." His voice reflected his confusion and his anger. "You want me to consider you when I make decisions. But you won't tell me what you think!" His voice had risen.

"Don't yell at me." Her green eyes flashed. "I was simply doing as you asked. I might have known that you would be angry. It's so typical of a man; tell him something, and if he doesn't like your remark, he grows angry."

"I am not angry," Stephen said in a roar.

"Listen to yourself. If I were one of your friends, you wouldn't speak to me so." Jane stared at him, willing him to disagree with her.

"No, madame, I wouldn't, but you are my wife." Stephen put his knife and fork carefully on his plate, got up from his chair, and came around the table. Jane's eyes widened nervously, wondering what he would do. He pulled her to her feet and kissed her passionately. "I will see you when you stop to change horses once more." He quickly left the room.

"Stephen!" she cried, running through the common room and outside. By the time she arrived in the yard, Stephen was nowhere to be found.

Jane kicked a rock in her path, sending it careening across the courtyard and into the wall. "I couldn't stay quiet, could I?" she asked. Had she realized that he was just inside the stable waiting for his horse to be saddled and watching her reaction she would not have blamed herself as she did.

As she bowled over the countryside that afternoon, Jane reminded herself that Stephen had asked her to tell him what was wrong. Remembering the kiss he had given her just before he had disappeared, she decided that he could not be too angry with her. But her feelings for him were still unsettled. What would happen at the inn that evening? she wondered.

Stephen, too, kept thinking about that kiss. Her lips had responded to his so sweetly. And she had not pushed him away whenever he had kissed her. Perhaps she would welcome further attentions. He urged his horse into a gallop, always in sight of the coach that carried the woman he longed to make completely his own.

Both Stephen and Jane were ready for a rest when they passed the signpost of the town where Jane's mother had always broken her journey to her brother's home. According to Mrs. Stanfield, it boasted the only posting house worthy of her patronage, the only one that provided a decent dinner and clean sheets.

Stephen arrived first and handed his horse over to a groom. As he entered the common room, the innkeeper, recognizing Quality when he saw it, hurried to his side. "We will need rooms for my wife and me, her maid, my valet, and my grooms. Also a private parlor where we can eat dinner," Stephen said, pulling off his gloves. He glanced around at the crowd, who by now was staring at him.

The innkeeper frowned. "No problem with the private parlor, sir. But—"

"But what?" Stephen fixed him with an icy stare.

"The grooms can sleep in the stables. Always have beds enough for them there. But your servants . . . I don't suppose they could sleep in the common room with this other lot?"

"Are you telling me I need to travel farther?" Stephen asked. Jane, who had entered the inn only moments before, stopped near the doorway. She held her breath.

"No, no, by no means, sir. But I have only two remaining rooms. Would your lady object to sharing with her maid? The room has a trundle bed, and your valet could sleep on the trundle bed in your room," the landlord suggested, mentally reviewing the amount of money he might make.

Jane walked up to her husband and put her hand through his arm. "You heard?" he asked. Because of his disappointment at the collapse of his plans, his voice was sharper than he had intended.

"Yes." She stifled a yawn. "Are you going to accept his offer?"

"Me? What do you think?" Stephen frowned slightly.

"I don't care. All I want is a place to wash my hands and face and sleep. Has no one dragged that road since the winter snows? The last five miles caused my bones to ache." She yawned again.

Her husband's frown grew deeper. The innkeeper looked nervously from one to the other. Finally, Stephen said, "We'll accept your offer. Show my wife to her room, and have the private parlor prepared for me." He walked with

Jane toward the stairs. "I'll send your maid up to you when she arrives. And don't come down without her." He lowered his voice until only she could hear him. "I don't like the look of this crew."

"Should we continue on?" she asked, her breath soft on his cheek. "I can, you know. I was only complaining." Her big green eyes stared into his. During her afternoon alone in the coach, she had admitted to herself that, whatever she had thought when she was younger, now it was Stephen that she wanted, Stephen, her husband. The memory of that realization caused her to blush.

Stephen caressed her cheek with his finger, certain she could read his love in his eyes. "No need for that. With your mother's recommendation, I am certain we will be all right."

"Whatever you wish." Jane longed to lay her aching head on his shoulder but resisted.

The innkeeper's wife bustled out of the kitchen, wiping her hands on her apron. "If you would come this way, madame," she said, leading the way up the stairs. Jane walked a few steps and then turned to look back at her husband.

"Order dinner," he suggested. He watched until she disappeared from sight. Then he sighed and walked across the common room, taking a seat until the innkeeper returned.

Almost two hours later, Stephen smiled at Jane across the table once more, wiped his mouth, and pushed back his chair. "Your mother was right."

"About what?" Jane put her glass down and smiled at her husband, her fingers longing to push back that lock of hair from his face once again.

"The food here. The rabbit fricassee was excellent. And the pear tarts were the best I have had in a long time. Don't you agree?"

His wife, who had been more selective than he, raised one eyebrow but didn't contradict him. "What does that face mean?" he asked.

"I was just wondering when you had grown so conscious of what you ate," Jane said. "When you were younger, you didn't care as long as there was enough." She put her elbows on the table and leaned forward. She was wearing the dress she had worn to her wedding without its spencer, and her hair was caught with green ribbons.

Stephen didn't say anything for a moment. Then he too leaned forward, his elbows on the table so that only a short distance separated them. "Maybe it is the company," he suggested. He smiled at her, and she felt herself grow warm. Then he held out a hand. "Come. We would be more comfortable sitting on the settee."

She put her hand in his and allowed him to lead her to the divan near the fireplace. Stephen seated her and then took his place beside her, keeping her hand in his. A comfortable silence fell between them as the maid scurried about the room clearing the table.

As soon as the door closed behind her, Stephen brought Jane's hand to his lips. She sighed. Her husband looked at her, trying to read her face. "Stephen," she whispered.

"What?"

"Nothing." Her fingers pulled free from his and stroked his cheek. He turned his head and placed a kiss in her palm. She closed her eyes for a moment and then opened them quickly when he nipped her finger with his teeth. "Stephen?"

"I want you to look at me," he whispered, his face close to her own. His blue eyes were intense.

"All right." She turned slightly, pulling back away from him just a little. He moved closer and put his other arm around her. She stared into his eyes, enjoying the excitement he was creating within her. Slowly, Stephen pulled her closer, ready to stop if she made any protest. She simply stared at him. He lowered his head to hers, his eyes fixed on hers.

At first, he barely touched his lips to hers. When she closed her eyes and leaned into him, her arms wrapping around his neck, he deepened the kiss, his lips opening slightly. Once again she sighed. As her lips parted, he ran his tongue over them, barely touching them. Following his lead, she explored his lips with her tongue. Stephen kissed her again, this time more passionately. He pulled her closer. Jane tightened her arms around his neck.

When he pulled back slightly, she sighed wistfully and let her arms go limp. He bent his head and caressed her neck and ear, sending shivers through her. Once again she followed his lead, kissing his chin. When she tried to kiss his neck, his neckcloth got in her way. Totally forgetting that they would have to cross the common room to get to their own rooms, Stephen reached up and pulled it free. He opened his top button. Jane's lips unerringly found the hollow beneath his Adam's apple, sending flames raging through him.

As she had done moments before, he closed his eyes, feeling the fire begin to build in him. He pulled her closer until she was sitting on his lap. As he felt her warmth next to him, he hesitated, fearing she would pull away when she felt his body's reaction to hers. Jane simply nestled closer to him, her hand undoing his buttons so that she could touch his chest although she had no conscious knowledge of doing so.

Taking advantage of her closeness, Stephen buried his face in her neck. Jane closed her eyes and let her head fall back, giving him more room to explore. He followed the line of her gown downward, his lips moving to learn her secrets. He released the ribbon that held her neckline in place and marveled as it fell back to reveal the tops of her breasts. She shivered once more.

"Do you want me to stop?" he asked, drawing on control he had not known he had. He moved back a little.

"No," she whispered and wrapped her arms around his neck and head, pulling him back to her eager embrace. Stephen smiled and kissed her breasts once more, pulling them free of her stays. He raised his head so that he could look at them, enjoying the way the blue veins showed through the creamy white skin with the rosy nipples waiting to be tasted. They spilled out into his hands, and he licked his lips and then took one nipple into his mouth, sucking slightly. "Ohhh," she moaned, pulling him closer still. One of her hands ran through his hair.

While his mouth caressed her breasts, his hands explored under her skirts. So caught up in the emotions he stirred within her, she was not aware of his hand creeping upward until he touched the inside of her thigh. She froze. As he paused, a raucous burst of laughter spilled over from the common room, reminding him where they were. Stephen closed his eyes and simply held her. Finally, he said, "I'm sorry."

Her eyes filled with tears, and she pulled away, turning her face away from his to try to hide the teardrops running down her cheeks. The abrupt transition from the passion they had just shared to his rejection left her limp.

Stephen tightened his arms around her. "Please. It's not you. Don't pull away," he begged.

She drew back far enough to see him clearly and blinked to clear her eyes. The look on his face reassured her slightly. She nestled back against his shoulder, allowing him to smooth back her hair that had tumbled free from its pins and ribbon. "What is wrong?" she asked as he took one of her hands in his and laced their fingers together. She tightened her fingers around his.

"I forgot where we were," he confessed.

"So did I."

"But I should have had better sense."

"I like you better this way," she teased, pushing his hair back once more.

He kissed her again, but before their emotions could flare out of control, he stopped. "Listen to them out there."

Jane breathed deeply, enjoying Stephen's warm scent. "Hmmm." She reached up and kissed his chin. As though he could not help himself, he bent his head and captured her lips once more, his tongue urging them to part. When they opened slightly, he slipped his tongue inside. She snuggled closer to him.

Once again, he pulled back. "Stephen?" his wife asked wistfully. The look on her face was almost his undoing.

"No. We must not."

She pouted. "Why not?"

"Listen to them out there. You have to walk through

them to get to your room. And they'll know exactly what we have been doing." He looked at his neckcloth lying on the floor nearby and wondered how he would ever make himself presentable. He glanced at Jane's skirts, aware of the wrinkles.

She pulled back from him slightly, the idea of everyone looking at her and knowing about their actions disturbing. "They will? How?"

"Jane, look at us." When she realized her state of undress with her top pushed down and her skirts pushed up, she blushed once more and tried to free herself.

"Not yet," he begged, knowing that he should allow her to go.

She subsided, hiding her face in his neck. "What can we do?" she asked, thinking that facing the eyes of the crowd outside would be much worse than facing her friends after she and Langston had parted.

For some time Stephen didn't answer her. Then he set her back on the settee beside him and crossed to the bellpull. Quickly, she rearranged her dress, smoothing her skirts and retying the ribbon that held her neckline in place. When the maid appeared, he told her, "Send my valet to me."

"Vernon? Why are you sending for him?" Jane protested when the woman had left, feeling almost more embarrassed at the thought of the valet's reaction than she would have at walking through the common room. She walked toward him, a frown creasing her forehead.

"I have an idea. Sit back down on the settee. And keep your back to the door," Stephen told her. Still frowning, she did as he said.

When Vernon appeared, Stephen told him, "Bring down our cloaks. We wish to talk a walk."

Vernon started to ask a question but, looking at his master, thought better of it. He nodded and hurried from the room.

"A walk?" Jane asked as Stephen took his place beside her once more.

"It gives us a reason to put on our cloaks. Yours does have a hood, doesn't it?"

She thought for a moment. Then her face broke into a smile. "Stephen, you're brilliant. Of course, our cloaks will cover everything." She leaned forward to kiss him.

His cheeks flushed, Stephen opened the door when Vernon scratched on it and took the cloaks. "When we return, we will go up to bed," he told him. "Have Annie wait for my wife in their room." Then he turned back to Jane.

As soon as they had hidden their disarray, they quickly made their way outside. Stephen looked around, trying to decide which way to go.

"Do you remember anything about the town?" he asked.

"I only came this way once," Jane admitted. "Usually Mama left us at home with our governess or my uncle visited us." She looked up and shivered.

"Are you cold?" Stephen asked, pulling her against him.

She shook her head, her eyes still fixed above. "They are so beautiful," she whispered.

His eyes fixed on her, he asked, "What?"

"The stars. There are so many of them." She turned her head and looked at him. "Do you ever wonder what they are?"

"Like the nursery rhyme, 'Twinkle, twinkle, little star. / How I wonder what you are'?"

"No, seriously. They are always there looking down on us. I sometimes wonder what they think of us."

"They would think you a beautiful lady." As they talked, they walked aimlessly down the road out into the countryside.

She stopped and looked at him, her green eyes wide. "You didn't have to say that."

"I wanted to. To me, you are the most beautiful lady I know." His voice was low and serious.

Jane lowered her eyelashes, hiding her eyes for a moment. Then she smiled at him. "Do you mean that?" she asked in a whisper.

He nodded and drew her arm through his once more.

"Yes. Even when I was a boy, I was fascinated by you, Miss Green Eyes," he admitted.

"That is the first time you have called me that in a long time."

"When you put up your hair and let down your skirts, it didn't seem right to call you that. Then when you said you would marry Langston, I felt it was not right for me to have a special name for you."

The mention of her former fiancé dampened her excitement. For a few minutes they continued on their walk without saying a word. Then Stephen pulled her to a halt. "We had better go back."

Silently, each wishing that somehow the evening could end differently, they walked back to the inn. Before they had reached the inn yard once more, Stephen pulled Jane to a stop. He turned to face her. She started to speak and then looked into his eyes. She stepped forward into his embrace, her lips pressing against his as passionately as his against hers. Then he stepped back once more, his face resolute. He pulled her hood over her head so that not even one strand of her hair showed.

"I'll see you to your room," he told her, tucking one last strand inside her gray hood. She ran her hand down his cheek, and he turned his head to kiss her hand. Slowly, reluctant to reenter the intruding world, they walked back into the inn and up the stairs to their room.

"Good night," she whispered, longing to pull him close. He simply smiled and turned away.

When Stephen handed Jane into the coach the next morning, there was no question about where he would ride. He followed her inside, the emotion in his eyes causing hers to fall.

"Will you be too unhappy if we do not arrive at your uncle's today?" he asked.

"Not arrive. But—?" She looked into his eyes and, recognizing the passion there, blushed. "Won't Mama worry when we don't arrive?"

"The message I sent told them not to expect us until at least tomorrow. If we are later, I can always send a groom with the change." He untied her bonnet and put it on the seat in front of them. "Or I can tell Jem Coachman to spring them and try to get there today." His voice told her what he thought of the last proposal.

"If she does not expect us . . ." Jane let her voice drift off. She lowered her eyes before the blaze in his.

"Good. I sent Vernon and Annie ahead to make certain we will have comfortable accommodations; so if we want to, we can stop occasionally. The innkeeper assured me that there are several lovely walks near the road." Stephen smiled at his wife. "He even had his wife pack a picnic lunch for us."

"A picnic! Remember how you . . ." As they traveled throughout the countryside, stopping now and again to walk to the edge of a nearby lake or look out over an overhang, Stephen and Jane recaptured the easy camaraderie that they had shared during those summers of their childhood. Stephen was ever careful to keep his passion under control while Jane, although longing for something more but unable to state what it was, simply enjoyed his company.

As they sat under a tree, the remainder of their luncheon uneaten, Stephen glanced around. The coachman and groom had unharnessed the horses and led them away to drink from the nearby stream. He could hear their voices in the distance. He looked back at his wife. She shook the crumbs from the cloth they had spread over the blanket and folded it neatly, replacing it in the basket. Gathering up the remnants of their meal, he helped her repack the basket.

As their fingers touched, both froze. Then they looked at each other, trying to read the other's face and eyes. They leaned forward and kissed hungrily. Stephen's arms drew Jane close, and her arms wrapped around his neck.

Once again the world intruded. All too clearly Stephen heard the sound of the returning men and horses. "We have to go," he murmured against her mouth. She nodded and pulled away from him. Standing up, he drew her up after him, holding her for a moment in the circle of his arms.

Then he stepped back and picked up the blanket. Jane kept her eyes on him as if afraid he would vanish.

When the horses were harnessed once more, Stephen handed his wife into the coach. His hand lingered on hers. Closing the door, he gave the order to start. "Spring 'em."

Jane looked at him, surprised. Only a short time earlier, they had discussed several other stops to make that afternoon. As the coach pulled back onto the road, Stephen moved closer to her, his eyes bluer than she had ever seen them. "Have our plans changed?" she asked.

He reached up to push a lock of her hair behind her ear, his finger a caress against her cheek. "There are too many people about when we stop," he told her. "I don't want to share you with anyone."

"There was no one to disturb us a few moments ago."

"Just the coachman and groom."

"Oh." In the light of the day, the passion in his eyes startled and excited her. She sat back in her corner and closed her eyes, drifting off to sleep, her hand still in his. He too sat back, his eyes on her.

When she awoke sometime later, she was nestled against her husband, her cheek resting on his chest, her hand holding his shirt. Slowly, she blinked her eyes, too comfortable and peaceful to want to move. She could hear the steady beat of Stephen's heart under her ear.

When he realized that her breathing had changed, Stephen's arms tightened around her. He lowered his head to hers, his chin resting on the top of her head. As he had watched her sleep, he had made some decisions. He took a deep breath. "Jane," he said softly.

She sighed and shifted against him, too comfortable even to want to talk. "Jane," he said again, this time more loudly.

"Hmmm."

"Are you awake?"

She stretched and pulled away from him. She shook her head to clear the last bits of sleep from her mind. "I suppose I must be," she admitted. Her smile was as sleepy as her voice.

"May we talk?"

She yawned. "I thought that was what we were doing," she said, smothering another yawn. She smiled at Stephen to soften her words.

He smiled back, enjoying the sight of her just waking up. "Seriously."

At once the sleepiness fell away from her. A frisson of fear laced through her. She searched his face, frightened of what she would find there. He smiled at her, and her fears disappeared. She nodded.

"Did I ever tell you why I really went to Canada?" he asked, knowing the answer.

"Really? You didn't go to inspect your uncle's investments?" she asked, her face puzzled.

"That was part of the reason. But I could have sent someone else to check on them for me."

"You didn't have to go?" She stared at him in amazement.

"No, but I wanted to."

"Why?"

He took a deep breath and said the words before he could call them back. "I didn't want to be here when you and Langston married." He looked at her, trying to gauge her reaction.

"What did Langston and I have to do with your going to Canada?" She turned slightly so that she could watch him more closely.

He squared his shoulders as though preparing to defend himself. "I am in love with you, have been in love with you since before you were presented," he admitted.

She stared at him, staggered by his admission. "But you—you never said—"

"How could I? It was always you and Langston. As long as I've known you." He let out his breath slowly, waiting for her to say something.

"But I didn't accept him until the beginning of my second Season," Jane said, still startled by his confession.

"He told me much earlier that he planned to ask you."

"But you should have—"

"Told you? What would you have said?" He looked her

in the face. "Think about the way we were then. What would have happened?" He took a deep breath. "I thought about it, thought about it all the time. Once I was ready to tell you; then you came in laughing about someone who had bored you to tears because he thought he was in love with you. I held my tongue."

"Oh, Stephen, if I had only known." She cradled his face in her hands. "How I must have hurt you." Her eyes filled with tears.

He brushed them away. "You didn't know how I felt. Then, you only had eyes for Langston."

Jane closed her eyes, trying to keep any more tears from falling. Then she opened them wide. "You said you are in love with me," she whispered. "Now? Do you mean now?" A glimmer of joy lit her eyes.

He nodded his head, his throat too full to speak. "You love me?" she asked again.

"For years," he said when he had cleared his throat.

"Oh, Stephen," she cried and reached out her arms to him. Eagerly, he pulled her close. His lips touched hers, and hers responded.

When she was flushed and rosy from his kisses and he needed to regain his control, he sat back. "Does this mean you care for me?" he asked with a twinkle in his eyes.

"Stephen!"

"I need the words, too," he admitted almost sheepishly.

She sat back, her face serious. "I didn't think I loved you then," she said. He braced himself. "In fact, until recently, when you kissed me"—she paused to smile at him and lean forward to kiss him, her lips soft and warm against his, giving him hope—"I was not sure what I felt about you. I missed you—more than you can imagine—when you went away. At first, I thought my unhappiness could be attributed to everything else that had happened to me. But I kept thinking about you, wondering how you were. And then to see you again with Langston." She looked up at him, begging him to understand. When his eyes darkened, she rushed on. "Then you asked me to marry you. I thought it was just because I was convenient."

"You said that before. I can assure you that it was not convenience. I love you."

"I am beginning to believe you do." Her lashes fluttered once more.

"And?" Stephen's eyes begged her not to keep him in suspense.

"I love you too." The smile that spread across Stephen's face lit the entire carriage. He reached out and pulled her into his arms, onto his lap. The next few minutes convinced Jane that she had never known how wonderful kisses could be.

When, sometime later, the carriage pulled into the yard of a quiet inn, Stephen handed Jane out. They walked into the building, their eyes on one another. "Your rooms are all arranged," the innkeeper assured them. "Shall I send for your servants?"

"We'll call for them when we need them," Stephen told him. "Show us to our rooms." He smiled fondly at his wife, and she smiled back.

When the door closed behind them, leaving them alone, Stephen walked slowly toward his wife, his eyes burning with a passion he had been hiding. "Come here, wife," he said in a husky voice.

Her veins singing, Jane met him halfway. "Yes, husband." The word thrilled Stephen. He wrapped his arms around her.

"You are certain?" he asked, the emotion in his voice giving it a quiver.

"Yes," she whispered, staring into his eyes. The sunlight caught her hair and made it glow. He kissed her again, took her hand, and led her into the bedroom.